THE LIONS OF JUDAH

THE LIONS OF JUDAH

Ted Willis

Holt, Rinehart and Winston New York

First published in the United States of America in 1980 by Holt, Rinehart and Winston, 383 Madison Avenue, New York, New York 10017.

Originally published in England.

LIBRARY OF CONGRESS CATALOGING IN PUBLICATION DATA
Willis, Ted, Baron Willis, 1918–
    The lions of Judah.
    1. World War, 1939–1945—Jews—Rescue—Fiction.
I. Title.
PZ4.W736Li   1980   [PR6045.I567]   823'.9'14   79–22703
ISBN: 0-03-053986-2

Designer: Susan Mitchell

Printed in the United States of America
10 9 8 7 6 5 4 3 2 1

This one is for Audrey.

FOREWORD

This is a work of fiction, but, like many stories, it was born out of a true incident. In 1965, in Gothenburg, Sweden, quite by chance, I met a middle-aged woman. She was married to a theater producer, and had Swedish citizenship, but she came originally from Germany, where her father had been a prominent member of the Jewish community. In the course of conversation over dinner one evening she told me of an incident at the end of 1938 in Berlin, when a young man called to seek help from her father. The story he had to tell, and the bizarre proposal he had to make, formed the germ of the idea for this book.

It is also true that shortly after the war, a unit of the Highland Light Infantry, attached to the Twenty-first Army Group in northwest Germany, discovered in the cellars of an old castle near Osnabrück certain documents that were afterward identified as the Blue Papers. These documents were prepared at monthly intervals by Bureau V of the Forschungsamt, an intelligence agency, which came under the control of Reichsmarschall Hermann Göring.

Many other incidents in this book are based on truth. It is, for example, a matter of record that in 1939 Albert Einstein wrote President Franklin Roosevelt a letter that was of decisive, not to say historic, importance.

—Ted Willis
Chislehurst, England

THE LIONS OF JUDAH

ONE

1

The young man lay still, pressing the whole weight of his body into the frozen earth. The frosted grass, sharp as thorns, scratched and prickled his face, but he greeted its chill sting with relief, closing his eyes, filling his throbbing lungs with the blessed air. Then, in the silence, above the anguished hammering of his heart, he heard the music begin.

Absurdly, a part of his mind registered the fact that the distant orchestra was playing the "Tritsch-Tratsch" Polka. It even told him, as though it were important, that the composer was Johann Strauss, Johann the Younger, born 1825, died 1899, and that the opus number was 214. It was all there, like the arithmetic tables he had once learned parrot fashion, by constant repetition.

And this thought brought in its train a memory of childhood: a small boy watching with wide eyes as his mother and father danced to this same tune, laughing and smiling at each other.

He remembered how, at first, he had been ashamed that they should behave in this astonishing way in front of other adults, and then how, carried away by the music and the gaiety, he had clapped and called for more. His mother had caught him up with a cry and had carried him off to bed; and, sharp as a photograph in his mind, he saw again the strand of hair that had escaped from its pins and was swinging across her face, and the small bead of perspiration sliding down from her forehead to the tip of her nose, where it hung like a dewdrop. He had lain awake for a long time listening to the music and laughter that drifted up from the parlor.

The memory brought him no pleasure; he felt the bitterness rise in his throat, like bile. He slid a hand over the spiky grass and touched the worn leather of the brown case. As if reassured by its presence, he lifted his head slowly.

The chateau lay immediately ahead of him at the top of a hill. Strings of colored lamps lined the balcony of the long terrace, arc lamps illuminated the twin towers, turning their dark gray stone to a gentle white, and the narrow windows of the main building glowed with light like bars of burnished bronze. From where the young man was lying, from the darkness of the meadow below, the chateau appeared to have no foothold in the earth; it seemed to float in a mist, like a castle in a fairy tale. The faint sound of the music, so sweet and inconsequential, only seemed to add substance to the illusion.

The cold was beginning to bite through his clothes into his flesh. He had to move on, keep the blood circulating, get closer to the house—perhaps, with luck, get inside it. And as if to emphasize that he was on open ground, exposed and vulnerable, the moon suddenly slipped its escort of clouds, flooding the meadow with amber light.

Clutching the heavy case, he stumbled forward in a crouching run toward a little copse of trees and shrubs that stood at the foot of the steep slope leading to the chateau. It was only about two hundred yards away, but by the time he reached its cover, he was once more gasping for air. You're not fit, my lad, he thought wryly, not fit at all. But that really wasn't surprising in the circumstances, considering how he had been forced to live during the past four or five months. If it could be called living. . . .

From somewhere to his right, a twig or branch snapped, sounding like a gunshot in his ears. He pressed back into the shadows, feeling the handle of the knife that hung in a sheath at his side. He heard the low murmur of voices, and then, their faces bright in the moonlight, he saw two guards. They were tall rugged young men, wrapped in heavy greatcoats, each with a rifle slung on his shoulder and a holstered pistol on his belt. They moved at a steady, relaxed pace, their breath making tiny clouds in the air, and as they skirted the copse, he caught a snatch of their conversation.

"No, the truth of the matter is, I stopped believing in God a long time ago."

"Ah, but there must be something. All this didn't start by itself."

"I don't know how it started . . ."

"There you are then!"

"My mother died of cancer when she was thirty-five. We prayed for her, did all the right things. Didn't do her any good. I stopped believing after that. I mean, what kind of God would do that to a person, tell me that?"

They passed on, their voices fading in the night, and for a moment the young man closed his eyes in relief. Yes, indeed, what kind of God would stand by and—

He cut off the thought. Halfway up the slope there was a crumbling stone wall; beyond that, he knew, there were terraces and ornamental gardens, sweeping up to the chateau. He had to reach the shelter of the wall before the guards came round again. There would probably be other patrols up there, but in the gardens, at least, there would be some cover. And he would be within two hundred yards of his target.

Above him, the orchestra was playing the "Delirien" Waltz, but this time his mind ignored the music. He knelt down and sprung the catches of the brown case. The rifle lay snug in a bed of black velvet; stock, barrel, and special telescopic sight, each in its separate compartment. The ammunition was in a small pouch in one corner.

He pulled the thick woolen gloves from his hands, dragging at the fingertips with his teeth; then, with deft, sure movements, he fitted the gun together, slid the telescopic attachment into place, and pulled off the protective end caps. He had trained himself to do this by touch, in complete darkness, but the spill of moonlight made it easier. He held the rifle to his shoulder, and the feel of the cheek rest against his face seemed to give him new strength and confidence; he noted with a touch of pride that his hands were rock steady.

It had been impossible for him to make any detailed plan. A preliminary reconnaissance of the ground or of the chateau would have been too dangerous. His only guide had been a local map, his only training an occasional foray into the countryside at night, to accustom himself to movement over rough ground in the dark. And when he got nearer to the chateau—*if* he got nearer—he would have to rely on luck and improvisation. But at least, so far his luck had held.

He lowered the rifle, took some ammunition from the pouch, and loaded the magazine, pressing each round in against the spring. It was designed to take six, but he put in four only, knowing from experience that a packed magazine could jam.

Four should be enough, he thought. Three for them and the last one for himself.

2

The Reichsmarschall paused at the top of the wide stairway, one hand on the marble balustrade, and looked down on the crowd below. Gradually, the guests became aware of his presence: heads were turned upward, the hubbub of conversation and laughter faded. A plump woman, her back to the stairs, cackled at some remark and was hushed reprovingly by her neighbors.

"What's the matter?" she asked indignantly. "Is it forbidden to laugh?" Her voice screeched in the growing silence.

"On the contrary!" said the Reichsmarschall, beaming down at her. "This is a party. You are positively commanded to enjoy yourself, madame!"

She turned quickly toward the sound, her face and neck reddened with embarrassment, but she was soon forgotten in the laughter and applause that swept through the hall.

"Heil Hitler!" said the Reichsmarschall, lifting a pudgy, beringed hand in a perfunctory salute. A hundred hands were raised in eager response.

"Heil Hitler!"

Four Luftwaffe officers cleared a space at the foot of the stairs, politely pushing the crowd back, and one of them, a major, called: "Will the ladies and gentlemen who are to be presented to His Excellency kindly form into line here." He indicated an area to the right of the stairs. "And would the other guests please pass into the ballroom."

The privileged ones came forward, while the others dispersed slowly, moving toward the music, casting a mixture of curious, respectful, and even adoring looks toward the Reichsmarschall, who remained standing at the head of the stairs, his large milk-white face set in a smile. A waiter with the insignia of the Luftwaffe, a swastika armband, and the stripes of a corporal on the sleeves of his white coat, appeared from one of the upper rooms carrying a small silver tray on which there stood a single glass of champagne. The Reichsmarschall sipped it tentatively and then held it up as though making a general toast to his guests.

The Major hurried up the stairs toward him, carrying a list of those who were to be presented, and stood at attention.

"All ready, sir."

The Reichsmarschall looked down at the long line of people waiting below.

"All that lot? God in heaven, Erich, what are you trying to do to me?" He spoke in a low voice, out of one side of his mouth, hardly disturbing the fixed smile.

"I've cut it down by more than half, sir. It's not my fault if everyone wants to shake your hand." The Major grinned easily. He was close enough to the Reichsmarschall to be allowed a certain degree of bluff familiarity, and he had remained close because he had never abused the privilege.

"Who are they?"

"The cream of the district, you might say. A couple of burgomasters, local party leaders, business men—"

The Reichsmarschall cut him short with a gesture. He was looking down at a tall elegant woman who was standing in the line at the foot of the stairs, alongside a sturdy, middle-aged man in a uniform of a party official. There was about her an air of sophistication that set her apart from the other women: she seemed calm, poised, almost bored with the ritual of the occasion.

"Who is that woman?" asked the Reichsmarschall.

She seemed to sense his interest, for at that moment she raised her head with its crown of copper-colored hair and looked upward. The face was attractive, yet something of a disappointment after the promise of her body in its low-cut, dark red dress; the lips were too thin, the eyes watchful and calculating, the sensuality seemed applied, superficial. She caught the Reichsmarschall's eye and gave him a small provocative smile.

The Major had been consulting his list. "Frau Raubel, sir. And her husband. He's one of our local people, a deputy gauleiter."

"With a wife like that, it's time he was promoted, don't you think?"

"I'm sure he would be grateful for your interest, sir." The Major grinned.

"Well, the night is young. We must see what we can do. Right, let's get it over with."

He handed his glass to the waiting corporal and descended until he reached the last stair, where he positioned himself for the introductions. He spoke to the Deputy Gauleiter at some length, keeping the others waiting. He said nothing to the man's wife, but from time to time their eyes met, and once again, with a sense of anticipation, he noted the small, almost imperceptible, yet impudent smile.

3

The young man had succeeded in reaching the stone wall without incident, and from there he easily gained the cover of a thick clump of rhododendrons to one side of the garden. He was little more than a hundred yards from the house, with a clear view of the terrace and of the two sentries who guarded it. From time to time the tall glass-paneled doors opened, releasing a burst of noisy conversation and music from within, and a solitary guest or sometimes a couple stepped out onto the terrace, but the cold night air quickly drove them back again. He could have picked any one of them easily, but he was looking for more important game.

The two sentries kept moving, as though they too

were conscious of the cold. Occasionally as they crossed, a few words were exchanged, and once an orderly brought them out two mugs of hot coffee. The young man fancied that he could smell its rich aroma and felt his empty stomach churn in envy.

The cold was everybody's enemy, but his most of all. The woolen gloves were soggy and damp; within them his fingers felt numb and stiff. He removed the right-hand glove and blew on the fingers, flexing them at the same time; when the moment came, he wanted them to be soft and supple, completely under control.

He knew now that he would not be able to get nearer to the house. All he could do was to wait, hoping that the man he had come to kill would step outside onto the terrace. And if that turned out to be a forlorn hope, he would try to work his way round to the front of the chateau and cover the departure of the guests; with luck, their host would appear to speed the most important of them on their way, and that would provide the opportunity he needed.

If the worst came to the worst, he thought, he could charge into the house and take his chances with the guards. Or settle for less than he had come for and simply pick off two or three of the VIPs as they moved to their cars.

Whatever happened, he had come too far to go back now. He was going to extract some payment in kind for all that had happened.

4

The Major could see that the Reichsmarschall was becoming bored and even irritated with the Deputy Gauleiter. For the past half hour they had been sitting apart from the other guests in a small anteroom, and

Herr Raubel, flattered by the attention lavished on him by the great man and misunderstanding its purpose, had gone on chattering in the most sycophantic way. At this moment he was boasting of the role he had played on November 9, the so-called Crystal Night, when anti-Jewish riots had been unleashed throughout the country.

"By the time we'd finished there wasn't a single Jewish shop left in business! Then we turned our attention to the rat holes they live in. You should have seen them scuttle, Your Excellency! We rounded up over two thousand of the vermin, gave them a good beating, and packed them off to the camps. All that's left in the town are a few old yids and some of their brats—and they won't last long, believe me! And afterwards, the next day, the air smelt fresher, purer! True! We'd got rid of all that Jewish subhuman stink! I said as much to my wife, isn't that so, Angela?"

His wife made a tiny gesture with her hands, but said nothing. Her eyes went briefly to the Reichsmarschall's face as though in apology for her husband's verbosity. The Reichsmarschall clicked his fingers, and an orderly refilled their glasses with brandy from a decanter. The glasses were long and narrow like those vases that are designed to hold a single rose, and decorated with a delicate pattern of flowers.

"Do you like the brandy?" asked the Reichsmarschall. He directed the question to the wife, but it was the husband who answered.

"Excellent. Simply superb, Your Excellency."

"And the glasses?" The Major could tell, by one look at the Reichsmarschall's face, that he had finally lost patience with the other man, that he was ready for mischief.

"Beautiful. Unusual."

"This is the only way to drink brandy. All that business of balloon glasses, all that is so much rubbish, sheer snobbery."

"Quite so, Your Excellency. You are quite right."

"How do you serve your brandy at home, Herr Raubel?" The Reichsmarschall leaned forward, his chair creaking, and looked directly at the Deputy Gauleiter, who wriggled slightly, his cheeks reddening.

"Well . . ." he said.

"In balloon glasses," answered the wife calmly.

"But I shall get some glasses like these as soon as possible," said her husband hastily.

"You will be unlucky," said the Reichsmarschall. "These were made in Munich, by a Jewish craftsman."

The Deputy Gauleiter opened his mouth to speak, but no sound came out. He looked at the glass in his hand as though he were holding a deadly snake.

"It was a family concern," went on the Reichsmarschall, "and it doesn't exist any longer. For obvious reasons."

"Exactly so," said the Deputy Gauleiter nervously, aware now that he had talked himself into a trap and trying desperately to think of a way out.

"But still, one has to admit, as you said, that the glasses are beautiful. Each one an exquisite work of art, isn't that so?"

"Indeed, Your Excellency, indeed."

"Which raises an interesting question, don't you think? How is it possible that subhuman vermin can produce work of such quality?" He twisted the glass in his hand, pursing his red, fleshy lips. "How would you answer that, Herr Raubel?"

The Deputy Gauleiter cleared his throat, making a little rasping noise. He glanced at his wife as if he hoped that she might help, but she remained silent, waiting for him to reply, and it seemed that she was mocking him with her eyes. And then, to his further consternation, he saw the Reichsmarschall put out a plump finger and run it down his wife's arm, from the shoulder to the wrist. She made no attempt to move and showed no surprise.

"The answer is, of course," he began. "The answer is . . ." The finger started once more on its casual downward course, leaving a faint line on the smooth brown skin, and he lost the thread of his thought.

The Reichsmarschall, as though tiring of the game, suddenly stood up and hurled his brandy glass into the fireplace, shattering it to pieces. "So much for the Jewish question," he said harshly. "I have other concerns. I must leave such problems to others, to men like yourself, Herr Deputy Gauleiter. You can rid us of our Jewish rubbish. But do it a little more quietly in the future, damn you!"

"I don't understand—" stammered the Deputy Gauleiter, who had leapt to his feet on the instant the Reichsmarschall had moved.

"Your famous Crystal Night—that is what I mean, man! In one night, with one stroke, you succeeded in putting half the world against us! The American and British newspapers were full of it, calling us barbarians. Even some of our closest sympathizers abroad have been antagonized. Some countries are even talking of a boycott of German goods. That's what you idiots achieved with your Crystal Night!" He glared at the Deputy Gauleiter as though he had carried out the pogrom single-handedly.

"Your Excellency must be aware that it was a spontaneous uprising of our people—"

"Spontaneous, my arse. The whole business was instigated by Goebbels, and you know it! Here I have been working my guts out, trying to prepare the nation for what is to come, asking the people to save every empty toothpaste tube, every rusty nail, every bit of scrap that can be turned into something useful for the war effort—and in one night you lot destroy property worth millions of marks!"

The Deputy Gauleiter shifted from one foot to the other and seemed to be about to speak. Instead, he looked at the brandy glass, which he still held in his left hand, as if this inanimate object were to blame for his present predicament. And then, quite unpredictably, the Reichsmarschall smiled and clapped a hand on the other man's shoulder.

"Don't look so scared, man. We're only talking between ourselves, between these four walls, as party men and comrades. Shall I tell you something to cheer you up? Listen. I've proposed to the Führer, and he has agreed, that we levy a fine of one billion marks on the Jewish community! We'll make them pay for the damage you did on Crystal Night—what do you say to that? A good twist, eh?"

"It's brilliant, Your Excellency—a brilliant idea!"

"Good. I'm glad we have your approval." He turned to his aide. "And now, Major, I'm sure Herr Raubel would like to see over the place. Perhaps you will show him round?" He turned back to the Deputy Gauleiter. "I can see that you are a man who takes an interest in the arts. I have an interesting collection here—pictures and so forth. Not yet complete, you understand, but coming on, coming on."

"I shall be honored, Your Excellency."

The Major stood by the open door. The Deputy Gauleiter looked at his wife, who simply lifted her glass in his direction and made no effort to join him.

"Enjoy yourself, darling," she said.

He stared at her, his lips trembling, but once again the words wouldn't come out.

"Tell me, Herr Raubel," said the Reichsmarschall, "tell me—how long have you been a Deputy Gauleiter?"

"Three years, Your Excellency, just over three years."

"Ridiculous that a man of your quality should still be only a ..." The Reichsmarschall spoke softly, as though thinking aloud, then continued more directly. "I must look into it."

"Your Excellency is very gracious, very kind."

"So everyone keeps telling me." He raised his hand in dismissal. "Heil Hitler!"

"Heil Hitler!" The Deputy Gauleiter clicked his heels smartly and returned his salute. He gave his wife a look of mute appeal, then stumbled out. The Reichsmarschall turned to the orderly.

"Bring Frau Raubel's wrap."

"Wrap?" she asked softly.

"It is a cold night," he said.

"Are we going out?"

"Only as far as the summer house. I think you'll like it—I had it specially built and furnished. It's very warm, very comfortable. I use it quite often."

5

The two sentries snapped to attention as the door opened and the Reichsmarschall stepped out onto the terrace, with the lady on his arm. He acknowledged them with a wave of the hand and a smile. He glanced up at the sky.

"Ah. A full moon. Very appropriate. But damned cold." He moved toward the steps and paused to address one of the guards, tapping his leg with a riding crop as he spoke. "How long have you been on duty out here?"

"Sir! We came on at ten hundred hours, sir."

"A four-hour watch?"

"Yes, sir!"

"Hmph. Two hours to go. Listen, tell the guard commander that all sentries are to be issued with a double brandy when they come off duty. With my compliments. He will draw the supplies from the wine orderly."

"Sir! Thank you, sir!"

The woman shivered under the fur wrap, and the Reichsmarschall moved on. The sentries saluted again and exchanged a grin, each thinking a similar thought. The Boss was a good fellow; he understood the feelings of the men in the ranks, unlike some of those toffee-nosed bureaucrats inside who wouldn't notice an ordinary man if he burst into flames in front of their eyes.

The young man, watching this scene from the screen of shrubs, could hardly believe his good fortune. There, a hundred yards distant, his white uniform glimmering in the moonlight, was the Reichsmarschall. He pulled the sodden gloves from his hands and dropped them at his feet. His fingers were trembling now, and he blew on them urgently. A shiver convulsed his whole body. Keep still, damn you, keep still, keep calm!

He raised the rifle to his shoulder and pushed the safety catch forward; the tiny click sounded like a whiplash in his ear, and the trembling began again. In spite of the cold, he could feel the sweat on his face; his blood seemed to be roaring like a torrent in its case of flesh. He moved to one side, steadied himself against a tree, and raised the rifle again. From somewhere, like an echo in his head, he heard a noise like the baying of dogs, but he ignored it.

The Reichsmarschall had descended the steps now and was moving across the first sloping stretch of lawn toward the summer house. But the woman at his side was obscuring him to some extent, screening the target. The young man waited, calmer now, the first shock over, panning the rifle to cover them. The distance was no more than eighty yards; soon he must be presented with a clear shot.

The couple paused, and the Reichsmarschall lifted his head, as though listening. He murmured something to the woman and moved to one side. The baying of the hounds sounded louder now, and the young man realized, with a surge of terror, that the sound spelled danger.

The Reichsmarschall was in his sights now, white and large. He could see the medals gleaming at his breast.

Finger on the trigger, the first even pressure . . .

And then the dogs came at him out of the shadows, bearing him down, snarling and tearing at his body like wolves. He pressed the trigger as he fell; the explosion shattered the night, and the bullet sped upward, as though to attack the stars.

Galvanized by pain and panic, he struck out blindly and managed to throw off one of the dogs. With the other still gripping his arm, he stumbled on to the open lawn, toward the figure in the white uniform. He almost reached him; his free hand was reaching for the knife, when the second dog brought him down once more. Three guards, with their revolvers drawn, came puffing up the slope.

"Call off those damned dogs!" ordered the Reichsmarschall harshly.

One of the guards barked a word of command, and the dogs backed off, still showing their teeth. The young man lay face downward at the Reichsmarschall's feet, blood bubbling from a gash in his right hand and through a jagged tear in the leg of his dark blue overalls. The moon, white and merciless, glared down upon the scene. The guests, who had come crowding out onto the terrace, fell silent.

A young Oberleutnant saluted the Reichsmarschall. "We picked up his scent down below, sir. Found this in the copse." His voice trembled with excitement as he held up the empty riflecase.

"And how was it you let him get so near? Another ten seconds or so and you might have had a dead Reichsmarschall on your hands." The Oberleutnant opened his mouth to reply, but he was cut short. "Never mind. I'll hear your explanation later. And it had better be convincing!"

The dogs snarled again as two of the guards jerked the young man to his feet. He hung between them like a puppet, his head sagging down, his body limp. The Reichsmarschall slashed at him with the riding crop, and the face came slowly upward. Their eyes met, and, strangely, at that moment, neither man looked with triumph or fear, anger or hatred, upon the other; the look was rather one of puzzled curiosity, as if each man was trying to look into the soul of his enemy.

The Reichsmarschall let the head drop. "Put him in the guardroom. Clean him up. I'll question him myself in the morning." He turned to the woman with the copper-colored hair. "Sorry about that, my dear. Shall we continue?"

He tapped her smartly on the bottom with the crop, and she giggled with pleasure. Taking her arm, he led her toward the summer house.

6

It was 5:00 A.M. before Frau Raubel left the chateau. All the other guests had long since departed, but her husband was waiting in the hall, a sullen, solitary figure, slumped in a chair by the door. The Major handed her over with scrupulous politeness, but there was a hint of contempt in his brown eyes.

As soon as they were in the car, the Deputy Gauleiter turned fiercely upon her. "Well?" he demanded.

She silenced him with a gesture of the hand toward

the driver and a tired frown. He sunk back in the corner away from her, chewing his lips and glaring straight ahead. Closing her eyes, his wife reflected that it had been an unusual and exciting evening. Painful in some ways, as she realized ruefully whenever the car ran over a bump and jarred her body; but on the other hand, she had given as good as she'd got in that direction. The reflection made her smile. There were few people who had seen the Reichsmarschall as she had seen him, naked as a fat cherub, on his knees like a suppliant! She understood now why he had chosen to take her to that luxurious summer house with its extraordinary pictures.

And beneath all this, there lay a special and private excitement, something that belonged to her alone. It was compounded partly of fear, and it added that extra dimension of tension that only fear can bring. She smiled again. What would the fat Reichsmarschall have said had he known that he had copulated and otherwise enjoyed himself with a woman who, according to the Nazi party's own Nuremberg Law for the Protection of German Blood and Honor, had polluted, unclean blood? She did not think of herself as Jewish; she did not follow the Jewish path or the Jewish religion. But her grandfather had been a Jew; one-quarter of her blood was Jewish. According to the law, that brought her into the category of those who were called the *Mischlinge*; she was a half-breed!

Thank God, she thought, that the old man, her grandfather, was dead. She had quite liked him in the old days, but now she hated him for the taint he had put upon her, the danger she faced because of him! Only her husband now knew the secret, and he would not, dare not, betray her because of his own position. He was implicated anyway, since he had himself removed some records and doctored others, so that the truth could not come out. For this reason, if for no other, they were inextricably bound to each other.

She put out her hand and touched his arm. He refused to look at her.

"You'll get your promotion," she said.

"Why did you do it?" he said softly. "Why did you have to shame me in front of everybody?"

"Why didn't you stop me? Why didn't you challenge him?"

He shook his head, unable to answer, and she saw tears glinting in his eyes.

She closed her eyes once more. "You'll get your promotion," she said again in a tired voice.

Back at the chateau, in his own bedroom, the Reichsmarschall slept soundly, his mind soothed by pleasing dreams. In the cell adjoining the guardroom, the young man lay on the bare-plank bed, aching with the pain of his failure.

TWO

1

The young man couldn't understand what was happening. After his capture he had steeled himself for the worst, expecting at any moment to be thrown to the Gestapo, with all that meant. Instead, his wounds had been dressed, and they had even gone so far as to give him an injection against tetanus.

The guards had been none too gentle; they had offered him no food or drink, but they hadn't actually beaten him up; and, more amazing still, no one had yet bothered to interrogate him. He had simply been bundled into the cell and left there as if he were of no concern, no importance, as if attempts on the life of the Reichsmarschall were an everyday, routine occurrence.

And then he began to consider whether this was not, after all, part of their technique. Perhaps the idea was to leave him in this state of suspended animation so that he would become disoriented and fear would feed on his imagination. Whatever their motive, the treatment was beginning to work. He was clearly an object of some interest, for at intervals during the night, different guards would peer into the cell through the observation slot and stare at him with unconcealed curiosity. Each time this happened, he felt his heart flutter with fear.

He had often wondered how he would react to capture and interrogation, even tried mentally to prepare himself for such a moment. In his imagination he had seen himself standing with dignity and contempt before his captors, buoyed up by his hatred. It was the dream of a romantic, he knew that now. The torture and brutality hadn't even begun yet, but inwardly he was already quaking with terror. Thank God, he thought, that I acted alone, that there are no associates to betray, for he felt certain that he would crack under the first blow. They would never believe that he had done all this on his own initiative; they would naturally assume that he was lying and pile on the pressure in an effort to make him disclose the names of his nonexistent comrades.

He closed his eyes, trying to shut out the thought of the nameless horrors that lay before him. He had read somewhere, or been told, that one should force the mind to concentrate on other things, and he paced the cell from door to window and back again, trying to dredge up something—anything—from his reluctant memory, but nothing would come. He began to count the triangular shapes in the thick wire netting that barred the window, but the numbers became a blur in his head.

He was on the verge of panic when he heard the bolts move in the heavy door, and it was almost with a sense of relief that he turned to face what was coming. An officer in the uniform of a major in the Luftwaffe entered the cell and motioned to the sentry to wait outside. The newcomer stood without speaking for a moment, wrinkling his nose a little as though he could scent the fear in the narrow room.

"How are your wounds?" he said, at last.

The voice was deep and quiet, without edge, but even so, the young man could not find the words with which to answer. He made a little gesture with his hands.

"What is your name?" asked the Major.

"Reiss." The reply came in a whisper.

"Speak up!" A sharper tone now.

"Reiss."

"First name?"

"Kurt."

"Where do you come from?"

"Hamburg."

"Address?"

"Thirty-one Struenseestrasse."

"Age?"

"Twenty-nine."

The Major took a small notebook from a pocket of his immaculate jacket and made a note of these details, repeating them aloud.

"Kurt Reiss, aged twenty-nine, Thirty-one Struenseestrasse, Hamburg. Is that right?"

"Yes."

"Who helped you?"

"No one."

"If you are lying—"

"It's the truth. I acted alone."

"Why did you do it?"

"I had my reasons."

"Hm. You had better be prepared to say more than that."

And to the young man's astonishment, the Major turned and left the cell without another word. He sat down on the bunk, surprised at his own calm. He hadn't done so badly after all; he had managed to hide his fear; he had not given way to panic. There was more to come, worse to come, of course, but the waiting was over, at least. And all they would find at Thirty-one Struenseestrasse was a small, almost-empty room from which they would learn nothing.

He was presented with another surprise a few minutes later, when one of the guards brought him some stale bread, a bit of sausage, and a mug of lukewarm coffee. The man banged the tray down on the bunk and said gruffly, though not unkindly: "Eat. It might be the last you get."

2

At eight o'clock the Reichsmarschall was awake and alert, and twenty minutes later he too sat down to breakfast, though his meal was somewhat more substantial and served with more grace. He began with his favorite bratwurst sausage, sliced and fried in butter and served with hot knödel—little balls of grated potatoes and white bread, stuffed with liver. Some fresh rye bread, Limburger cheese, a bowl of Australian peaches, a pot of coffee, and a stein of Einbecker beer waited upon the dispatch of the first course.

Tucking a white napkin into the high collar of his gold-braided smoking jacket, he attacked the food with enormous speed and gusto, shoveling great forkfuls into his mouth and chewing noisily. When he had finished the sausage and knödel, he wiped his lips and sat back while the orderly removed the plate. He then started to eat again, but at a more leisurely pace. He was now ready to begin the business of the day, and promptly at 8:30, the Major arrived with the newspapers, the more pressing items of mail, a note of messages received, and various reports.

Each newspaper had been carefully scanned and marked; references to the Reichsmarschall were ringed in red and other important news items in blue. The Reichsmarschall waved the Major to a seat at the table, indicated that he should help himself to coffee, and then flicked through the papers, studying only those parts that were marked in red. He seemed pleased with what he found, for as he turned the pages, he nodded his head in approval and smiled.

The Major stirred his coffee and waited, watching the other man. It was odd, he thought, that even after two years the Reichsmarschall was still capable of surprising him. Last night the man had come within a few seconds of death, yet he seemed unshaken; he had spent hours with the Raubel woman, getting up to God knows what antics, yet he looked as fresh as if he had slept a whole night alone in his own bed.

When he had first been offered the post of personal aide to the Reichsmarschall, the Major had accepted with a certain secret reluctance. He had agreed mainly because it might have been dangerous to refuse.

His reservations had no political foundation, for he had no deep convictions in that direction; he was, after all, a military man, first and last. Like many others, he had been doubtful about the Nazis in the beginning, believing their methods to be dubious and vulgar, but now he shared the general enthusiasm. He believed that Hitler had stopped the rot, given the nation a new and vibrant spirit. And most of all, he had freed the armed forces from the shackles of Versailles, wiped out the bitter memory of defeat, and restored to the soldier a sense of national pride.

The Major had two reasons for his private doubts. The first was simply that he did not see himself as an armchair flyer. Before taking the staff job he had been Deputy Kommandeur of a Luftwaffe Gruppe at Mainz, and it was his ambition to get back into active service as soon as possible. He had twice applied to be returned to his Gruppe and had been met with a brusque refusal on each occasion. The Reichsmarschall seemed upset, even hurt, that one of his staff should want to leave his personal service.

His other main reservations about the job were less clear, and he would have found them difficult to put into words, but in essence they stemmed from the extravagant character of the Reichsmarschall. The Major had been wary of him two years before, and he was even more wary now. His personality, like his body, was too gross; it repelled and attracted in equal measure, and it was almost impossible to remain untouched by its force. Moreover, he was not one man, but several, one, as it were, inside the other, like a set of Russian dolls.

In two years, he reckoned that he had seen the Reichsmarschall in all his various manifestations. The war hero, beloved of the men in the ranks because he seemed to understand their problems—the strutting peacock; the fat clown, chest rattling with medals, lips and cheeks touched with rouge; the sly and ruthless politician, playing his colleagues at their own game and, more often than not, emerging as the winner; the hard-line Nazi, terrible in anger, pitiless in action; the courteous and witty diplomat, charming even his enemies; the relaxed host; the gourmet; the ladies' man; the devoted husband. What disconcerted the Major was his own inability to establish which of the dozen or so different people who seemed to inhabit that huge body was the real man.

He watched as the Reichsmarschall turned the pages. Peach juice oozed from his mouth and splashed onto the paper, but he read on, still smiling.

At this moment he was showing the face of the commander, relaxing with a trusted subordinate. But what other faces shall we see today, the Major wondered. For the most terrifying feature of the man was his unpredictability; he could change in a moment from good humor to towering rage, from kindness to cruelty, from human being to gangster. And it was impossible to anticipate these changes. All one could do was to watch, remain constantly on guard. He remembered, with a certain wistfulness, the straightforward and uncomplicated life at his Gruppe in Mainz, and wondered whether he should risk making yet another application for transfer.

The Reichsmarschall dropped the last of the papers onto the floor, picked up another peach, and looked at the Major. "Well, Erich, what have you got for me this morning?"

"There's the man in the guardroom—"

"Later. We can enjoy ourselves with that one later." He squashed a thumb into the peach, smiled, and began to tear the fruit with his teeth and suck up the juice.

"Why not just hand him over to the Gestapo?"

"Are you mad? It's not every day that someone takes a pot shot at me. Oh, no—he's mine." He paused. "What else is there?"

"A few telegrams from Berlin. Nothing urgent. And the monthly Blue Paper from Bureau Five of the Forschungsamt."

That should please him, thought the Major. The Forschungsamt was close to the heart of the Reichsmarschall, who had been responsible for its formation in 1933 and still controlled it. Disguised as a research office, the Forschungsamt was, in fact, a highly developed intelligence operation. Among other things it organized wiretapping on a huge scale; friend and foe alike came under its surveillance, and some of the more personal reports, on people like Goebbels and his various mistresses, for instance, were a source of great amusement to the Reichsmarschall. He also used them to astute political effect.

The more serious aspect of the work of the Forschungsamt lay in its ability to tap the telephone lines of foreign embassies in Germany. Thousands of messages and conversations were intercepted, recorded, and decoded. The Major had never been allowed to see anything of this side of the work; the reports, printed on brown paper, were distributed in sealed boxes to

Hitler, the Reichsmarschall, and a few selected ministers.

However, the Blue Papers were a different matter. In 1937, the Reichsmarschall had set up Bureau V of the Forschungsamt, which he described, in private, as his personal crystal ball. Its task was, literally, to look into the future, to try to anticipate how the leading politicians in Britain, France, the United States and Russia would react in any given circumstances. Bureau V's estimate of world reaction to Hitler's take-over of Austria and the Sudetenland, made some months before the actual events, had proved to be amazingly accurate.

"Ah, at last!" said the Reichsmarschall. He clicked his fingers, and on the instant, the orderly brought a hot, perfumed towel with which he wiped his face and hands. He picked up the Blue Paper and leafed through it eagerly, grunting with satisfaction. He studied the last page carefully, rubbing the tip of his nose with a forefinger in a characteristic gesture, then he turned back to the beginning and began to read with more care.

After a while he glanced at the Major, as if surprised to find him still there. "You can clear off now, Erich. I want to study this." The Major picked up the remaining papers, clicked his heels, and as he reached the door, the Reichsmarschall added: "I'll see the prisoner in an hour. You did have him cleaned up?"

"Yes, sir."

"Good. I can't stand the stink of stale sweat. Turns my stomach."

When the Major had gone, the Reichsmarschall went back to the Blue Paper. An idea was beginning to form in his mind; it was vague as yet, and as elusive as a shadow, but it was there, and he read on with a growing sense of excitement.

3

Kurt's bewilderment increased as the time passed. After eating his meager meal, he was taken by a tough-looking warrant officer to a first-aid room, where a doctor examined his wounds and redressed them. The nasty gashes in his leg and hand had been stitched and were still very painful, but the other injuries were of a minor character only. The doctor smiled at the Warrant Officer.

"He'll live, eh, Herr Stabsfeldwebel?" he said dryly.

"I wouldn't bet on it, doctor," said the man, grinning back. He gave Kurt a push and propelled him out into a passage; but instead of leading him back to the cell, he took him into a washroom.

"Strip off," he ordered, "and wash. All over. When you leave here, I want you smelling as fresh as a rosebud." He went out, locking the door.

Kurt thought for a moment of escape, but the two windows were too high and too small and he could see no other way out. Slowly, and with great difficulty, using his one good hand, he peeled off the torn overalls. There was soap and a towel at one of the basins and he washed and dried himself as best he could, glad of the sharp, refreshing touch of the water on his skin.

It did something to revive his spirits too, for the old, familiar anger, the bitterness that had led him to this place, began to surge within him. He felt ashamed of his earlier fear, of his meek compliance to their orders. Hadn't he always been the one to tell people that they should stand and fight, that it was better to die than to live in the shadows like a rat or to rot in a camp? What right did we have to criticize the weakness of others if, when put to the test, he also responded to the oppressor's orders with passive obedience?

An image of his father's face came into his mind, an image so agonizing that it was almost too painful to bear. He shook his head, as if this would clear the picture away, but it would not go. The dark eyes, eloquent with hopelessness, haunted him, and he felt his guts tighten with hatred.

The key turned in the lock, and he stepped quickly to the door. As the Warrant Officer came in, hesitating for a second at the sight of what seemed to be an empty room, Kurt launched himself, circling the thick neck with his uninjured arm, trying to bring the big man down. He was taller than his opponent and had the element of surprise on his side, but the other man was built like an ox and refused to go down. After a few moments of desperate, gasping struggle, the Warrant Officer managed to loosen the grip; he raised his right arm and smashed the elbow into Kurt's ribs with crunching force.

Kurt doubled up, gasping; the Warrant Officer wheeled round and struck him again, bringing a huge fist down on the exposed neck. As Kurt fell, his head a whirling kaleidoscope of color, he heard a voice that seemed to reverberate in his ears like an echo in a distant canyon.

"No, Herr Stabsfeldwebel! No!"

He opened his eyes and saw, as in a mist, the Warrant Officer standing over him with a drawn revolver. The gun loomed before him, huge and menacing, filling his field of vision, and in that moment he longed to hear it speak, prayed for the simple mercy of a bullet. But it remained tantalizingly silent. Slowly the mist cleared, and he saw that another man had entered the room; he raised his head and recognized the Major.

"The bastard jumped me—tried to strangle me!" said the Warrant Officer.

"Your own fault. Put that thing away."

Kurt saw the revolver retreat and disappear into its holster. The Major moved forward and looked down at him, a glint of amusement in his eyes.

"You're a regular fighting cock, aren't you? Get up!"

"Up!" shouted the Warrant Officer, and suiting the deed to the word, he hauled the prisoner roughly to his feet.

"You'll need to get him cleaned up again," said the Major.

"What for? Why don't we just shoot the bastard?"

The Major turned to him with narrowed eyes. "You will stand to attention when you address me, Herr Stabsfeldwebel, and you will ask permission to speak. You will also place yourself on a charge for neglect of duty. The prisoner should not have been left alone."

"Sir!" The Warrant Officer stiffened like a ramrod, but the look he gave Kurt was as menacing as that of a cornered wolf.

The Major looked at his watch. "In forty minutes, you will conduct the prisoner to my office. Clean and in good condition!"

"Sir!" As the door closed behind the Major, the Warrant Officer turned to Kurt and indicated a shirt and a pair of trousers that had fallen to the floor during the struggle. "Pick 'em up!" he snarled. Kurt did so, the pain shooting through his bruised neck as he bent over.

"Now, you pig bastard, get washed again and put those on. And don't try any funny business, or Major or no Major, I'll kick your head in!"

4

"Have you ever read Heine, Major?"

"I don't think so, sir."

"Heinrich Heine, the poet."

"I read him at school, sir, I believe. But not since. Poetry isn't in my line. Besides, aren't his books—"

"Banned? Oh, yes. He was a Jew." The Reichsmarschall, still in a good humor, smiled. "Can I trust you, Major?"

"The Reichsmarschall knows—"

"Of course. A rhetorical question. Years ago, I also read Heine. And I came across something he had written that is very interesting. I even made a note of it for future reference. This morning I found that note tucked away in a drawer." He passed a small filing card across to the Major. "Read it, Major. Don't worry, it isn't poetry. Read it aloud—that way you'll get the full quality."

The Major glanced at the quotation typed on the card. It gave no indication of the source or the author. He began to read, murmuring the words in a flat voice.

"No, no!" said the Reichsmarschall. "Have you no feeling for words? Give it to me!" He took the card and delivered the quotation in a full, rich, dramatic tone.

"German thunder is truly German: it takes its time. But it will come, and when it crashes it will crash as nothing in history crashed before. A drama will be performed which will make the French Revolution seem like a pretty idyll."

The Reichsmarschall leaned back and surveyed his one-man audience, awaiting a reaction. The Major hesitated, like a man at a crossroads, wondering what way to take. In the end, he settled for the tactful, noncommittal answer.

"As you said, sir—very interesting."

"Interesting? It's amazing. That was written almost a hundred years ago, man. An amazing prophecy, don't you think?"

"Remarkable."

"And it's all happening now, Erich. German thunder, roaring in the ears of the world. A drama that has a whole nation as its players and an audience that one can count in the billions." He shook his head. "What a pity that one can't quote that, eh? What a point that would make on a platform! German thunder!"

He stood up, moved to the window and stood there looking out, deep in thought. The Major waited patiently, guessing correctly that the Reichsmarschall was, for the moment, in one of his sentimental, reminiscent moods.

"It's ours now, Erich. Germany. All ours. Today, Germany. Tomorrow, the world. German thunder. And we've achieved it in a few short years, less than one tiny tick of the cosmic clock." He swung round on the Major. "Do you know the reason for our success, Erich? I'll tell you. In two words. Political will. Think about it. *Political will.* All the rest flows from that. Look at France. When the time comes we will cut through her like a hot knife through butter. Why? Because she has no leaders, no one with the political will to fight. Look at the other democracies. Who is there with the will to oppose us? Chamberlain in Britain? Well, we know what happened to him at Munich. The moment his Czech friends were under threat, he handed them to us on a platter! Churchill would have been a different proposition, but he is a voice crying in the wilderness. Apart from him, there is only Roosevelt." He checked suddenly and glared fiercely at the Major, his mood veering once more. "Am I boring you, Major?"

"No, sir. I find it fascinating."

"You are not a political animal, are you?"

"Not really, sir."

"I know. I know the military mind. You have a contempt for politics and politicians, isn't that so?" Without waiting for a reply he went on accusingly, his voice edged with anger. "Tell me, tell me, Herr Major, what your generals did to save Germany after Versailles! Who united the Reich, cleared out the rubbish, and started us on the road to victory? Was it the generals? No! Ludendorff and Hindenburg apart, they did nothing! It was a politician, the supreme politician, a man with iron determination and the political will to conquer. Adolf Hitler. The Führer. He led us out of the darkness, Herr Major!"

"With you at his side, sir," said the Major quickly.

The flattery was intentional. He could sense that the Reichsmarschall was on the verge of one of his unpredictable rages, that any moment the storm might break. He had seen it so often before; this was a man who could lash himself into a fury that fed on his own rhetoric and grew with each word. But his vanity had stronger roots, and the Major was playing on that.

The Reichsmarschall looked at him sharply, as though he had read the other man's mind. And then, suddenly, he thumped the Major on the shoulder and his face split into a huge smile.

"With me at his side! Bravo, Erich. Quite right. With me always at the Führer's side!" He wagged a finger in the Major's face. "You'd have made a good diplomat, you know."

"I doubt it, sir," said the Major, hiding his relief.

"Oh, yes. You came in exactly on cue and said exactly the right thing."

He sat down at the desk. "Now—what about this fellow who tried to take a shot at me last night? I said I'd see him in an hour."

"We're getting him cleaned up again, sir."

"Again?"

"He attacked Stabsfeldwebel Frentz."

"He did, did he! A man of initiative and spirit, it seems." His voice hardened. "The guards are getting careless. I want a full inquiry into what happened last night, Major. I want to know why this assassin was allowed to get so near the chateau."

"I've already taken the necessary steps. Four men are under close arrest." The Major handed the Reichsmarschall a sheet of typed notes. "The prisoner comes from the Altona district of Hamburg. His name is Kurt Reiss."

"Jewish?" The Reichsmarschall's head went up.

"Yes, sir. I've been on to the police in Hamburg and to the Gestapo. That's all they've given me on him at the moment."

"A nice young Jew before lunch, eh? Nothing I like better. Give me five minutes, then wheel him in."

THREE

1

The Reichsmarschall reached for a pipe from the rack
on the desk and filled it with tobacco from a blue Dres-
den jar. He did it automatically, without thinking, for
his eyes were on the sheet of paper that lay on the desk
before him. And all the time the idea that had begun to
form in his mind earlier that morning was growing,
taking firmer shape.

He lit the pipe, blew out a plume of smoke, and went
over the notes yet again. They were plain and impersonal, like an entry in a reference book, yet the feel of
the paper alone seemed to add to his sense of excitement.

Kurt Reiss (alias, Fritz Eckart, Wilhelm Dietl), born
1909 in Berlin. Address given as: 31 Struenseestrasse, Altona, Hamburg. Jewish. Only child of Dr.
Alfred Reiss, former Professor of Philosophy at
Humboldt University, Berlin. Mother: Lillian, née
Lichenstein. Both parents active members of the
former Social Democratic party. They were arrested
for activities against the State on August 23, 1937,
and sent to the Correction and Re-education Camp
at Dachau. Kurt Reiss was educated in Berlin and at
Kings College, Cambridge, England, from 1928 to
1930, where he studied politics and languages. Left
Cambridge after two years without completing the
degree course and returned to Berlin. Joined the Social Democratic party. Active in the Reichsbanner,

the paramilitary organization set up to combat the Sturmabteilung. In 1931 formed the Jüdische Schutzkorps, also paramilitary, to organize defense of Jewish synagogues and property. After 1934, Reiss was associated with Neu-Beginnen, the underground opposition movement, using various assumed names. Escaped capture in Cologne when four of his associates were arrested. Next heard of in Spain, where he joined the Thaelmann Centuria of the International Brigade using the name Wilhelm Dietl. Later became Deputy Commander of the Fourth Company of the Thaelmann Battalion. Wounded at Las Rozas, in Battle of Madrid. Known to have been in Britain from October 1937 to July 1938. Nothing known since. Inquiries at 31 Struenseestrasse indicate that he arrived there on November 16, 1938, posing as a merchant seaman and stayed for six days, until November 22. Registered as Fritz Eckart and produced identification papers in that name. Inquiries proceeding.

Physical characteristics: Height: 5 ft. 11 in.; weight: 186 lbs.; dark brown hair, brown eyes, broad features, could pass as Aryan. Distinguishing marks: small scar crescent shaped on lower left side of chin, and scar on left thigh.

Note: Reiss, senior died in Dachau on October 4, 1937. Cause of death: heart failure. His wife, Lillian, died one day later on October 5. Cause of death: self-inflicted injuries.

The Reichsmarschall leaned back and relit the pipe. There was a knock at the door, but he ignored it. He watched the blue-gray smoke float upward, clenching his teeth on the stem of the pipe as the thoughts tumbled and roared in his head. What had begun as an idea, a wild and improbable idea, was now taking shape as a plan. A plan so incredible and outrageous yet so simple and beautiful that he felt an extraordinary sense of exhilaration. He laid the pipe in a large glass ashtray and ran his fingers along the edges of the desk in a little dance of delight.

The knock was repeated, and he steadied himself. He took a mirror from the center drawer of the desk and studied his face, sticking an eyebrow back with a damp finger, wiping the moisture from his lips. Composing his face into a stern, austere expression he covered the sheet of notes with some other documents and lowered his head over them.

"Come in," he said, in a voice that was little more than a murmur.

The door opened and the Major appeared. "The prisoner, sir."

"What?" The Reichsmarschall managed to sound surprised. "Ah, yes. Bring him in." He sighed heavily, as if this were yet one more burden to carry.

The Major stepped to one side, snapped out an order, and Kurt was pushed into the room by a guard. A second guard followed immediately and joined his colleague on the other side of the prisoner. There followed a very long and deliberate silence, as the Reichsmarschall continued to study the papers on the desk. At last, at long last, he raised his head and looked directly at Kurt.

"We can dispense with the guard, Major," he said quietly.

The guards saluted and marched out. The Reichsmarschall rose from the desk and circled the prisoner, appraising him. He plucked at the flaxen hair and smiled. "Ah. Marvelous what a little bleach will do." Then, to Kurt's surprise, he indicated a chair. "Sit."

When Kurt hesitated, he said, with more edge, "Sit down! I'm not going to eat you." He chuckled, and added: "Not yet, at any rate."

The Reichsmarschall went back to his seat, picked up the pipe, and lit it once again. He tilted himself back and looked at Kurt with the air of an affable uncle.

"Now, let's have it, my lad. Why did you try to kill me, eh?"

2

The man named Zochert had come to the headquarters of the Free German Movement in Hampstead, London, in June 1938. He was one of the lucky ones. He had once been a minor official of the Social Democratic party in Frankfurt, and for this crime the Nazis sent him to Dachau. After nine months, in March 1938, he had been released without reason or warning. He discovered subsequently that his wife had gone to an uncle with money and certain Nazi connections, and with his help had bribed a succession of officials. Zochert wasn't Jewish and he wasn't important; the money had done the trick. Terrified by his experiences in the camp, Zochert had taken the first possible opportunity to get himself and his wife out of Germany.

None of this was unusual. It was well known that many officers in the Tötenkopfverbaende, the so-called Death's Head units of the SS, which were responsible for the camps, used the prisoners in their hands as commodities, to be exchanged for cash under the counter. Quite often they simply arrested someone, dumped him in a camp without trial, and then let the distraught relatives of the victim know that the release could be arranged on certain financial conditions. It had become a thriving business; it was even said that the SS kept a secret list that set out the range of prices for such transactions.

Nevertheless, Zochert was treated cautiously at first. Gestapo agents, posing as refugees, had attempted to join the Free German Movement on several occasions, and prospective members were carefully screened. Eventually he was able to prove his story and was admitted to provisional membership.

It was in the clubroom of the movement that Zochert met Kurt Reiss. Kurt had learned through the underground network of Neu-Beginnen that his parents had been taken to Dachau, and he was desperate for news of them.

Zochert, a shaken man, still with the quick look of fear in his eyes, was reluctant to speak at first. The nightmare of the camp was behind him now; he did not wish to be reminded of it but Kurt persisted.

"Reiss," he said. "Alfred. Dr. Alfred Reiss. And my mother, Lillian. They were sent to Dachau in September—that much I know. You must have been there at the same time."

Zochert looked round furtively, as though he feared the Gestapo were watching. "There were so many . . . . " he said weakly.

"Reiss!" urged Kurt. "A tall man, slightly stooped, with longish hair going gray and a short pointed beard."

"They were all shaved," muttered Zochert. "The first day, everybody. Hair clipped to the skull, no beards allowed."

"He was well known," said Kurt. "My father was well known. You must have heard something."

"I can't remember." Zochert gave him a quick, frightened glance, then looked quickly down at his coffee. His wife, sitting silently beside him, touched his arm. Her eyes, glittering with tears, begged Kurt to press the matter no further.

Later, as Kurt was putting on his coat at the front entrance, the wife came to him. "Please," she said, "you must forgive my husband." Kurt made a little helpless gesture with his hands in reply. "It was a terrible time for him," she went on. "He is not yet himself. Perhaps he will never be the same again."

A week or so later Kurt was at the club once more, and this time Zochert's wife sought him out. "I have spoken with my husband. It is difficult for him as I told you. But he would like to see you. Not here—tonight, perhaps, at our room?"

She gave him the address, and that evening he found his way to the shabby basement flat in Swiss Cottage where the Zocherts lived. He spent a half hour there, thirty minutes that he was to remember all his life.

"You wish to know about your father?" asked Zochert.

"Yes, yes."

"Everything?"

"Everything."

"It is not good."

"For God's sake, it couldn't be worse than it is now. Not knowing." He paused, lowered his voice. "Is he dead—is that what you want to tell me?"

Zochert nodded. "Believe me, it was better for him. It was a release, you understand?"

"My mother?"

"She was in the women's camp."

"I know, I know!"

"She is also—it happened the day after the death of your father. . . . " His voice faltered.

"She is dead?"

"Yes. She killed herself. They are both . . . both . . . I think it is better that you know this."

"How did my mother die?"

"Isn't it enough that you know—isn't this enough?" asked the wife gently.

"I want to know everything!" said Kurt savagely. "Everything!"

"I was told—I heard—that your mother cut her

wrists with a piece of hacksaw blade," said Zochert.

Kurt closed his eyes and shook his head from side to side. That sweet, gentle woman who had never committed the slightest act of violence against another human soul! How had she found the strength thus to savage herself? Once, as a child on holiday he had almost drowned, exhausting his strength in the struggle against an unexpected current that threatened to carry him out to sea. He could feel the same choking sensation in his lungs now, as though any moment he would drown in grief.

He heard Zochert's voice, as from a long way off. "You wished to know," he said defensively. And added, as if it were a consolation: "There were many others who did the same. Every day. You have to understand the despair. . . ."

"My father? Tell me about him." The words rasped in his throat.

"He was—I told you—he was killed."

"How?"

"Why torture yourself?" asked the woman awkwardly, gently.

"I want to know."

"The commandant at the camp—Obersturmbannführer Stutz—he—" Zochert gave Kurt a pitiful look. "Please," he begged, "please." It was as if the name, just the sound of the name, terrified him still, as if he were afraid that Stutz could reach out and pluck him back to the camp.

"Tell me, you have to tell me," Kurt pleaded. "I know, I know how hard it is for you, but you must understand—"

Zochert nodded. "You see, Stutz . . . you see, he made the prisoners build this kennel."

"Kennel?"

"Yes. Like a dog kennel only a little bigger. It was

put in the yard, near the SS barracks. And Stutz then took a Jewish prisoner—usually someone of former importance—put a leather collar around his neck . . . and chained him up by the Kennel."

"Like a dog?"

"Yes. Like that. Exactly like that. The prisoner was forced to remain on his hands and knees, to bark like a dog, eat scraps from a bowl, do . . . do certain tricks. Sometimes Stutz would give the order 'Die for Germany,' which meant that the prisoner would have to roll over on his back like . . . like . . ." He drew a hand slowly across his damp forehead. "If he refused or did not respond when ordered, he was whipped, kicked, beaten. Stutz would . . . he used to show . . . show all this to special visitors. It was his showpiece. Usually the prisoner died after two or three days or went mad and was shot. Very few survived the Kennel."

"And my father?" Kurt's voice was a whisper.

"He was taken to the Kennel one evening. He refused to . . . he refused to obey Stutz. They kept him chained there for three days and nights. On the fourth day, when he still refused, they took him to the *Bock*. A whipping rack. We were ordered to parade to watch the punishment. Stutz ordered fifty strokes of the whip—a death sentence. A death sentence. Your father did not cry out. That night the prisoners honored his memory by standing for two minutes in silence."

After a long pause the woman sighed deeply. "All these things . . . these terrible things are happening over there . . . and the world does nothing."

"The world doesn't care!" said Kurt.

3

The Reichsmarschall smiled tolerantly. "All right. I understand. It was a foolish question. You are a Jew, correct? So you wished to kill me for obvious reasons. And I must congratulate you. You came very near. Too close for comfort."

"Not close enough," Kurt said.

He was surprised by his own boldness; it was almost as if another person were speaking through his lips. For the fear still lay deep within him. He could feel his leg trembling, the pain from the old wound throbbing in his thigh. He pressed down on the knee with his hand, urging it to be still.

The Major took a step toward him, his arm raised in anger, but the Reichsmarschall waved him back. "No, Major, no! The young man has courage; we have to admit that, at least." He beamed at Kurt. "Still, it was a little unfair to pick on me. I wasn't responsible for Crystal Night, you know. Actually, I opposed it, though you won't believe that, I'm sure. You should have aimed your rifle at the learned Dr. Goebbels."

"He was to be next," Kurt said.

The Reichsmarschall exploded with laughter, rocking in his seat for a full twenty seconds before he replied. "Oh, we have a rich one here, Erich. A real find. A Jew who refuses to lie down. You see—the age of miracles is still with us!" He laughed again and then said, with heavy, exaggerated politeness: "Forgive me, Herr Reiss, but I do find it amusing. I can't wait to tell Joseph that you put me first on your list, above him."

"No," said Kurt, "you were not the first name on the list."

4

It had taken Kurt the best part of three months to make his preparations. After his conversation with Zochert he dropped out of the Free German Movement, allowed himself to be seen there no longer. His most pressing need was for money to finance his plans, so he went north to Manchester and took a job as an unskilled worker in an engineering factory. In the evenings he earned additional money as a barman in a local public house.

When he judged that he had enough saved, he went back to London, and through his connections with Neu-Beginnen, the anti-Nazi underground opposition, he secured a British passport in the name of Richard Lloyd. It was now September. He booked quite openly with a travel agency in Kensington and managed to get himself attached to a group of outdoor enthusiasts who were going to Germany on a walking holiday.

He spoke good colloquial English without trace of an accent, and with his hair dyed to the color of straw, he looked the perfect Aryan type. The SS man who checked his passport at the frontier gave it only a perfunctory glance and said, with a smile, "Welcome to Germany." The rifle in its brown case, bundled up in a blanket and stowed with the tents and camping equipment of the entire party, went through on the nod without mishap.

After two days he told the tour leader that he would catch up with the group later and headed for Munich alone. Still using his English identity, he put up in a small hotel on the fringe of the city. On the first Sunday after his arrival, he joined an excursion to the Dachauer Moos, a stretch of moorland outside Munich. For the passengers, the real attraction of the trip was that the coach passed the entrance to the concentration camp, and Kurt's neighbor was courteous enough to point this out to him.

There was little to be seen except the watchtowers, the high-perimeter fence, the distant outline of huts. Apart from the SS guards at the gate, there was no sign of human activity; indeed, the silence, the feeling of stillness, was the most striking feature of the place. The flowering shrubs in the neat beds by the gates were just beginning to put on their rich autumn colors, and a flight of birds in neat formation flew high across the camp.

Some of the passengers half averted their eyes and began quick, inconsequential conversations; others stared with unconcealed interest, looking back long after the coach had passed the camp. Kurt felt his heart quicken with pain and closed his eyes for a moment, dipping his head slightly in a small salute to his dead parents, but otherwise he showed nothing of his inner feelings. It had been like that ever since that evening with Zochert in the room at Swiss Cottage. He was like an actor who, stricken by some personal and private grief, has, nevertheless, to put on a public show, to speak certain lines, to smile, to behave more or less like a human being. Thus he went through the superficial routine of everyday social intercourse, astonished at his own ability to mask his emotions and equally astonished that, as yet, no one had been able to recognize the masquerade, to look beyond the small talk, the careful smile and see the dead heart that lay beneath.

He had to wait longer than expected in Munich, and during that period, as a safety precaution, he changed his lodgings three times. He also bought himself a black leather coat and a hat with a wide brim. During the day he divided his time between the State library on the Ludwigstrasse, posing as an English student working on a historical thesis, and the smaller cafés of the *Schwabing* quarter of the town. Zochert had provided him with two vital pieces of information, and by catching the odd bit of gossip and by a little discreet questioning, he was able to move closer to his objective.

He began to keep watch on a small house on the corner of a quiet residential street. On the third evening of the second week, a car drew up and a burly man in civilian clothes got out. The car drove away, and the man, using a key, entered the house.

Kurt waited for twenty minutes, walked to the front door, and rang the bell. There was no answer, and he rang again, more insistently. After a moment or two, a light went on in the hall and a woman in a silk kimono opened the door three or four inches. It took Kurt a little time to realize that the woman was, in fact, a painted boy.

"Yes?" asked the boy.

"I have an urgent message for Obersturmbann-führer Stutz." Kurt jammed the door open with his foot and held out an envelope, but as the boy tried to take it, he added sternly: "I have to give it to him personally."

"He isn't here."

"Look, I know he's upstairs. Get him! It's urgent."

The boy fled back inside, and Kurt heard voices raised in argument. Eventually Stutz appeared, buttoning his jacket. The anger that showed on his face faded a little as he took in the black leather coat and the hat with the brim pulled down over the face.

"What is it?" he blustered.

"An urgent message for you, Herr Obersturmbann-führer."

He held out the envelope and waited for the other man to open it. As he did so, Kurt plunged the knife deep and hard into his guts. Stutz screamed and fell across the threshold. With the cool precision of a surgeon, Kurt bent over him, retrieved the knife, and drove the blade into his heart.

"Die for Germany," he said, as the body rolled over in its final convulsion.

5

"Not the first?" said the Reichsmarschall. "How disappointing." He gave the prisoner a sharp look, and then his eyes went to the sheet of notes on the desk. After a moment he shook his head, as though in disbelief, and looked up.

"Stutz?" he asked. Kurt said nothing, and the Reichsmarschall shook his head again. "They'll hang you alive on a butcher's hook for that," he murmured, a trace of wonder in his voice. "What have you done—appointed yourself as a one-man execution squad?" When Kurt still remained silent, he continued: "Tell me, tell me this. What did you hope to achieve by killing me?"

"Satisfaction," said Kurt. "One less Nazi." Again, he had the feeling that another voice was speaking, and he was astonished at its audacity. It was as though he, the real Kurt Reiss, were simply an observer of this strange and grotesque confrontation.

The Reichsmarschall nodded, puffing at his pipe. They might, Kurt thought, have been discussing the weather or the price of bread. The Major, for his part, stood there nonplussed, marveling at the recklessness of this young man, wondering when the explosion would come.

"Of course," said the Reichsmarschall, "I can understand that. But consider this. Would you have saved a single Jew? On the contrary, if your bullet had found its mark, you would have unleashed a pogrom against your people beside which Crystal Night would have seemed like a Sunday-school picnic."

"What difference?" said Kurt. "My people are doomed anyway. So far they've submitted, bowed their heads, in the hope that all this—all this will pass. But it won't. And once they realize that fact, perhaps some of them may choose to resist, to fight."

"You are a romantic!" said the Reichsmarschall. "The Jews won't fight. And if they tried it, we would snuff them out like that!" He snapped a thumb and finger together.

"Better a quick death on the streets than a slow one in Dachau," said Kurt. Even as the words came out he was conscious that they sounded absurdly melodramatic; and that other part of him, which was listening, shrank inwardly a little with embarrassment. Yet, on the other hand, this whole situation was unreal, a sort of melodrama that provoked its own melodramatic responses. What was he doing here at all? What game was this? Was the man at the desk, the man he had come to kill, simply indulging his sadistic impulses, toying with him, as a cat with a mouse, before showing his claws and making the final, deadly strike? And this thought somehow strengthened him, bringing with it a new surge of defiance. What had he to lose?

But suddenly, after a long, thoughtful silence, the Reichsmarschall surprised him by going off on another tack. "You were in England, I see," he said. "What are things like there?"

"At least there are no pogroms," Kurt replied.

The Reichsmarschall smiled. "But they don't seem very anxious to help you, do they? Not exactly rushing forward with offers of hospitality, eh? Neither in Britain nor America." He leaned forward. "What do you think they'd say if we offered to let them have all our Jews, everyone of them, the whole lot? I'll tell you. First, there'd be a public outcry. The people would scream out that they'd already got enough Jews of their own. And the governments would make a lot of sweet, democratic noises; they'd hum and they'd ha, and it would all add up to one word. No. *No.* Correct?"

Kurt said nothing. The Reichsmarschall's eyes hardened, as though he were annoyed at this lack of response, and his voice took on a shriller note.

"The truth is, nobody wants you! Nobody! Britain is closing the door on Palestine, America refuses to increase its quota. Secretly, they all agree with us. They all think you should go somewhere else, Herr Reiss! Roosevelt suggested that you be dumped down in Ethiopia, Angola or the Central African highlands. Did you know that? Are you listening? Venezuela, Kenya, Alaska, Madagascar—they've all been put forward by your so-called friends as ideal homelands for the Jews. Of course, nothing has been done, and it never will be. The great big bleeding heart of democracy in action! They're hypocrites, all of them!"

Kurt still remained silent. None of this was new to him, and though there was an element of exaggeration in what the other man had said, it was the truth. The bitter, painful truth. But to have admitted it in these circumstances would have seemed like an act of collaboration with the enemy.

"Hmph!" grunted the Reichsmarschall contemptuously. "Nothing to say now, eh? Lost your tongue! No word of defense for your democratic friends?"

"We have no friends," said Kurt quietly. "The only people who can or will help the Jews are the Jews themselves."

6

Ten minutes later a bewildered Kurt was back in the cell, and the Reichsmarschall was giving instructions to an equally bewildered Major.

"I want that man looked after, Major. No rough treatment, decent food, exercise. Is that understood?"

"Yes, sir."

"I will hold you personally responsible."

"Yes, sir. What am I to tell the local SS? They've heard about last night; they want to take charge of the prisoner."

"Tell them he's in our custody and we'll deal with him. And listen, play down this attempted assassination business. Tell them—tell them the man is a bit of a crank, that it's not serious. If they get awkward, tell them that we might let them have a crack at him later."

"Yes, sir. Heil Hitler!" The Major saluted and went out. As soon as he had gone, the Reichsmarschall picked up the red telephone, with the direct line to Berlin. When a voice answered he said curtly: "Put me on to Reichsführer Himmler."

The man at the other end recognized the voice immediately and said respectfully, "He is not here at the moment, Your Excellency. He is in conference with the Führer."

"Tell him to call me as soon as he returns. Tell him it is urgent. I am at the chateau."

He hung up, and once again his face widened in a slow, self-satisfied smile. Another thought crossed his mind, and he pressed a bell that brought his secretary, a plain girl wearing the uniform of an auxiliary in the Luftwaffe, hurrying into the office.

"Yes, Your Excellency?"

"My wife's Christmas present—what is happening?"

"Herr Steiner is driving down this afternoon with a selection of necklaces for your inspection, Your Excellency."

"Good. Now we must try and think of something for the Führer." He sighed. "But what can you get for a man who has everything?"

FOUR

1

For the next three days, Kurt experienced a strange and unexpected calm. The hatred was still ticking in his heart, but it was less obsessive, and the images of fear no longer haunted his mind. It was as though he were surrounded by a gentle mist through which past, present, and future were seen in softer focus. It was the past that chiefly occupied his mind, since the present was a sort of limbo, and the future was not in his own keeping. He no longer cared what they had in store for him; he knew that, in the end, it would be death, and in the meantime he was content to drift along on these peaceful, borrowed hours.

His food was adequate, his wounds were healing, and for a half hour or so each morning he was taken for a walk in the grounds of the chateau, accompanied by the Major and followed by two guards. He was even issued with a short padded jacket as a protection against the bitter cold. The Major, austere and correct, gave him a warning when he was allowed out for the first time.

"Don't try anything foolish. The guards have orders to shoot to kill."

"Don't tempt me," Kurt said dryly.

No other words were exchanged, and the Major kept his distance. Kurt was content to walk in silence, enveloped in his own thoughts, invigorated by the touch of the cold, clean air on his skin. The routine was the same each day; they crossed the terrace at the back of the chateau and followed a gravel path that circled that part of the grounds that was known as the English Garden. They walked briskly, completing the circuit three times before Kurt returned to his cell.

The garden, neat and well tended, its smooth lawn and banks of evergreen shrubs glittering with frost, inevitably reminded him of the gardens he had known in Cambridge. He had always loved nature in a distant sort of way, but he knew nothing about the outdoors: he could scarcely tell one tree or one bird from another. In Berlin, the small family garden had been kept in trim by a handyman who came in one day each week. His parents seldom used it; they were always too busy, and their interests lay elsewhere. Like them, he had come to take its green welcome for granted.

Now, on these morning walks, he began to regret his ignorance. He longed to know the name of each plant and tree, of each bird, of every living creature. It occurred to him that this was the first time for years that his life had taken pause; up to this moment it had been filled with clamorous action, with a constant, unceasing battle for one objective or another. There had been no relief; except for an hour stolen here and there, he had turned his back on nature, art, poetry, music, the theater, literature—on all those pleasures that were covered by the one word his enemies hated: *culture*. It was ironic, he thought, that he should have devoted his adult life to fighting the Philistines, and in the process, had become one himself!

In the old days, he had been content to make the sacrifice, to concentrate all his energies on the cause. Tomorrow, he had told himself, tomorrow or the day after, when the battle has been won and we have built a brave new world, there will be time enough to enjoy the pleasures that nature and the arts had to offer. In the meantime, struggle and organization were the order of the day; everything else had to be set aside.

Everything else, even love. Of course, there had

been times, moments, interludes he had not lived like a monk. But equally, he had kept his personal feelings at arm's length, resisting any deep involvement. As he trod the gravel path, he recalled an afternoon in the Tiergarten in Berlin with a girl called Eva. They had walked hand in hand, two people in love, the dry autumn leaves crackling and shuffling beneath their feet, discussing the future with all the solemnity of youth. Marriage, they decided, was out of the question; this was not time to settle down to family life, to raise children. The cause needed all their capacity for love, every ounce of their strength, complete and utter dedication. Subjective feelings had to be set sternly aside because they could divert the mind, create divided loyalties, weaken the will.

He remembered all this with a wry, inner smile. What had happened over the years to that great leaping flame of idealism by which he had warmed and sustained his life? That brave new world had not materialized; there had been no dawn, only this long black night that grew increasingly more terrible.

Now, once again, time was his enemy. His flickering faith had died in Zochert's room in Swiss Cottage, and since his days and even his hours were numbered, there was no way in which he could fill the empty spaces in his life.

So, what was left?

And then he realized, as he paced around the garden, that only one thing remained. He was a Jew. He had been stripped of everything except his Jewishness. It was a startling thought, a paradox that both intrigued and mocked him. He had never sought to hide his background, but he had always thought of himself, first and foremost, as a German, no more, no less. And like his parents, he had followed no religious beliefs, embraced no man's God. This had not changed—how could it in the face of all that had happened?

No, it was something deeper still, something to do, perhaps, with blood, with roots, with elemental loyalty. The masses, in whom he had placed all his hopes, had deserted the Jews, and the world outside had turned its face away. The people who were under siege, the scorned, the rejected, the people hemmed in with hate, were his people. They were his family, all he had left.

He tried to put the thought aside, but it would not be silenced; it echoed and reverberated in his mind with all the force of revelation.

That evening, the guards were surprised to hear the prisoner singing in his cell. They were not to know that this old Russian-Jewish folksong had sprung unbidden from some recess in Kurt's memory, nor were they to know that he was as surprised as they that the past should choose to surface at such a moment and in such a way. He had last heard the song from his grandmother, and as the words came struggling back, he could hear her clear voice mixed with the busy rattle of crockery as she moved around the kitchen.

Stabsfeldwebel Frentz hammered on the cell door, shouting for silence, but Kurt ignored the interruption. Frentz tried once more and then gave up in disgust. In ordinary circumstances he would have gone in and given the prisoner a good beating up, but he was bound by the Major's order that the man should not be harmed. The whole thing was crazy, he told himself savagely. The fellow was a Jew and an assassin, so what the hell were they saving him for? As he walked angrily away, Kurt continued to croon the half-forgotten words.

Time is only a lantern,
Lighting man on his way.
The future lies in the shadows,
So sing your songs today.

The other guards listened, caught up in spite of themselves; and there were those among them who avoided Frentz's eye, afraid that he might find a hint of pity on their faces.

2

"Five hundred years ago, in this castle, the Teutonic knights of old dedicated themselves to the conquest of the Slavic lands to the east. You are the heirs of that Teutonic order. The day will come when, under the leadership of the Führer, you will fulfill once and for all that ancient dream of living space for the German people. Learn the lesson well, young comrades! Absolute obedience to your leaders, boldness in action, ruthlessness toward the enemy—let these be your watchwords! Maintain at all times a pure Aryan spirit! Young knights of the Schutzstaffel—I salute you! Heil Hitler!"

There was a moment of silence as the Reichsmarschall finished speaking, and then the response came as with one thunderous voice from the two hundred young men who stood facing him in the great hall.

"Heil Hitler! Heil Hitler!"

"Sieg Heil!" shouted the Reichsmarschall. "Sieg Heil Hitler!"

"Sieg Heil! Sieg Heil! Sieg Heil Hitler!"

The Reichsmarschall stepped back, and Himmler saw, with a delight that he did not show, that his eyes were glittering with emotion. It had not been easy to persuade the man to make the journey to the castle at Marienburg in East Prussia, but the place had, once again, worked its magic. From now on, he was sure that the Reichsmarschall would lend his full support to the *Ordensburgen*, the "order castles," in which the young elite of the SS were trained. This was his creation, his passion, his joy. These fine virile young men—they were truly his knights, the future leaders of the race. And the generals, those stiff-necked nincompoops who led the Reichswehr, were trying to close down his *Ordensburgen*, intriguing against him! Now, at least, he could rely on the Reichsmarschall!

He touched the Reichsmarschall's arm, and together they left the stage, as the students once more took up the chant.

"Sieg Heil Hitler! Sieg Heil Hitler! Sieg Heil Hitler!"

The Reichsmarschall was still in a sentimental mood when they sat down together for lunch in a room in the west tower.

"Incredible, Heinrich," he said, shaking his head, "incredible. It's the—it's the spirit. You can feel it everywhere."

"I'm glad you could come," said Himmler dryly. Other thoughts were clicking in his mind. He knew that the Reichsmarschall had only agreed to make the trip because he was anxious for a private talk. What was on his mind? And hard on the heels of this question came others. Why had he played down the attempt on his life, and why was he keeping the assassin a private prisoner at the chateau?

But the Reichsmarschall seemed to be in no hurry to disclose his intentions. "It took me back to the old days, Heinrich, I mean, the real old days, before all the riff-raff jumped on the bandwagon. We had the same spirit then."

"They were good days. But these are good days also. To see the fulfillment of a dream . . . "

"Of course. My God, we've come a long way, eh? When did you first take over the SS?"

"In 1929." Himmler allowed himself a thin smile. "I had less than two hundred men in those days, and a staff of five!" And he added, tactfully, "I've never forgotten that you were responsible for giving me my first real chance."

"There was some opposition at the time, I don't mind telling you. No names, no pack drill. But the Führer took my word on it and—well—the rest speaks for itself." The Reichsmarschall grinned affably. "Anyway, it's better than being a chicken farmer, eh?"

Himmler smiled again, but with the muscles of his face only this time; the eyes behind the silver-rimmed pince-nez were cold. He did not like to be reminded of his obscure agricultural beginnings.

"Still," said the Reichsmarschall with a chuckle, "twisting the necks of all those chickens must have been good experience, eh? I mean, now you do it with people. And very well too, if I may say so."

"I hear," said Himmler carefully, "I hear that you had a very interesting party the other night."

"Interesting? I'd hardly say that." The Reichsmarschall cut himself a slice of cheese and began to nibble at it. "It was one of those duty affairs, for the locals."

"How well do you know Frau Raubel?"

"Never heard of her." The big man continued to eat. "This is a fine cheese. Beautiful flavor."

Himmler took a small black pad from his pocket and made a note. "English red Leicester," he said. "I will see that some is sent to you." He put the pad away and continued: "Frau Raubel was at your party with her husband. He's a Deputy Gauleiter."

"Ah, yes. I know the one you mean. Attractive woman." The Reichsmarschall ran a finger round his upper gum and then wiped it on his napkin.

"Did you know she is a *Mischling*?"

"Really?" The big man seemed quite unconcerned. "I must say, she doesn't look it."

"She had a Jewish grandfather."

"Did she? What a cow!"

"We have been checking. Certain records were removed or destroyed, but we are pretty sure of our facts."

"Is there anything you don't know, Heinrich?"

"It is my job."

"Of course. Thank you for telling me. I am delighted to know that you are so—so vigilant." The words were polite enough, but there was an edge to the voice.

"I heard that you also had another rather special visitor," said Himmler quietly. He leaned across and refilled his visitor's glass. "You like this wine?"

"Excellent." The Reichsmarschall sipped the Hock appreciatively. "Another visitor? Oh, yes. Now that was interesting."

"I was wondering why your people are still holding on to him?"

"They are acting on my orders." He pulled a case to his knees, opened it, and took out a large official buff envelope. "I have my reasons." He slid the envelope across the table to Himmler. "Read that."

Himmler glanced at him and opened the envelope. "Ah, your famous Blue Papers. Bureau Five."

"Read it. Won't take you long."

As the other man polished his pince-nez and started to read, the Reichsmarschall took a pipe from the case and packed it with tobacco. He strolled to one of the narrow windows, puffing out smoke. The sky had darkened to a somber gray and it was beginning to snow. Down below, in the cobbled courtyard, a squad of young SS officers was being drilled by a giant sergeant, the snowflakes speckling their caps and shoulders.

"Fascinating," said Himmler at last.

"Isn't it!"

"But I don't see—"

The Reichsmarschall came back to the table, his face bright with enthusiasm. "Listen, Heinrich, listen carefully. I've got an idea, a tremendous idea. And I need your help."

"If it is within my power ... " Himmler spread his hands.

"It is, it is. What I need from you are some Jews."

"Jews?"

"About one thousand, give or take." He laughed. "That's not much to ask, is it? After all, you've plenty to spare."

3

Before leaving for Marienburg, the Reichsmarschall had left certain instructions with the Major. They were as explicit as they were puzzling, and he found them distasteful and unpleasant; but they were orders nonetheless and had to be obeyed. So on the morning of the fourth day the Major went to the cell.

"Come with me," he said abruptly.

Kurt was expecting the usual walk, but to his surprise, he was taken round to the front of the chateau, where a small camouflaged truck was waiting. He was bundled into the rear, and they manacled his wrist to an iron ring on one of the truck-body struts. Two guards sat on a wooden seat that ran along the other side, and the back flaps were closed. Through a cellophane panel in the canvas at the front, Kurt saw the Major get in with Stabsfeldwebel Frentz, who took the wheel.

The two guards stared at him impassively, as if he were some inanimate object; as soon as the truck bumped away one lit a cigarette. The light, seeping from the window and a slight opening at the back, was an eerie yellow. The guard with the cigarette coughed, the sound rasping from his throat. The faint sickly smell of oil and gasoline crept up through the floorboards.

Kurt felt the fear tighten in his stomach, felt the strength and calm that had come in the past three days ebbing away. The strange interlude was over. There could only be one explanation for this unexpected journey: he was to be handed over to the Gestapo. All the old terrors stampeded through his mind, black unspeakable images that set his heart thudding. He fought against the fear, nails gritting into his palms, teeth clenched, and slowly the moments of panic passed.

He stood in silence, bracing his body against the lurching movements of the truck, and eventually he gathered the courage to speak.

"Where are you taking me?"

"To the cinema. Where else?" said the older of the two guards.

"We didn't want you to get bored," said his companion. Both men laughed. The older guard took the half-smoked cigarette from his lips, glancing quickly toward the front of the truck, then held it out.

"Here," he said, "shut your mouth with this. And watch the front. If the Herr Stabsfeldwebel sees you smoking, he'll have our guts for garters. And yours too, my lad!"

Kurt reached out and took the cigarette. He drew on it too eagerly and felt the smoke scour his throat and his stomach heave. Watching him, the two guards looked at each other and grinned.

"Tell me," said the younger guard, "are you a proper Jew?"

"I'm a Jew," said Kurt.

"I mean, what I mean is—did you have it cut? What's the word?"

"Circumcised, you stupid sod," said the other guard.

"Well, have you?" asked the younger man.

"Yes," said Kurt.

"Did it hurt?"

"I don't remember. It's done soon after you're born."

"Why?"

"I don't know. Custom, I suppose." It was a curious and unreal conversation, but he was glad to talk, to have even this degree of human contact. Anything was better than silence and the dark thoughts that came with it.

"I wouldn't like to be a Jew in Germany today," said the younger man, and shaking his head he repeated emphatically, "I certainly wouldn't like to be a Jew in Germany today."

"I've got nothing against them personally," said his friend, as though Kurt were not present. "Not personally. Once worked for a Jew-boy. He was a good boss."

"Bet he had money, though," said the young guard.

"He had a bit, I suppose. I told you, I worked for him. He had a business. A small business. Not a big business. Small."

"There you are then. It's right what they say. Where there's Jews, there's money."

"Did you never see a poor Jew?" Kurt asked quietly.

"Yes," answered the younger guard, with a laugh. "We're looking at one now."

"Ah, leave the poor sod alone," said the other man.

The truck began to slow down at that moment, and the young guard seized the cigarette end from Kurt and, pulling the rear canvas flap aside, he tossed it out.

Kurt heard the sudden, shattering roar of an engine gathering pace and force, then another, and another, and another, the sound swelling into a great deep-throated chorus. Some five hundred yards from the truck he saw a flight of Messerschmitts lined up to one side of an airfield in preparation for takeoff, their propellers lifting and whirling the dust into angry clouds. And then the guard closed the flap, shutting out the view.

Once again, tension gripped Kurt's stomach with iron fingers and the thoughts and fears churned frantically in his mind. An airfield? Why an airfield? Why here? Where were they going to take him now? What weird and terrible game were they playing with him?

4

Himmler left East Prussia in his private plane in the early hours of the morning after his meeting with the Reichsmarschall. He was a ceaseless worker, and his staff thought it strange that on this occasion he ignored the heavy black box with its bold SS seal, which was full of reports and documents for his attention. Instead, he sat for most of the journey with his eyes closed and his hands pressed together, as though in prayer, with the fingertips against his lips.

When they landed at Berlin's Tempelhof Airport, he drove straight to his office on Prinz Albrechtstrasse, and sent for Reinhard Heydrich, head of the Security Service Department of the SS and his most trusted associate. When Heydrich, tall, blond, and looking superbly fit, entered the big room on the first floor, Himmler greeted him brusquely, pressed a button on a tape recorder that stood ready on the desk, and said, "Listen."

For the next fifteen minutes Heydrich listened to the voice of the Reichsmarschall, interrupted occasionally by a question or comment from Himmler. As the tape whirred round, he glanced at the other man from time to time, mainly with an expression of amused surprise on his face. When the recorded conversation finished, he switched off the machine and looked up at Himmler.

"So that's what he wanted!" he said softly.

"What do you think?"

"It's crazy. A crazy idea."

"Is it? That was my first reaction. But the more I think about it—"

"Did you agree?"

"I said I'd give him an answer within twenty-four hours."

Heydrich nodded, and began to pace the carpet. "I see your point, Herr Reichsführer. There is something appealing about the idea. It has shape, even a certain beauty."

"What it comes down to, Reinhard, what it comes down to, is this. What have we got to lose?"

"A few Jews."

"Exactly."

"And good riddance. But what about the political implications?"

"There will be none. We stand well back, we have no open involvement, we keep our hands clean. In fact, as the Reichsmarschall said, we can make immense political capital out of the situation."

"The Führer will have to give his approval."

"Naturally. Since the Reichsmarschall dreamed up the idea, he can have the job of selling it to him."

"And Goebbels?"

"Let's leave him out of it!" Himmler snorted. "The man is disaster prone. First, that affair with the Czech actress and then Crystal Night! No, if he sticks his dirty thumb in the pie, he'll ruin everything."

"What about Admiral Canaris and the Intelligence Service?"

"We shan't need him or his Abwehr either. The Reichsmarschall doesn't like him, and I don't trust him. We have our own SS agents abroad; they can supply whatever information we need."

"Of course. I understand. And it will be much better if we keep tight control of the operation."

"Exactly so." Himmler nodded, and his face eased into something like a smile. "We might get a little bonus for ourselves out of this, Reinhard. Can you guess what?"

The tall man considered a moment. He had a shrewd idea of what was in his master's mind, but he was too wily to put it into words. Himmler did not like his subordinates to anticipate him, or to appear too clever. "I'm afraid I can't, Herr Reichsführer," he said after a decent interval.

"The Forschungsamt, Reinhard!"

"Ah. I begin to understand."

"It is ridiculous that the Reichsmarschall should have control of such an organization! Logically, it ought to be in our hands since it is an internal intelligence operation. So, if we play the Reichsmarschall's little game on this occasion, it may help us later, do you see?"

"It's a brilliant idea, Herr Reichsführer."

"Think, Reinhard. The Forschungsamt! What we could do with it, eh? A wiretap on any telephone, on all the foreign embassies—on anyone who interested us, anyone at all!" The pale eyes gleamed behind the pince-nez in a moment of pure rapture, then he straightened his shoulders and strode briskly to the desk. He picked up his copy of the Blue Paper.

"Here, you'd better study this. But it is for your eyes only. Then set to work on a feasibility report about this whole project. Transport and so forth. It will be a complicated business. And send signals to Buttmann in America and Cuno in London. Get them back here quickly for a briefing."

As soon as Heydrich had gone, Himmler picked up the telephone. "Get me the headquarters of Luftflotte Two at Brunswick. Find out if the Reichsmarschall has arrived there from Marienburg yet. If he has, put me on to him. If not, leave word that he should call the moment he arrives."

He put the phone back on its cradle and leaned forward on the desk. Once again he pressed his hands together and held the tips of his fingers to his lips. He was a devout believer, and this time he actually was offering up a silent prayer.

One hour later the Reichsmarschall came on the line. After a brief exchange of courtesies, Himmler said: "I have considered your proposal. If the Führer agrees, I will give it my full support."

5

Through the window in the front flap Kurt could see part of a building, which, from its location, he took to be a Luftwaffe barracks. The Major had left the truck as soon as it stopped, and Kurt presumed that he had gone inside.

Otherwise, nothing had happened. Frentz remained silent behind the wheel, and the two guards sat huddled in their greatcoats watching the prisoner with eyes that showed their boredom. A chill wind bustled the canvas covering on the truck, and little eddies of fiercely cold air forced their way into the interior. Kurt felt as though his body had been drained of all life and warmth; his teeth were chattering, and the manacled hand, blue and mottled with cold, seemed to have turned to ice.

After about ten minutes the Major returned and got into the front next to Frentz. Still they waited, and then Kurt caught a glimpse of another, larger truck, which drew up behind the first. The driver gave two blasts on his horn, and they began to move off.

Kurt's field of vision was limited to what he could see through the window in the front flap and an occasional opening at the rear, which appeared whenever a gust of wind hit the canvas. He saw that they had left the vicinity of the airfield and were moving into open country; and after a while he could feel from the motion of the truck that they had left the road and were bumping and lurching over a rough track.

They began to climb, the engine growling in lower gear, and then stopped. Silence. Then, strangely, the almost unbelievable sound of a bird singing. After this the rumble of men's voices, the harsh, metallic crash of studded boots stamping the frozen earth, a shouted order, a subdued shuffling.

Silence again.

Another shouted order. The sound of feet, moving in regular rhythm, marching away, receding. The Major's voice now, and a heavy tread approaching the rear of the truck. The canvas flap was pulled aside and Frentz appeared, flapping his arms, a grin on his square, craggy face. He held out a hand, and one of the guards pulled him up. In the other hand he held a folded black bag.

"Right!" he said. "Let's be having him."

It happened in a moment. The younger guard pinioned Kurt from the front, enclosing his free arm. Frentz moved behind him, and there was a crackle of canvas. Kurt waited as though stunned, staring at the guard, seeing as in closeup the pastry-colored cheeks, the black wart on the tip of the chin.

Then the bag was dragged over his head and shoulders, the harsh material scouring his skin, the gritty smell of coal dust rasping his nostrils.

Darkness.

He fought frantically, twisting and squirming, and felt release as the guard staggered back. Pain, sharp as fire, stabbed at his wrist and arm, as he tugged at the manacle, struggling like an animal caught in a snare. Then, as from a long way off, he heard a curse and doubled up in wretching agony as a great fist thudded into his stomach.

Particles of coal dust fouled his throat; his lungs

heaved. But for the manacle, he would have fallen; as it was, he hung there, fighting for air, waiting with part of his consciousness for the next blow to fall.

The grating of a key. The sudden, blessed relief of the pressure on his arm. He sunk to his knees, only to be hauled up again and to be bundled out of the truck.

He felt frozen ground beneath his feet, felt himself stumbling around in drunken, erratic circles, heard the muffled sound of laughter. Anger rose above the panic, and, tearing himself free, he charged, head down, toward the laughter, only to trip and fall. He scrambled to his feet, tearing at the coarse cloth that imprisoned his head, but he was seized again.

Arms twisted behind his back, he was propelled forward, feet slithering on the icy ground. Still the throbbing darkness, the feeling that time had stopped; and rising above the musty stink of the bag, the heavy scent of his own fear. His wrist and hand prickled with pain as the blood began to course back.

He was jerked to a halt, unseen hands twisted him round, and he felt the roundness of a tree against his back. The hands released their hold, and he leaned against the tree, trying desperately to bring some order to the thoughts that roared and whirled in his mind.

The murmur of voices, a moment of silence, a louder voice barking an order. Then a sound he recognized: the harsh snap of rifle magazines. He stiffened, the sound booming in his head, driving all the other dark images before it.

Its echoes died away, and suddenly, quite suddenly, he felt calm. A strange, empty, rootless calm, as if he were without weight or substance, a shadow in a dream. This, he thought, is what death is like, or the moment before death. And in the stifling darkness faces flickered through his mind—his parents, his grandmother, Eva, his friend Hans, who had died at his side in the Park of El Pardo during the battle for Madrid. . . .

Light flooded in, prickling his eyes, as the bag was lifted from his head. He closed them for a moment, and when he looked again, he saw Frentz standing before him. For the moment, even he did not matter. Kurt gulped in the clean, sharp air filling his lungs. Gradually he adjusted to the scene, taking it all in little by little.

They were on a stretch of moorland, thick with gorse and studded with boulders. Beyond Frentz there was a line of men in the uniform of one of the Fliegerdivisions, the elite parachute troops, holding automatic weapons. The Major stood to one side talking with an Oberleutnant from the Fliegerdivision.

And farther back still, looming over it all, was the Reichsmarschall himself, the wintry sun striking fire from the diamonds on the *Ritterkreuz* that hung around his neck.

Time stopped once more. Kurt leaned back, glad of the support of the tree, hearing only the renewed thudding of his heart.

The Major moved toward him with measured stride. Frentz stepped back a pace, jolted a rifle into Kurt's ribs, and froze into immobility. The Major stopped, straddled his legs, and said quietly: "Would you like a cigarette?"

Kurt made an almost imperceptible negative motion of his head.

"Any message or request?" He looked down at his gloved hand as he spoke, as if he did not want to meet Kurt's eye.

Kurt shivered in spite of himself. Again, the slight motion of the hand.

The Major made a little gesture with his hands, as though apologizing for what he was about to say. "I have orders from the Reichsmarschall. He . . . he wishes ... " He stopped, glanced at Frentz, and then began again in a flat unemotional voice, hurrying the words. "Listen. Behind you is the open moor, plenty of cover. You will be given five minutes start and then we shall come after you. If you remain at large for two hours, your life will be spared." And he added again, as though it needed emphasis, "Those are the Reichsmarschall's orders."

Still Kurt was silent, though the thoughts tumbled and danced in his mind. A hunt? He remembered seeing a press photograph of the Reichsmarschall at a hunting party, standing with a triumphant smile over a dead chamois. Was he to be hunted also, like an animal? Madmen had taken over the world; he was living in a madhouse!

"If you refuse this opportunity—" The Major waved a hand toward the line of troops, then glanced at his watch.

"I am not a chamois," Kurt said. His voice was almost inaudible, and as the Major looked at him, his head cocked in a query, he repeated more firmly, "Tell the Reichsmarschall that I am not a chamois. I am not an animal to be hunted." He felt suddenly weary, drained of all energy; the words and the defiance seemed to be coming from another person.

Frentz stabbed the rifle harder into Kurt's body and scowled, resenting this impudence, but the Major checked him with an angry gesture.

"I will ask you once more—" he began.

But Kurt was already shaking his head. "No. I won't make sport for you. I will not run, Major." He felt a stir of anger and tried to shout so that the Reichsmarschall would hear, but his voice sounded cracked and shrill. "I'm not running. I will not run!"

"We shall see!" The Major nodded brusquely and stepped back.

The next few moments were a blur. Through misted eyes Kurt saw the Major move behind the line of troops, heard him murmur something to the Reichsmarschall. A word of command, the rifles raised.

Don't run! Don't run! Don't run! The words screamed in his head.

Bracing himself against the tree, his hands touching the rough bark, he closed his eyes and clamped his teeth over the lower lip.

A thundering crash of fire echoed in his head. A branch creaked above him; foliage fell across his face. And then a kinder darkness enveloped him, and, dipping forward, he slid to the ground.

6

He heard, as from the bottom of a pit, the murmur of voices, felt a trickle like fire scorch his mouth and burn his body. Opening his eyes in slow wonder, he saw that he was being supported by the two guards while the Major held a brandy flask to his lips. He shook his head, trying to think, to focus, and as the Major stepped back, the face of the Reichsmarschall filled his field of vision.

"Welcome back!" said the Reichsmarschall. "Don't worry, you're not dead. They fired high. It was just a rehearsal. And a sort of examination. Which you passed, I'm glad to say. I'm sure you must be too."

With a great shout of anger Kurt launched himself at the bland white face. It took the Major and the two guards to hold back the writhing, frenzied figure, and four men altogether to get him back to the truck.

As he was dragged away, the Reichsmarschall turned to the Major with a smile. "Pity he robbed us of the hunt. It would have been interesting. What do you make of him?"

"I would like a thousand men with his guts," said the Major bluntly.

The Reichsmarschall nodded. "That's what I needed to find out. Was he just a fanatic, a madman, simply out for revenge, or did he have true courage? Now we know. He'll do, he'll do very well, I think."

The Major did not know what the Reichsmarschall was talking about, but he did know that in his own mind there was a consciousness of shame, and in his mouth, a taste like vomit.

FIVE

1

The narrow street, with its huddled, drunken-looking houses, was deserted. The streetlamps illuminated only the emptiness of the uneven broken sidewalks and the rutted roadway. Each window was shuttered and barred; the only sounds were the rustle of scraps of paper and garbage in the gutter, stirred into movement by the chill wind, and the echo of Kurt's footsteps.

Behind these windows, behind every door, there were human beings, people, families, yet not even the cry of a baby or the bark of a dog intruded on the silence. It was like walking in a cemetery at night; it even had the smell of a cemetery.

He stopped at one of the doors, peered at the number, and knocked. The noise seemed to roll round the street, but it evoked no response. He waited, and then knocked again, more insistently.

A narrow strip of light appeared at the bottom of the door, and he heard a cautious whisper.

"Who is it?"

"I wish to speak to Herr Gelder. Hugo Gelder."

"Who is it?"

"Kurt Reiss. He knows me. He was a friend of my father."

The door opened to the extent of the security chain, and a woman's face looked out at him. Her face was shadowed; he had only the impression of large, luminous dark eyes, glistening in the half-light.

"Kurt? Kurt Reiss?"

"Yes."

A long pause. "What do you want?"

"To see Herr Gelder."

"We have nothing, we can give you nothing." She tried to close the door, but he gripped it with his hand and held it fast.

"I don't want anything," he said. "Only to speak to Herr Gelder for a few minutes."

"What about?"

"It is a private matter."

"I am his daughter. You can tell me what it is."

"His daughter? Emmy?"

Another pause. "Yes. I am Emmy."

"I'm sorry. It's dark, I didn't recognize—" The apology sounded foolish, incongruous, and he stopped. "Emmy, you must remember me. We met often, at your house, our house. Kurt! Kurt Reiss!"

"Kurt Reiss was killed in Spain."

"I was wounded, that's all."

"He had dark hair."

"It is dyed. Emmy, I have to see your father!"

"Go away! We can't help you, we have enough trouble! Don't you know there is a curfew for Jews in this area? If the Gestapo find you on the street, if they saw you here in this doorway—" She checked, stared at him for a moment and then quickly released the chain. "Come in, quickly. Quick, quick!"

He stepped into the narrow dimly lit passage, and she closed the door, refastening the chain and sliding home a bolt. A dank smell hung in the air, the dark brown paper was peeling away from the walls revealing patches of damp.

She peered at him for a moment. "You've changed. Not just the hair ... "

"Haven't we all?"

In the weak light from the unshaded bulb, she

looked thin and shapeless; her short hair was lank and untidy, her dark eyes seemed too big for her sallow face. In daylight, he thought, in daylight, I would have passed her on the street, I would not have recognized her.

As if she had read his mind, she stroked the hair back from her forehead, and said in a softer tone: "I'm sorry if I—" She made an ineffectual gesture with her hands. "We have to be careful."

"Of course, I understand."

"Kurt! Kurt Reiss! Is it really you?" She held out her hands, and her laughing smile reminded him for the first time of the Emmy he had known four or five years before. Well, he hadn't really known her, she had been a figure scampering through the background, a laughing schoolgirl who seemed never to be serious, never to grow up. She must have been fifteen then, he thought, and now—oh, God, she looks thirty-five!

"It's really me," he said, trying to return her smile.

"Are they . . . are they after you?" she whispered. A door creaked in the passage, and a gaunt face peered out cautiously, curiously, dark eyes flickering from left to right.

"This way," said Emmy quickly. She took Kurt's hand and led him up the rickety stairs to a front room on the first floor.

It was a small room with a sagging ceiling, and Kurt's first impression was of clutter. In an alcove to one side there was a single bed covered with a worn dark blue blanket; near this stood an old sewing machine, some unfinished work still under the needle, and beside this, a large cardboard box half filled with garments that looked like work shirts. The other part of the room contained a dresser, a table, two wooden chairs, and a depressed-looking armchair. It would have been all too much even for a larger room, but he saw, at second glance, that it was clean and ordered; moreover, the bright checkered cloth on the table, the arrangement of evergreen twigs in a vase on the shelf suggested that whatever else had gone, there was still some pride left.

"Sit down, please." She removed the half-finished shirt from the machine, dropped it in the box, and slid this under the bed. "I'm sorry, we don't have visitors these days...."

"It's fine," he said. He sat down on one of the wooden chairs by the table.

"We have some coffee. Would you like some coffee?" She smiled shyly, like a young housewife entertaining for the first time and anxious to please.

"No, thanks. I have only a few minutes."

"Are—are they after you?"

"It's a long story," he said. He caught the quick familiar gleam of fear in her eyes and added, "Look, you're in no danger. I mean, I haven't put you in danger by coming here. I wouldn't do that."

"How can you be so sure?"

"You have nothing to worry about." But as he spoke, he too wondered how he could be so certain.

The Major and the SS officer were waiting for him in the big black car on the corner of the street. How was it possible to trust such people? What was to prevent them picking up Emmy Gelder and her parents after he'd left? On the other hand, if he tried to make a dash for it, to escape into the nearby rabbit warren of streets and alleys, that would guarantee a visit from the SS and the arrest of the Gelder family. He'd been a fool to come—it was unfair to them, criminally unfair; yet he had been driven to it by desperation. He had to make a terrible decision, and he could not make it alone.

"Why do you want to see my father?" She searched his face with her eyes, and the look of fear had given way to one of suspicion.

"I need his help."

"He has done enough. He has no more to give."

"Advice. I meant advice. That's all."

She hesitated for a moment and then dropped into a chair across the table from him. "He is not the man you knew."

"No one is the same," he said, and regretted the words at once. They sounded too pat, too easy.

"He was in Buchenwald for two years. Up to two months ago. I bought him out. I gave the house, the furniture, the workshop, my father's tools to an SS official in exchange for his freedom. If that's the word for—for this." She indicated the room with a tired gesture of the hand. "That's why we're living here—" She checked suddenly then went on sharply: "How did you know where to find us?"

"I heard you'd moved."

She searched his face again. In a flat voice, she continued: "My mother is in Prague. She was Czech, they made her go back. I haven't heard from her for almost a year."

"Your sister—you had a sister, didn't you?"

"She got false papers—don't ask me how—took an Aryan name. I don't know where she is. She went over to them—we call it crossing the lake. In a way, I don't blame her. That's what it's all about, isn't that so? Survival." She sighed. "So, you see how it is with us. No better, no worse than for thousands of others. We rub along. The worst problem is not knowing when the next blow will fall or where."

He nodded. There was no way he could console her, and words of sympathy would not help either. At least, she had a father left.

"And you?"

"After Spain, after I was wounded, I got to England."

"England!" Her eyes widened in astonishment. "You were in England and you came back here! Why? Why?"

"It was necessary."

"Are you mad?"

"Sometimes, yes, I think so."

She stood up, her chair scraping on the wooden floor. Her voice was a whisper. "Go away! Leave us! I don't want to know what you are doing; I don't want you to involve my father. I told you, he has given enough. Leave us alone, please, please."

She was on the verge of tears, her lips trembling. He reached out and gripped her arm. "It isn't like that, Emmy, it isn't what you think." And it was in his mind then to tell her that he might be able to help them both, but he held back the thought. It was too soon to speak of such a thing: to raise her hopes would be an outrageous act of cruelty. Instead, he said, "I have to come to a decision. I need to speak to your father. Just for a minute or so. Emmy—I have to talk to someone."

"You have to make a decision? About what?"

"Someone has ... someone has put a certain ... " He hesitated, trying to find the right word. "A certain proposal. A sort of bargain. And I don't know what to do."

2

It had happened on the sixth day after Kurt's capture.

Rain, heavy and incessant, beat at the windows and hammered on the roof. Although it was still early afternoon, the heavy gold curtains were drawn and the lamps were on, dividing the library of the chateau into pools of mellow light. When the Reichsmarschall leaned back from the desk and lifted his head, his face, normally as white as lard, seemed to have taken on the color of saffron.

A high-ranking SS officer, wearing the Sicherheitsdienst insignia of the Security Service on his sleeve, stood at ease beside the Reichsmarschall. He was a short, well-muscled man, built like a bull, with strong features and eyebrows that bristled fiercely. His eyes seldom left Kurt, and in them there seemed to be only one expression—contempt. Kurt faced the desk with the Major behind him.

"Well, what do you think of him, Herr Brigadeführer?" asked the Reichsmarschall.

The SS officer smiled and sniffed the air. "He has the look and the smell of a Jew, Your Excellency."

"Don't say that!" said the Reichsmarschall in a pained voice. "I had him specially scrubbed down for this meeting."

"You can't scrub away that sort of stink. I can smell it a mile away."

"Careful," warned the Reichsmarschall, "this one bites."

"Does he? I like the ones who do that. They make the job more interesting." The officer grinned and cracked the knuckles of his left hand. The grin vanished as he caught a look from Kurt. "Don't look at me, Jew! Keep your eyes down. Down, do you hear!"

As Kurt continued to stare at him, he took a threatening step forward. The Reichsmarschall put up a casual restraining hand. "Easy, easy, Herr Brigadeführer. This one is mine." He chuckled as the officer stepped back, then suddenly changing his mood, he said sharply: "God, do all you people in the SD have one-track minds! You are not here to beat up Jews, man! You are here as a liaison officer on a project of the highest importance, a project that the Führer and I discussed yesterday and to which he has given his full approval. You will remember that. If you're not happy with your position, you can go back to Himmler and ask him to send someone else. Do I make myself clear?"

"Of course, Your Excellency. I am honored to have been selected by the Reichsführer and to serve you."

"Good." Again the tone changed, and he continued

affably: "Don't worry, you may still have him in the end. Herr Reiss might refuse our proposition after all."

Kurt heard his name sound in his ears like a small echo. Ever since the mock execution, he had felt more than ever as if he were, in some way, two people. There was the physical Kurt, the body that went through the motions of living, and another Kurt who seemed not to inhabit his flesh but to be watching the other self from a distance. These two selves had been in the room from the beginning, the one standing before the desk and the other, so to speak, in some other spot, looking on, listening but not really hearing, like a disinterested spectator at a dull play. Now, at the mention of his name, the second half sprang to the alert, as though realizing that he, too, was part of the action.

"Tell me, Herr Reiss," said the Reichsmarschall with exaggerated politeness, "tell me, do you think of yourself as a German?"

"I did once," Kurt replied quietly.

"Not anymore?"

"No."

"As what then?"

"As a Jew."

"Good. That is a beginning. You understand, then, the position of the Jews in Germany today?"

"The Jews have no position in Germany today."

"Good again. Well put. So let us come directly to the point. When we first talked you said—let me get it right—you said that the only people who could help the Jews were the Jews themselves. Correct?"

"Yes."

"Do you still believe that?"

"Yes."

"Would you help them if you were in a position to do so?"

Kurt could only stare at them in bewilderment. He

had the feeling that he was walking through a long black tunnel that was filled with strange echoes and to which there was no ending.

"Let me repeat the question. Would you—you personally—help the Jews if you were in a position to do so?" The Reichsmarschall leaned forward. For a moment or two, the only sound was the monotonous drumming of the rain.

"Why do you ask such a question?" said Kurt. The words seemed to crackle in his throat. "If you wish to torment me—"

"If we wished to torment you, we have better ways," said the Reichsmarschall. He cut short the Brigadeführer's incipient chortle with an angry, impatient movement of the hand. "Answer the question. Would you be willing to help your people?"

Again, Kurt seemed unable to tear his eyes away from the face that swum before him, half in light, half in shadow. The thoughts were still tumbling around in the tunnel of his mind, but there was a little light now, and he said at last: "Since it is you that asks the question, I can only reply by asking one in return. What is the price?"

"Your life, perhaps?"

"That isn't worth much."

"True. But if I make you a present of it? If I give it back to you?"

"Why would you do that?"

"We are going round in circles. I ask you once again, would you be willing to help your people?"

"Yes."

"Ah." The Reichsmarschall sat back with a sigh. "A straight answer at last." He drummed his fingers on the desk as though gathering his thoughts for the next assault.

"Listen," he said, "this is the proposal. You will undertake a mission for us. A mission of some danger, but you will have, perhaps, a fifty-fifty chance of survival. If you survive you will not only have your life but your freedom also. Do you understand?"

"A mission—for you?" Kurt could feel the blood burning in his cheeks, and a sense of humiliation overwhelmed him. Nothing they had said to him up to this point, not one of their insults, had touched him. But this had gone into him like a dagger thrust. Did they really think he could be bought?

"Wait," said the Reichsmarschall mildly. "Wait. I haven't finished yet."

"I don't want to listen!" Kurt's voice trembled, and to add to his shame, he felt tears prick at his eyelids. At this moment, when he ought to be strong, defiant, scornful!

The Brigadeführer moved restlessly. "Let me have him for ten minutes. I'll make him listen!"

"Shut up! Shut up!" The Reichsmarschall's voice exploded with anger, and the SS man stiffened into silence. Turning back to Kurt, the Reichsmarschall continued in a more reasonable tone. "Listen. I am not a fool. I know enough of you to understand that you cannot be bought. You are not the man to make a bargain with us for your own life. But suppose I offered you ten thousand lives in exchange?"

"Ten thou—" The Brigadeführer bit back the interruption.

"Ten thousand Jewish lives," said the Reichsmarschall slowly, weighing each word. "If you undertake this mission and carry it through to success, I will give you the lives of ten thousand Jews."

3

Hugo Gelder sat in the worn armchair listening hard, trying to follow what the young man was saying, but there was this mist in his mind in which his thoughts were forever getting lost and kept wandering down the wrong road. He wondered about the twigs in the vase, about the hole in his slipper, about the damp patch on the ceiling, which, if you looked at it in certain ways, seemed just like a map of Australia. And because of this, he thought about his brother in Melbourne, and then his sister in Budapest, and what had happened to the dollhouse he had once made for her, the dollhouse that had three floors and a roof that opened. . . .

From time to time he looked down to his lap at the hands that he did not recognize as his own and that never stopped trembling. He found that he could hold one with the other, but then they trembled and shook together, dancing gently on his legs.

"Papa, listen, this is important." When Emmy spoke like this he sat up and looked at the young man with a stern, serious expression to indicate that he was taking in every word, but after a little while his mind slipped away again, his eyes went to the patch on the ceiling, and he wondered once more about his brother and the dollhouse and a dozen other things.

Kurt continued, out of respect, but eventually he turned to Emmy and said softly: "I don't think—"

"I did warn you," she said. Standing up, she took her father's arm and raised him from the chair. "Come along, papa, you're tired. Back to bed."

As she touched his arm, Kurt saw the old man pull away at first and look up fearfully: then, seeing it was Emmy, he got up with a smile of relief. Old man? Kurt shook his head at the thought. Gelder was fifty-one, the same age as his own father would have been had he. . . .

Yet the man was old; the juice of life, which had once coursed so energetically through his veins, had been sucked out of him. In the old days—strange how his mind kept going back to the old days—Gelder had been a fierce and vibrant man, a keen Zionist and a leading, if tempermental, member of the Jewish community. He was at his happiest in an argument; Kurt's father would debate politics and religion with him for hours on end, and Gelder's voice would rock the house. But underneath the explosive exterior there lay a kind, warm, and gentle heart.

Gelder was a carpenter, and sometimes Kurt would be allowed to visit the tiny workshop where he kept his tools with loving care and made simple, beautiful furniture. Once he flew into a rage when he found Kurt using a chisel as a screwdriver, and he had lectured the boy on the sanctity of the craftsman's tools. And as Kurt remembered, the clean fresh scent of newly planed pine came floating back to him. . . .

He heard Emmy's voice. "Say goodnight to Kurt, papa."

"Goodnight, young man," her father said with grave politeness. "Most interesting, most interesting." And as she led him into the other room he continued to mutter: "Interesting, most interesting."

When she came back, Kurt was standing up. "I'm sorry," he said, and moved toward the door.

"He's only been home a few weeks," she said. "He's getting better all the time. Every day there's an improvement."

"I didn't know. I didn't realize," he said. "I thought—"

"That he would help you with your moral dilemma?"

He gave her a quick angry glance, resenting the note of sarcasm in her voice. "It wasn't easy for me to come here; I told them—I had to argue—that I couldn't make the decision alone. I thought of your father because—because I respect his judgment."

"Wait." She touched his arm, her voice softening. "I will tell you what my father would have said, if he had been himself. He would have said, 'Do as they ask.' Do it!"

"Work for *them*? How can they be trusted? How do I know that they will keep their side of the bargain?"

"Listen. Sit down." And as he hesitated, she pleaded: "Please. Look, I speak as my father would have spoken. First, whatever they want, it must be important, isn't that so?"

"Important. And evil."

"Yes. You are probably right. Nevertheless, good can sometimes come from evil. And God looks first at a man's heart, then at his mind. Isn't that what they say? He will know what is in your heart." He made a small impatient gesture. "All right. Sorry. Forget God. But listen. They captured you eight days ago, correct?"

"Yes."

"Then why aren't you dead? Why aren't you in Buchenwald or Dachau? Because they need you alive. Why did they allow you to come here to consult my father? Because they need you. They *need* you, Kurt. And they are prepared to pay for your cooperation."

"It's monstrous . . . to use people . . . like counters on a board, like slaves."

"Everything about our lives is monstrous. We live in a monstrous society, ruled by monsters. They wish to destroy us. Our only answer to that is what I said before—survival. If you can help ten thousand Jews to survive—a thousand, a hundred, even ten—you will be winning a small victory." She shook her head. "I wish I had the chance! I would not hesitate for a moment."

"I don't know, I don't know." He shook his head unhappily.

"Who will help us if we don't help ourselves?" she

said bitterly. "Do you see a queue of good Germans at the door, holding out their hands to us? And the English, the Americans, what are they doing, apart from passing resolutions of protest?"

"Isn't that the point?" he asked. "Even if I accepted their—their Nazi bargain, and even if they kept their word, who would take ten thousand Jews? Where would they go?"

"If the Jews were free to leave, if they had exit visas, the world would have to take them, don't you see? They would be shamed into taking them, forced to live up to their pious resolutions."

"I wish I could believe that, Emmy."

"Tomorrow," she said, "tomorrow I'll see the Jewish Council. They must approach England, America, other countries. Go to the embassies. Go on their hands and knees if necessary."

"We've had enough of that!" he said sharply. "Enough of crawling on our knees!"

"Wait!" she said suddenly, eagerly, as an idea came to her. "I have it! Suppose, suppose the ten thousand were children?"

"Children?"

"Yes! Yes, that's it." She clapped her hands together in excitement. "How could they refuse to take our children, how could anyone refuse them?"

He looked at her thoughtfully. "Children," he murmured, half to himself. "Children. Would their parents let them go?"

"Let them leave this—this prison? You can't be serious. Besides, there are many who have no parents."

"If it were possible—" he said.

"Make it possible!" She took his hand, her eyes shining. "Make it possible."

"I don't even know what it is they want me to do," he said.

"Does it matter? Whatever they want, it must be

worth ten thousand children, isn't that right?"

"Yes." He nodded, feeling some of her enthusiasm warm his blood.

From below there came an urgent, heavy hammering on the door. "It's for me," he said. "I've been too long."

"You will do it?" she said.

"I will think about it. You've helped, Emmy, it's been good to talk."

"You will let me know?"

"Soon. Tomorrow perhaps." He moved to the door. "Go and speak to the council anyway. It can't hurt. But they must not know the background; you must not mention me or any sort of bargain. Say—say simply that you have heard through a friend of your father that the Nazis might—might—just possibly allow a number of children to leave."

"I'll find a way," she said.

The hammering at the front door was renewed with greater force. "If I don't go," he said, "they'll break in." They embraced impulsively and kissed cheeks.

At the top of the stairs, her mind racing, she said softly: "Kurt. I've remembered something my father used to tell us—about making a deal."

"What?"

"He used to say, 'if you want to make a deal with someone you don't trust, always ask him for a deposit, something on account.' "

When he reached the door, he looked back at her. She was standing on the top stair; she waved a hand to him and called in a whisper: "Shalom."

The Major was waiting outside. "One more minute," he said, "and I was coming in to get you."

Kurt ignored him, saying nothing as they walked up the street to the car. The Brigadeführer, seated in the back, scowled at him, but he ignored that also.

Beyond the Jewish quarter, the Berlin streets were

bright with light, the shops decorated for Christmas, the cafés and bars crowded with people. It was another world, but Kurt scarcely noticed it.

He was thinking about the remark Emmy had made at the top of the stairs, and he was still thinking about it when, to his surprise, they arrived at the Air Ministry building.

4

Kurt was led up the wide stairway to the first floor and taken into a small anteroom, where two secretaries were at work. One of them lifted her head and smiled.

"Ah. Go through, Major. The Reichsmarschall is expecting you." She gave Kurt a look that was half curious, half hostile.

The Reichsmarschall was standing by a large wall map as they entered, and it was at once obvious that this was not one of his more affable evenings. He swung round impatiently as the two officers clicked to attention, made a perfunctory response, and then, without moving from his position on the other side of the large room, he snapped out a single word.

"Well?"

"I beg to report, Herr Reichsmarschall, that—" began the Brigadeführer, but he was cut short.

"Keep your trap shut! When I want you to speak, I'll tell you." He strode across the wide carpet and planted himself in front of Kurt, glowering at him. "You. No more games. I've been patient enough. What have you decided?"

"I will do what you ask," Kurt said.

"Thank you," said the Reichsmarschall dryly. "Thank you so much."

"There are two conditions," Kurt continued.

"Oh? And what may they be, my Jewish friend?" There was a dangerous edge to the voice, and hearing it, the Major stiffened.

"First, as to the ten thousand Jews you have agreed to release—they must be children between the ages of five and sixteen." Kurt spoke quietly, nervously.

"Children. Interesting. I can see how your mind has been working. You want to preserve the stock, is that it? So that you can pollute the earth with new generations of Jews! And your next condition?"

"I want you to release five hundred children at once."

"At once?"

"Within the next week or month—before I carry out the mission."

"I see. Why may I ask?"

"As an assurance of your good faith in this matter."

"You mean you want a little on account, is that it?" Kurt nodded, thinking how odd it was that this man should use almost the same words as Emmy. "Five percent of the price in advance," continued the Reichsmarschall. "Well, you're a Jew, I should have expected it. And if I comply, what guarantee have I that you will perform your part of the bargain?"

"You have my promise."

"Your promise! Your promise!" The Reichsmarschall exploded into anger. His arm went up, and he hit Kurt across the face with the back of his hand, using all his force. One of his rings dug into the cheek, bringing a trickle of blood.

The Reichsmarschall's red lips glistened with moisture as his voice rose to a scream: "I am expected to take the promise of Jewish scum like you, but my word—the word of a Reichsmarschall—my word isn't good enough! You want an assurance of my good faith. Right, you shall have it!" He turned on the SS officer.

"Take him, Herr Brigadeführer! He's all yours! There will be no deal, no assurances. I've lost interest. Take him, I said, take him!"

"Yes, Herr Reichsmarschall." The flustered Brigadeführer grabbed Kurt and bundled him from the room.

"Did you hear him, did you hear that Jew! Questioning my word! Offering me his promises!" The Reichsmarschall raged on for a moment, and then, quite suddenly and in characteristic fashion, his mood veered round again. Perhaps it was because of what he read in the Major's eyes, for he grinned in the sheepish manner of a schoolboy who had been caught out in some offense.

"I suppose you have to hand it to the cheeky bastard," he said. He pushed the Major aside and hurried from the room.

Kurt and the Brigadeführer were halfway down the stairs. "I've been waiting for this," said the SS man. "I've been waiting for you to fall into my lap. And while we're about it, we'll pick up those Jew friends you paid a call on. Have a nice little Christmas party!"

It had all happened so quickly, so unexpectedly that Kurt's mind was still half numb with shock. It had all been a dream, a stupid dream! And he had, after all, put Emmy and her father into real danger.

They had reached the bottom of the stairs now, and as they turned toward the street, the realization of his own plight stabbed him like a spear. This was his last chance to make a break. Once they got him to Gestapo HQ on Prinz Albrechtstrasse he would be finished. If he could get free there might even be a chance to warn the Gelders.

"Hold it, hold it!" As he tensed himself the voice of the Reichsmarschall came roaring down from above, bouncing back off the walls. The sentries in the entrance hall went rigid; the Brigadeführer looked up in surprise then stiffened also, tightening his grip on Kurt's arm.

The Reichsmarschall leaned over the balustrade. "Major Keller will take charge of the prisoner, Herr Brigadeführer." He turned to the Major, who had appeared beside him. "Take him to the barracks at Luft-flotte One and lock him up. We don't want to make any hasty decisions, do we?"

It was as near as that.

SIX

1

Once more, time seemed to have come to a halt.

Kurt remained locked in the cell with its Luftwaffe-gray walls, and apart from the guards who brought him food and the same lukewarm gritty coffee twice each day, he saw no one except a doctor who removed the stitches from his wounds, and put on a new dressing. Even the Major seemed to have deserted him, and he was allowed no exercise. The cell was equipped with its own lavatory and hand basin, and each morning he washed both himself and the floor all over: it was good discipline, it was hygienic, and it was something to do.

He remembered how his mother, whenever she felt depressed or in an ill temper, would attack the house with soap, water, scrubbing brush, and broom, scouring and cleaning it from top to bottom. She claimed that the exercise always made her feel better, and, indeed, she usually ended up singing her favorite Strauss songs in her rather tuneless voice. But the daily washing of his cell brought him little comfort.

Almost two weeks passed in this sluggish fashion, and each day was worse than the last. He felt lost, desperate, forgotten. Why was the Reichsmarschall taking so long to reach a decision? Did the delay mean that he had rejected the terms? If he had, why were they still holding him, why hadn't he been handed over to the Gestapo? Above all, he was concerned about Emmy and her father. He had rashly told her that he would talk to her again in a day or so; but time was slipping by and he had made no contact. What would she be thinking? And was she safe?

So his thoughts veered between hope and despair, his spirits rose and fell. He made an effort to think of other things, to recite or sing half-remembered poems and songs, but he could not maintain the necessary concentration; inevitably his mind found its way back to the same well-beaten track.

The only break in this torpid routine came one evening when the guards brought his meal. Instead of the tin plate with its usual scrap of sausage or cheese and black bread, they brought in a tray from which there rose the teasing aroma of hot food. One guard set it down on the table, while the other dropped a pack of cigarettes and a box of matches on the bunk. Kurt looked from one face to the other in surprise, but they remained impassive.

As they went out, he asked: "What's this?"

"Orders from Major Keller," said one of the guards. There was a glint of amusement in his eyes.

For a moment Kurt was chilled by the thought that this unexpected bounty was a prelude to the firing squad or worse. Was it not the custom of all executioners to feed their victims a hearty breakfast or supper, to provide them with a last cigarette? But the idea did not take root: he no longer thought in terms of a personal future, one way or the other.

It was so long since he had eaten a hot meal, or a meal of any variety and taste, that for a moment or two he could only stare at the tray in wonder. From the larger of two dishes there rose the succulent smell of roast goose blended with the spiky scent of apple stuffing; alongside the helping of goose, there were two mounds, one of boiled potatoes and the other of red cabbage. On the smaller dish there lay a thick chunk of

Schwarzwalderkirschentorte, rich chocolate cake with cherries, topped with a blob of cream. There was an enamel mug filled with beer, a spoon, but no knife or fork.

In the past few weeks he had learned to live with a feeling of perpetual emptiness: hunger had ceased to worry him. But now, triggered by the sight and smell of food, his stomach churned and heaved, and the saliva drenched his mouth and throat.

He fell on the meal like a ravenous animal, tearing the goose apart with his hands, packing the pieces of pink flesh into his mouth along with spoonfuls of potato and cabbage. Little trickles of fatty juice oozed from between his lips and splashed onto the table, but he ignored them. For the next few minutes nothing else existed but what lay in front of him; he almost laughed with joy as he felt his body expand and glow with an unfamiliar warmth. A tiny warning voice told him to slow down, but temptation and appetite were too strong, and when the goose and vegetables had gone, he began at once on the chocolate cake and cream.

Suddenly he dropped the spoon as his body revolted against the rich, unfamiliar fare and a great swell of nausea rose from his guts. He clamped a hand to his mouth as it filled with bile, staggered to the lavatory, and was violently and wretchedly sick. He was pale and damp with sweat when he came back at last to the table and freshened his throat with a little of the beer. He lay back on the bunk filled with a sense of self-disgust and lit a cigarette, but its acrid taste turned his stomach over again, and he laid it aside. He rested for a few minutes; slowly his aching body settled down again and the nausea passed.

And then he remembered the newspaper. The battered tray on which they had brought his food was lined with newspaper, and in his haste to fill his stomach he had forgotten it! His appetite for news was almost as powerful as his physical hunger, and with eager hands he lifted the dishes and removed the precious sheets.

It was a complete, if crumpled and grease-stained, copy of the *Volkischer Beobachter*, and as far as he could tell, it was about a week old. Like all newspapers in Germany it was controlled and run by the Nazis, but it was something at least, better than nothing. Calculating from the date of the paper he suddenly realized the significance of the goose, the beer, the chocolate cake. It was Christmas Eve, and with typical sentimentality they had remembered their prisoner! He shook his head: how was it possible to understand such people? He relit the cigarette and settled back, determined not to make the same mistake as he had with the food: he would read slowly, take his time, make the words last. But all the anger, bitterness, hatred came surging back as he turned the pages. One of the leading articles reported a new speech by Hitler in which he called on the other European nations to eliminate their Jewish population. No German support would be given to any state that refused to follow this path. The article quoted the Führer as saying: "This vermin must be destroyed. The Jews are our sworn enemies, and at the end of the year there will not be a Jew left in Germany."

Another prominently placed report announced that the German government had imposed a fine of one billion marks on the Jewish community to pay the cost of the damage done on Crystal Night.

And in the overseas-news section it was mockingly reported, in item after item, that Britain was further restricting the entry of Jews into Palestine; that Roosevelt had turned down a proposal that the annual quota of Germans, including Jews, to be admitted to the United States, be increased; that anti-Jewish laws were to be enacted in Hungary and Rumania. It seemed to Kurt that the whole world had rejected his people, closed ranks against them!

And it was in that moment, as he crumpled the newspaper in disgust, that he heard the voices. The men in the mess hall across the yard had finished their dinner and were softly singing the traditional Christmas hymn.

Silent night, holy night.
All is calm, all is bright . . .

Kurt picked up the tray and hurled it with all his strength against the barred window, in the direction of the sound.

2

The truth was that the Reichsmarschall's plan had, to a certain extent, lost impetus. He was a man of impulse, and it was part of his nature to embrace an idea with enormous enthusiasm one day and to go cold on the next, and while he had not exactly abandoned Kurt, he had relegated him to the back of his mind while he concentrated on what he regarded as a more urgent matter.

Hjalmar Schacht, president of the Reichsbank, had composed a memorandum attacking "the reckless expenditures" of the Nazi government, which he maintained were driving the country "to the brink of ruin." He urged that there should be a cutback on military expenditure and that plans for the expansion of the Reichsmarschall's beloved Luftwaffe should be modified drastically.

It was a weighty document, made all the more

threatening by the fact that it had been signed not only by Schacht, but by all the other governors of the Reichsbank. Its specific references to the Luftwaffe had driven the Reichsmarschall into a fury, and for the past few days he had been fully occupied in drumming up opposition to the proposals.

He was able to celebrate New Year's Eve at the chateau in a more equable frame of mind, having heard from the Führer earlier that day that he intended to fire Schacht and replace him with someone who, in Nazi terms, had a less-conservative financial approach. No brake was to be put on the expansion of the Luftwaffe; indeed, production of both the fighter and bomber forces was to be greatly increased.

Delighted with this triumph, the Reichsmarschall greeted the guests at his New Year's Eve party in jovial mood. On this occasion he had invited only a few special friends, and there was none of the formality that had attended the previous party.

Shortly after midnight, when the conventional greetings had been exchanged and the appropriate toasts to the Führer, the Reich, and the future dispensed with, the Reichsmarschall performed an old Teutonic ceremony. A basin of water was placed on a table, and to the applause of the guests, an officer brought in a small ladle that contained molten lead.

"Now," said the Reichsmarschall with a smile, "let us see the shape of the future."

He took the ladle and poured the thick, bubbling liquid into the water. There was a sharp hiss, a burst of steam rose from the basin, and the lead solidified into an odd, irregular pattern. The Reichsmarschall studied this thoughtfully for a few moments.

"Hmph," he grunted, and turned to one of the women. "Come, Ilse, you're supposed to be the expert. Tell us what that means."

A plump woman with a pale, dramatic face and large eyes, hands glittering with rings, wrists jangling with bracelets, stepped forward and examined the basin. She looked up with a smile. "Oh, it's good. It's very good!"

"Don't keep us in suspense."

"Well," she said, "the old Teutonic knights believed that one could foretell the future from the pattern taken by the lead. Now, you see here, at this side, that the metal has formed into the shape of a spear. That means there will be war."

As they crowded round to stare down at the basin, the Reichsmarschall said: "War, eh? Well, one doesn't have to be a genius to see that on the horizon. The point is—how will it turn out for us?"

"Victory!" she crowed. "Complete victory! You can see, the spear is firm and unbroken." This statement was greeted with cheers and applause.

"What else?" asked the Reichsmarschall.

"You will enjoy a great personal triumph," she said. "See, here the lead has formed into a sort of star."

"I like it, I like it," chuckled the Reichsmarschall.

"It looks a bit like the Jewish star to me," muttered one of the guests tactlessly.

"Then it is possible that His Excellency's personal triumph may be connected with the Jewish problem," she said calmly.

"You're going to get rid of them for us, sir!" said one of the officers. "Time somebody did."

"That's Himmler's job," said the Reichsmarschall modestly, and added, with a mischievous smile, "Mustn't tread on the Reichsführer's toes, must we?" They laughed dutifully. But at that moment the Reichsmarschall remembered Kurt Reiss, the prisoner he was still holding at Luftflotte I, the man whom he had begun to think of as his own special Jew. He felt a surge of renewed interest in the plan that had excited him so much a few weeks earlier.

Later, he went into the library and made several telephone calls on the private, scrambled line. He spoke to the Führer at the Berghof in Berchtesgaden, to Rudolf Hess, and to the Generalobersts in command of the four main air fleets, conveying New Year greetings and discussing various problems of a political and military nature. As he finished these calls, and was about to rejoin his guests, the telephone rang. He picked up the receiver again to find Himmler on the line.

"A happy New Year," said the Reichsführer.

"And the same to you," replied the Reichsmarschall.

"How is it all going with you?"

"Fine. Couldn't be better."

"I hear that Schacht is on the way out."

He hears everything, thought the Reichsmarschall. Aloud, he said, "Not before time. He is a clerk, a bookkeeper. He has no character, no understanding of politics. All he knows are figures, balances."

"Quite so." A pause. "What about the other little project we discussed at Marienburg?"

"Project?"

"Concerning that Jew."

"Ah. It's in hand."

"You haven't abandoned the idea?"

"Naturally not."

"Excellent. You see, I have some rather interesting information that may have a bearing on our plans." *Our* plans, thought the Reichsmarschall. Already he is putting himself in a position to take credit for the operation. But again he made no comment.

"Following our conversation at Marienburg," Himmler continued, "I recalled Buttmann from Washington and Cuno from London. Both excellent men, as you know. I saw them both this morning. What Cuno had to tell me was of special importance. With respect, I think you should see him before you proceed any further."

"He's in Berlin?"

"Yes."

"I shall be coming back tomorrow afternoon. Ask him to be available in the evening."

"Excellent. Will you come here?"

"It isn't possible. Ask him to be at the Air Ministry at seven P.M."

"I will bring him myself."

"There is no need—"

"It will be my pleasure."

"That is very good of you, Heinrich," said the Reichsmarschall with a politeness he did not feel.

"And how is the Jew?" asked Himmler.

"We're looking after him. He's in good hands."

"I understand that he had the impudence to ask for an assurance of good faith on our part." A dry, cold chuckle came down the line.

"He has a well-developed sense of humor," said the Reichsmarschall.

"Do you intend to meet his so-called terms?"

"I'll decide that after I've spoken to you and Cuno. In any case, the man is a Jew: bargaining is second nature to him."

When the conversation had finished, the Reichsmarschall went to join his guests. Some of them were still studying the pattern of the lead, reading all manner of things into the tangled shape.

"Look!" said one of the women excitedly. "Look here. Isn't that the letter *R*?"

"I can't see it," said her husband, moving his head from one side to the other.

"You're blind! Look, it's in two pieces. The letter *R*— but it's broken by the point of the sword."

"You're right!" he exclaimed. He turned to the plump woman with the rings and bangles. "Well, what do you make of that? Is that an omen or not?"

"I think we should ask the Reichsmarschall," she said.

"You have only to read *Mein Kampf* to learn the answer to that one," said the Reichsmarschall. "*R* for Russia."

As they laughed and applauded, another name occurred to him but he did not mention it. The Star of David, the pointed sword, the broken letter *R*. He was not a superstitious man, but it was amusing and interesting that his own projections for the future should be confirmed in this bizarre fashion.

Perhaps there was something in it after all.

3

At about this time, the Major was sleeping with his mistress in her apartment at Wriezen, a few miles northeast of Berlin. To be exact, he was asleep and she was lying awake by his side, watching the slow measured movements of his chest, studying his face with a mixture of tenderness and bewilderment. It was always like this after they had made love.

She loved him, she was in no doubt about that, but he disconcerted her. They had been together for almost a year, seeing each other whenever he could get away, yet there were times when she felt she hardly knew him at all. He was a paradox. Naked he was a gentle and tender lover, oddly childlike and innocent in his delight of her body, so that at such moments her heart overflowed with a warmth and love that was almost maternal; but in his clothes, in his uniform, he became another person—stern, awkward, reticent.

When they talked it was of trivialities, everyday things. He never mentioned the Reichsmarschall or his work, never expressed an opinion one way or another on what was happening in the world. All their conversations were skin-deep, and when she touched on other more serious matters, he would turn her remarks aside, divert them to some lighter topic. Yet she knew with absolute certainty that he was not a superficial man. He did not treat her in this way because she was a woman whose proper place was in the kitchen or in bed and nowhere else. No, she was sure that for some reason he was afraid to show his real self, that from within the invisible armor a man unknown to her watched the world with cautious eyes.

He stirred and woke and, after a moment, smiled at her.

"What are you doing?"

"Looking at you."

"Well?"

"I've decided that you are quite handsome in a rugged, craggy sort of way."

"Thank you."

"Would you like some coffee, a cognac?"

"Nothing, thank you."

She settled back, resting her head on her hands and sighed. "The New Year. What will it bring?"

"God knows." He had a sudden mental vision of Kurt Reiss with a black coal sack over his head, running in furious circles, trying to attack his tormentors.

"Do you ever feel guilty, ashamed?"

"Why do you ask?" Had she read his thoughts?

"Because that is how I feel a lot of the time."

"About us?"

"No, no. About that least of all. I meant—about other things, all that is happening."

"You shouldn't worry about it, Leni."

But this time she refused to be turned aside. "A week ago they took away Mr. Engelhardt from the flat below. The day before Christmas. He isn't a Jew or anything. They just carted him off, and his wife doesn't know where he is."

"They must have had a reason."

"Years ago he was a Social Democrat, one of their local councillors. That's the only reason Mrs. Engelhardt could think of."

"That's all they need. One has to accept such things."

"Why?"

"Oh, Leni . . ." He sighed.

"No, I mean it. Suppose he has done something wrong—though I find that hard to believe. Isn't he entitled to a proper trial? And his wife—surely she is entitled to know where he is, to see him?"

"Leni, I know nothing of politics."

"This isn't politics! Why do you say that? I'm not political either, come to that. But I am speaking about people, good people. Mr. Engelhardt never hurt anyone in his life. Why should he be made to suffer in this terrible way? Surely he has some rights?"

"Perhaps." He sighed again.

"Perhaps?" she said angrily. "Is that all you can say?"

"I'm in the Luftwaffe," he said stubbornly. "I know about flying and airplanes, that's all."

"But you must have an opinion!"

"No," he said, "no opinions."

"I don't believe it. I can't believe it." She turned on her side and, propping herself up on an elbow, looked down at him. "Answer me a direct question. Do you agree with what they have done to Mr. Engelhardt?"

He considered this for a moment, twisting a lock of her blonde hair in his fingers. "No," he said at last.

"But on the other hand I am not surprised. There is the difference between us." Once again, and for no reason that he could understand, the picture of Kurt with the sack over his head flashed into his mind.

She was quick to read the pain in his eyes and pressed her lips against his hand. "Is there nothing one can do?" she murmured. "Nothing?"

"When you are caught in a storm, the only thing to do is to keep your head down and wait for it to pass." He pressed a finger against her cheek, and his voice took on a firmer, warning note. "I mean that, Leni. Be careful. Watch what you say. Don't get involved. Keep your head down." He smiled. "You're all I've got."

"Couldn't you—couldn't you speak to the Reichsmarschall about Mr. Engelhardt?"

"And say what?"

"That it was a mistake, that he isn't an enemy or anything like that. He's only one man; he's not young anymore. One old man can't be important to them."

"You're an innocent. Shall I tell you something about the Reichsmarschall? Some time ago he slept with a certain woman. Her name doesn't matter, but she is married to a high party official, a deputy gauleiter. The Reichsmarschall shamed the man openly; he took the wife away from under his nose simply because he wanted her. To be truthful, she wasn't unwilling. They spent half the night together. Then a few days later he somehow discovered that she was part Jewish. That's not all. To protect her and himself, the husband had destroyed certain documents and falsified others. The Reichsmarschall ordered their immediate arrest. She was bundled off to a camp, and the husband is in a civil prison, charged with forgery and conspiracy. And I am speaking of a man who was a loyal party servant. One of his friends, also a senior party official, came to the chateau to appeal on his behalf. The Reichsmarschall simply laughed in his face, told him to get out or he'd have him thrown in jail also."

It was almost the first time that he had spoken to her at such length and so seriously. "What are you trying to say—that he is incapable of pity?" she asked.

"I don't know," he said. "I think he might pity an injured dog or a chamois. But as for the rest . . . "

"How can you bear to work with such a man?"

"I have no choice. It's a job. And in some ways he is a brilliant person. Fascinating." He paused as his thoughts drifted off, then added: "I want to get back to flying. That's what I know. And it's a different world, different people." It suddenly occurred to him that he had said too much, and he went on quickly: "What I've told you about the Reichsmarschall is confidential. Don't speak of it to anyone."

She drew back a little, and the hurt showed in her voice. "Has it come to this, then—that you can't even trust me?"

"I didn't mean it like that, Leni." He pulled her to him.

"It's true, though, isn't it?" she whispered. "It's getting so that one is afraid to speak."

"I'll have that coffee and cognac now," he said.

"You will not," she said, and pushing herself up, she straddled his body.

"You're insatiable," he said happily.

"And a happy New Year to you too," she said.

Afterward, as they sipped cognac together, he said: "What I will do is try and find out where they have taken Mr. Engelhardt."

She did not seem to be listening. "Did you mean it," she asked, "did you mean it when you said that I was all you've got?"

"You and the Luftwaffe," he said. "I've nothing else."

4

What the Reichsmarschall heard from Himmler and his British agent, Cuno, rekindled all his enthusiasm for the project. As soon as the two SS men had gone, he gave instructions that Kurt should be brought before him immediately.

"Right," he said briskly. "We've wasted enough time on this matter. First, as to your request that five hundred Jews should be granted immediate exit visas. I tell you straightaway, that is impossible."

"But—" began Kurt.

"Wait!" The Reichsmarschall cut him off. "However, as a humanitarian gesture, we are prepared to allow not more than one hundred to leave. Whether they are children or not is immaterial. And it must be arranged within seven days. Each person will be allowed to take one case containing personal possessions and a sum not exceeding two hundred marks. I warn you, there will be no further bargaining on this matter. One hundred. Take it or leave it. What is your answer?"

Kurt looked into the big, bland face, his mind racing. How much further could he press it? Dare he take the risk of losing all? He remembered Emmy's words: "something on account." They had offered less, far less than he'd hoped for, but at least something had been conceded. And it meant that the Reichsmarschall was still serious about this mysterious mission, and that could mean safety for another ten thousand people.

"I accept," he said quietly.

"Good. Now we can proceed to the next step. Within the next week you will recruit a team of three people. All Jews, young men. They will need to be tough and dedicated, ready to operate under your command. Arrangements will be made for the entire group, including yourself, to receive special training. When that has been completed to our satisfaction—and yours—you will receive further instructions. Is that understood?"

Beyond the window behind the Reichsmarschall, snow billowed gently down onto the city; the roofs were already layered with glittering white sheets, and the sounds from the street below were quiet, muffled. Watching it, trying to bring some order to his tangled thoughts, Kurt felt as if he were trapped in a dream, a nightmare from which there was no escape.

The Reichsmarschall, watching Kurt, clicked his fingers impatiently, and the Major stepped behind him and drew the curtains, closing off the room.

"Do you understand?" asked the Reichsmarschall tersely.

"Yes," said Kurt mechanically. "I think so. Three men, Jews. A squad. Yes."

The Reichsmarschall indicated the Brigadeführer of the SD, who as before was standing beside the desk, scowling at Kurt. "Choose the men you want. If there are any difficulties, consult the Brigadeführer."

"Why do you need other people? Why can't I carry out the operation alone?"

"Call it insurance," said the Reichsmarschall, smiling for the first time. "Any more questions?"

"Who is the target?" asked Kurt.

"What?" The Reichsmarschall stared at him in surprise.

"The target," said Kurt calmly. "You want someone killed, correct? Who is it?"

The Reichsmarschall slapped the desk and laughed openly. "I told you he was a bright one!" He shook his head. "We'll tell you what it's all about when we're good and ready, not before." He laughed again. "Do you know, if you weren't what you are, I could get to like you!"

"That makes me glad to be a Jew," said Kurt evenly.

The Reichsmarschall's eyes gleamed like ice, the muscles of his neck tightened. "Take him away," he snapped. "Get on with it, get on with it!"

The Major, who had been standing by the door, stepped forward and took the prisoner's arm. Kurt shook himself free. "There is one other thing," he said. The Reichsmarschall looked up sharply but did not reply. "If I am to recruit this team you speak of and make the other arrangements, I must have freedom of movement."

"For the next week, one week, you may come and go as you wish, within reason."

"I don't want an SS man at my elbow wherever I go." Kurt looked at the Brigadeführer. "Especially that one."

"Watch that tongue of yours, Jew, or I'll pull it out with my own hands!" snarled the Brigadeführer.

"Well, now," said the Reichsmarschall silkily, "you have presented us with a problem. If we let you move around freely, without an escort, what guarantee have we that you might not cut and run? Don't say you'll give me your word—that currency is counterfeit."

"You have offered to release ten thousand Jews if I carry through this mission. That is your guarantee."

"Perhaps. Perhaps." The Reichsmarschall paused, and then his voice quickened. "In ordinary circumstances, our normal practice would be to take your family into protective custody, simply as a precautionary measure, you understand. Hostages, if you like, though I don't much care for the term myself. Unfortunately, in your case, there is no family to fall back on."

"You should have thought of that before you murdered them," said Kurt bitterly.

"One can never foresee these things," said the Reichsmarschall reasonably. He spoke as if he were considering a chess problem, regretting a mistaken move earlier in the game. "However, we anticipated that this situation might arise, and we've done the best we could, in the circumstances. You will have your freedom of movement for one week. Without escort. You will, of course, report back to Luftflotte One and the Major each evening, and you will give him details of all your proposed movements in advance. Transport, a little money—all that will be arranged. As surety, the Brigadeführer has taken into custody your friends Fraulein Gelder and her father. Providing you behave yourself, they will be released unharmed as soon as you have recruited your team and are ready for training."

The room seemed to tilt sharply, and Kurt felt as if he were lurching with it, sliding down an invisible slope. He felt the Major's hand on his arm as he fought to keep his balance. The Reichsmarschall's face, the mocking face of the Brigadeführer swam before his eyes, each merging with the other for a moment and then floating off to continue its separate existence.

Slowly the sensation passed. The room settled itself; the floor beneath his feet became stable. He saw the Reichsmarschall's lips move and, straining to concentrate, he heard: "You have something further to say?"

"Yes." The word came out in a hoarse whisper, and as he repeated it his voice went to the other extreme and he shouted: "Yes!"

"Well?"

"The Gelders have done nothing—nothing! You have no right—" Even as he spoke he knew that such argument was useless, but he was fighting for time, searching his mind to find some way to counter this new threat. And all the time, a pulse of guilt and shame throbbed in his head; he was responsible; he and he alone had exposed Emmy and her father to this new danger.

"They have associated with a known criminal—

yourself," said the Reichsmarschall, as though surprised by Kurt's objections. The Brigadeführer nodded vigorous agreement. "But whether they have done anything or not is immaterial—you must see that, surely? The point is that they are your friends and I don't imagine that you would wish them to suffer because of any failure on your part. Correct?"

"I want to see them."

"The Reichsmarschall glanced at the SS man. "I imagine you can arrange that, Herr Brigadeführer?"

"If you think it necessary, Your Excellency."

"Arrange it." The Reichsmarschall waved a nonchalant hand. "It is of no consequence."

"And the Gelders will be allowed to leave within seven days, as part of the one hundred Jews who are to be given exit visas," said Kurt.

"Don't push your luck!" said the Brigadeführer viciously.

Kurt ignored him and looked directly at the Reichsmarschall. "You said you would release them in one week, when I have recruited this—this squad. When that happens, I want them to go with the others."

"A matter of conscience, is it?" asked the Reichsmarschall shrewdly. He opened his hands. "Very well. I am a reasonable man. It is agreed."

"In the meantime, they will not be harmed?"

"In the meantime, they will not be harmed!" The Reichsmarschall raised his voice. "Are you satisfied now? For God's sake, get the bastard out of here before he asks me for blood!"

Kurt turned away, the tension flooding from his body as relief took over. The feeling of guilt no longer hammered in his head, and he even felt a sense of elation. He had won a tiny victory in spite of everything, and the thought cheered him.

SEVEN

1

"Haven't you done enough?"

It was not so much a question as a statement, and it was accompanied by a look of such contempt and bitterness that Kurt flinched, as from a blow. They had brought Emmy up from the grim depths of the cells at Gestapo headquarters, and she now faced him across the wooden table in the detention room with its dark green walls and barred window.

He had rehearsed in his mind, over and over again, the things he would say to her, but now that the moment had come none of the words seemed adequate. She felt betrayed, she thought that he had betrayed her, and how could he make her think otherwise?

"It isn't like you think, Emmy," he muttered.

"No?" She wore a loose brown prison dress within which her body sagged and her thin shoulders drooped; in her face only the eyes had life and color.

He pulled a wooden chair across to her, the legs squeaking on the stone floor. "Sit down," he pleaded. She crossed her arms, hugging her body as if for comfort or support, and, without answering, moved toward the door.

"Your father will be here presently," he said.

"My father?" She turned back to him, her head tilted to one side in surprise.

"It's been arranged, I—I mean, it's been arranged that you are not to be harmed, you understand?" He blundered on quickly, desperate to hold her attention.

"It's hard to explain ... but what I told you the other night still stands. You ... it was you who gave me the idea. Do you remember? Ask for something on account, you said. That's what I did. They've agreed to release one hundred people providing it can be arranged in one week. Most of them to be children. That's why I had to see you."

"You said we were in no danger. I asked you to go away, not to trouble us. I begged you." She shivered and tightened the arms around her body. He saw the knuckles of her hands stand out, white under the pressure.

"They arrested you without my knowledge," he said. "You have to believe me." He saw the disbelief on her face and brought his fists down on the table in frustration. "Look, look, I'm sorry. I'm sorry. And I know that sounds stupid and it doesn't help. I shouldn't have involved you. But your father was the only one I could think of, the only one I could turn to. They've promised me—it's part of the deal—that neither of you will be harmed, that you'll be freed in a week, provided I fulfill certain conditions. Don't ask me what that promise is worth, because I don't know ... I don't know. All I do know is that they seem to want me badly enough to agree. If all goes well, you'll be out of here in a few days and you'll get exit visas. You and your father. What's more, if we can find a place, a country that will take a hundred people, you can be part of the group. That's all agreed. But I have only seven days to do it in, don't you see? That's all. Who can I go to? Did you speak to the Jewish Council? Tell me, Emmy, tell me! For God's sake—help me!"

The flood of words stopped at last. Her large dark eyes were blank, showing no feeling, and then her lips quivered and she suddenly sat down. He put a hand on her shoulder and she grasped it fiercely; her fingers were thin and hard, biting into his flesh.

The door opened and her father came in. He walked like a puppet, with small stiff steps, his eyes on the ground, and he stopped as though someone had jerked a string when the door slammed behind him. He did not lift his head until Emmy touched his arm, and eased him into a chair.

Without looking at Kurt, she said: "Go and see Mr. Zellner of the Jewish Council. Joseph Zellner. I spoke with him the day after I saw you. Perhaps he will be able to do something."

"Can I trust him, absolutely trust him?"

"You can trust him," she said, and this time she looked at Kurt directly. "I hope he can trust you."

2

Zellner was a small, brisk, keen-eyed man with a lean, melancholy face and an unprepossessing appearance. The truth of the matter was that he had once been very fat; however, the recent years of privation and persecution had seen to that, and now his clothes flapped around his bones like those of a scarecrow, and on his cheeks and neck, where there had once been generous folds of flesh, there was a pattern of deep lines.

The impression of melancholy vanished as soon as he opened his mouth to speak. By some miracle he managed to retain his sense of humor, and the eyes told Kurt that this man was, as yet, undefeated. He had already made the round of the various embassies, not once but many times, and he had at his fingertips the information Kurt needed.

"One hundred people, mainly children? That can be handled, I think. But the ten thousand to follow? More difficult. At the moment, we are working on a plan to get our people into Cuba. The regime there is corrupt, and entry visas may be bought—at a price. From Cuba it may be possible for them to get into the United States later."

"But how can the other countries refuse to take in our children? If we appealed to them—"

"It would do about as much good as bleeding a corpse. You want to know the truth? The truth is that they are bored by our constant appeals. We are a nuisance. They don't believe that things are as bad as we say, and they believe even less when we say they will get worse. That's the truth. We embarrass them by our cries for help, we remind them of something they'd rather forget—their consciences. But we will keep trying. Even quiet waters can wash down a cliff, isn't that what they say?"

They met again the next morning in the same little café in the Jewish quarter, and Zellner had some interesting news. "There is a Jewish orphanage just outside Wittenberg. They have a big old house there—beautiful. Too beautiful! The Nazis want to take it over for themselves, they've given us two weeks to get out."

"How many people?"

"Eighty children, sixteen staff. There is nowhere they can go. But I have seen the Swedish Red Cross and they are prepared to take them to Malmö, in Sweden. The Swedish government has agreed, and we are working like crazy on the arrangements. In two days, maybe three, they will be ready to leave.

"Then that's it," said Kurt. "Ninety-six in all. Plus the Gelders—ninety-eight people. You could nominate two other people to make up the hundred?"

"Can a fish swim?" said Zellner. "Can a bird fly?"

Kurt took a document from his pocket and handed it to Zellner. "Here is all the authorization you need. Signed by the Reichsmarschall and countersigned by Heydrich."

"For such signatures," said Zellner, "I could get a fortune." He studied the paper, shaking his head. "O, Lord," he whispered, "if you can spare a moment, glance down from heaven and take a look at your world! We have a paper like this and it makes us happy! I ask you, in all humility, is that reasonable?" He folded the document with great care and put it in his pocket."Not many, but it is something. One log won't make a fire maybe, but it helps, eh?"

"Can you arrange everything?" asked Kurt. "I have other things to do."

"Leave it with me," said Zellner, "leave it with me." He sucked his teeth thoughtfully. "Now, as to the other matter we discussed."

"Yes?"

"More difficult."

"To find three people who will help me to buy the freedom of ten thousand?" said Kurt angrily.

"I said difficult, not impossible. A tree can't be felled with one stroke. What did you expect—I should call a public meeting and ask for volunteers?"

"I mentioned some names—people who were in the defense group with me years ago—the Jüdische Schutzkorps. What about them?"

"You gave me five names. Two of them can't be traced. Disappeared. To our certain knowledge, two of the others have gone abroad. The fifth, Wolf Goldberg, is in Sachsenhausen."

"The camp?"

"What else? He was taken a year ago."

"Why?"

"Who needs a reason?" Zellner shrugged, lifting his shoulders inside the loose coat. "But I have to confess that in this instance, Goldberg committed a heinous crime. He refused to step into the gutter to make way for three Brownshirts. Can you imagine? A Jew refusing to give way?" He smiled, and more creases appeared on his lined face. "A foolish gesture. The action of a *meshugener!*"

"Maybe we need more of such foolishness!" said Kurt.

"That is also a point of view," said Zellner reasonably. "On the other hand, there are those who say, 'to endure, be obscure.' Who is to say which is right? You know Goldberg?"

"I knew him," said Kurt.

"I heard that he was a criminal, with a record. A gangster." Zellner spoke carefully, watching Kurt's eyes.

3

Kurt could even remember the smell of those days.

It was in March 1931. Winter still gripped Berlin in its relentless hands, as if determined not to give way to spring; day followed day without a break in the monotony of leaden skies and misty drizzling rain. The chill moisture seemed to have soaked into the skin of the city, down to its very bones, so that the streets, houses, and offices were filled with the rotting odor of dampness.

On one such morning, Wolf Goldberg came to the small overcrowded office of the Jewish defense organization, the Jüdische Schutzkorps. Kurt, Eva, and other members of the committee were gathered round the table discussing the events of the previous evening. There had been yet another clash with the Brownshirts, in which a Jew and a young member of the Reichsbanner had been killed and several others injured; one Nazi Stormtrooper had also died. This was the latest in a series of violent confrontations that had been inspired by Goebbels and deliberately provoked by the Nazis; Kurt was planning a massive march of protest to the civic authorities.

It was in the middle of the discussion that Wolf walked in. He didn't knock, he simply pushed open the door and stood glowering at Kurt and the others. He was a huge, stocky man, and in his presence the room seemed to shrink. Everything about him suggested that he had deliberately modeled himself on the image of a Hollywood gangster: the hat pulled down over the slow, deep-set eyes, the cigarette dangling from the full lips, the scar on his right cheek, which divided the blue swarthiness of the skin. It was so near caricature that Kurt was too amazed to laugh, and the feeling of parody continued when the man spoke, for this also was like a moment from one of the new talking pictures.

"Who's the boss here?" The voice was low and deep, the eyes moved carefully from face to face.

"What do you want?" asked Kurt.

"I told you, I want to see the boss. Are you the boss?"

"I'm the organizer," said Kurt.

The big man moved forward and stubbed out his cigarette in the tin lid that served as an ashtray. Kurt saw then that his hands were as big as bricks.

"Goldberg's the name, Wolf Goldberg." He seemed a little disappointed that there was no reaction to this. "You've heard of me, maybe?"

"No. I don't think I have," said Kurt. "Look, Mr. Goldberg, we are in the middle of a meeting—"

"What's the matter, you don't want to talk to me?"

"It's not that—"

"Listen, that boy who was killed last night. Do you know who he was? My nephew, that's who he was."

"Jakob Ekstein?"

"A good Jewish boy. A little crazy, maybe, but a fine boy, may he rest in peace."

"I'm sorry."

"Sorry? What's that? Sorry is worth as much as an

empty egg. Correct me if I'm wrong—you fight the Nazis?"

"We defend Jewish lives, property."

"But you fight the Nazis?"

"If they attack us—yes."

"You need money?"

"We can always use—"

The big man reached into the pockets of his raincoat and his jacket and dropped four wads of notes on the table. "There's four thousand marks. If you want more, just ask. I'll get it."

"That's marvelous!" Eva said. "Wonderful!"

Wolf looked at her. "You want more?"

"This will do for the present, Mr. Goldberg," said Kurt quickly. "Eva, make out a receipt."

"A receipt I don't want," said Wolf. "Do me a favor—if somebody asks, don't say where it came from."

"Where did it come from?" asked Kurt.

"You see, somebody's already asking! It came from my pockets. You were watching. Didn't you see?"

"Thank you very much," said Kurt tactfully.

"You're welcome. Use it well." He moved to the door, then turned to face them again. "Another thing. I got friends, a few friends, you understand? No offense, but they're not like you—they're professionals, real pro's. Next time there's trouble, let me know. We'll be glad to help."

That was how it began. Only later did Kurt learn that Wolf was indeed a sort of gangster, a man who had carved out a small underworld empire for himself and who had already served one prison sentence. In the days and weeks that followed they struck up a strange but firm friendship, and, though Kurt was wary of accepting further donations, there were many times when he was glad to have the big man battling at his side.

Slowly, too, the real character of the man emerged from beneath the mask: it was as if, lacking an identity of his own, he had assumed the outward trappings of the gangster, believing that this alone would win him respect and status. But gradually, as he became more and more involved with the work of the Jüdische Schutzkorps and saw that he was respected for his own sake, he relaxed and allowed his own more natural personality to take over. The caution went out of his eyes, and he began to smile, revealing an impish sense of humor.

There was still a side of his life that he kept hidden and about which Kurt asked no questions. It was enough for him that Wolf was content to serve and that toward the organization his attitude was one of scrupulous honesty and dedication. He seemed to have contacts everywhere, and was constantly coming up with inside information that Kurt was able to turn to good use; and he proved to be one of those extraordinary people who have the ability to fix almost anything. He would disappear for a few hours, and, on his return, the shortage, whatever its nature, would be filled. It was said of Wolf that if a rescue party went to look for him in the middle of the Sahara they would find him sitting under a palm tree with a stein of his favorite Einbecker beer in his hand and a girl at his side.

On political issues he showed a childlike eagerness to learn, though he remained naïve. He would plague Kurt with questions and then sit through the answers, his brow furrowed with the effort to follow the argument.

Once he said to Kurt: "Listen, I've got an idea. How many Jews in Germany?"

"About a half million."

"And how many anti-Nazis?"

"Millions."

"Then that's it! What we do is tell each man to kill one Nazi. Wouldn't that do the trick? No more Nazis, end of problem!"

"You're not serious!" But looking at him, Kurt saw that he was.

"Serious? Of course, I'm serious. We start with Hitler and work downward."

"That's not the answer, Wolf."

"No? Well, you're the one with the brains. But I tell you this, man. If we don't cut their throats, they'll cut ours, as sure as bagels have holes and sun blackens the gypsies."

4

And now Wolf was in Sachsenhausen concentration camp, and Kurt wondered if they had been able to break his spirit, as they had broken Hugo Gelder and Zochert and so many others.

The drift of his thoughts was checked as, through the window, he saw a car brake to a halt outside the café. Two boyish-looking SA men in brown uniforms got out, laughing together as they moved forward; in the same moment three people made a hurried exit through a rear door. The murmur of conversation ceased, and the remaining customers kept their eyes down over their coffee cups as the front door burst open and the Stormtroopers appeared in the entrance. The café owner, an elderly woman, came across to them, wiping her hands nervously. She took an envelope from her apron pocket and held it out.

The taller of the two snatched the envelope and shoved her aside. Both men looked around with studied arrogance, their eyes moving from table to table.

"Two more coffees, please," said Kurt clearly. He picked up a newspaper and began to read it, rustling the pages noisily. "And two pieces of cheesecake," he added, in a louder voice.

Heads went up and down again quickly, someone coughed, a cup rattled. Then a heavy stillness, which was more than a silence, in which the woman looked from Kurt to the SA men and back again, and wiped her hands yet again.

The tall Stormtrooper smiled, showing firm white teeth, and waggled a finger at Kurt. "You. Here. Come here," he said softly.

Kurt ignored him, his eyes on the newspaper. Another silence, which was broken by a long sigh, half sad, half fearful, from another part of the room.

"You—I'm talking to you!" The words grated between the teeth, heavy with menace.

Kurt lowered the newspaper in a slow, deliberate movement and looked at the SA man as though in surprise. "Me?"

"Come here!" But the SA man's voice held a note of bluster now. He had become accustomed to instant obedience and humility from these people, and this man's cool insolence was disconcerting.

Kurt folded the paper, pressed it flat, and laid it on the table. Zellner looked at him, his eyes pleading, but said nothing. Pushing back his chair, Kurt rose, took a small imitation-leather wallet from his pocket, and strolled toward the SA men. He flipped the wallet open and dangled a sheet of notepaper in front of them; they stiffened as they saw the distinctive crest and the bold signature, and the arrogance left their faces.

"What are you doing here?" said Kurt sharply.

"We came—well—to check on the Jews, to see if their papers were in order," stammered the taller man.

"And to collect a little protection money?" Kurt took

the envelope and opened the flap; it contained a small wad of marks.

"Donation to the local party funds," said the second man.

"Don't lie to me," said Kurt, lowering his voice. "Don't you think I know what goes on?" He tossed the envelope onto the counter. "That was for your own pockets, right?"

"You know how it is," said the tall one. "And they can afford it."

"Is that what you learned in the Hitler Youth? Didn't they teach you about National Socialist morality?" he asked dryly. "Leave this place alone in the future. It has been placed in Special Category Four as a protected business. Clear?"

"Yes, sir."

"Good. Now, piss off, pig scum, before I change my mind and report you to your gauleiter!"

"Heil Hitler!" They raised their hands in salute and hurried from the café. Kurt watched from the doorway as the car drove away, then went back to the table. Zellner saw that his hands were shaking. One by one the other customers got up, paid their bills and left, casting furtive looks in his direction.

"It's all right!" Kurt assured them as they passed. "No need to leave now. They won't be back." But they ignored him, and soon only Zellner and he remained.

"What did you expect?" said Zellner bitterly, "a round of applause? Listen, my friend, we have to live here. We haven't got a pass signed by the Reichsmarschall to protect our skins! Give me such a letter and I will be brave also, I will crow in their faces like a rooster. You haven't one to spare? What a pity! I shall have to survive the only way I know. I shall continue to lower my eyes, bend my neck, and press my lips together in silence."

"And if we don't survive? If they take even that from us?"

Zellner shrugged. "Every man knows he will die, but no man wants to believe it. As long as a man breathes, he should not lose hope."

"Hitler has said that by the end of the year there will not be a Jew left in Germany. 'The vermin must be destroyed'—that's what he said."

"I read the speech."

"If it came to that, would you fight? Or would you still lower your eyes?"

"How can I answer such a question? The future— who knows what it holds? For me the future is the present. And I do what I can."

Kurt thought again of that conversation with Wolf, all those years before. "Someone once told me that the only solution was to kill every Nazi. I said it was impossible."

"You were right."

"Perhaps. But I am not so sure now. I think, if I had the chance, I would do just that."

Zellner shook his head. "Then you are the same as the Nazis. You have the same taint."

"They made me that way."

"Has it occurred to you that perhaps all this may be necessary?" As Kurt opened his mouth to protest, Zellner held up a hand. "Wait, let me finish. Maybe this is necessary to purge the German people, to show them and the world the deep pit to which persecution and prejudice can lead. I believe that when it is over, finally over, the German people will look back in horror at these times, that they will resolve never again to take the same road. They will have a purer spirit."

"And we are to be the lambs led to slaughter, so that this may be achieved?"

"If that is the only way. It is written that as everyone

treads on dust, so does every nation tread on Israel; but dust lasts longer than metal, and so shall Israel survive."

"It is also written that the minced beef does not love the butcher."

"If we lose the power of forgiveness, we lose the best of our hearts. Why did Hitler grow strong? Because the victorious nations imposed a treaty of hatred at Versailles, they could not find the spirit of forgiveness. They nourished the soil from which the Nazis sprung. If you survive, my friend, remember that. Hatred is like a noose: it can hang your enemy, but in the end it will strangle you also."

"Perhaps," said Kurt. "But as far as I can see, hatred is all we have left."

5

To Kurt's astonishment and relief, Wolf Goldberg had hardly changed at all. He was thinner, of course, and the thick, curly black hair had been shaved to the skull; but he was still big enough to fill out the blue mechanic's overalls with which they had replaced the striped camp uniform, and lurking in his eyes there was the same impish humor.

He had been brought from Sachsenhausen to the barracks of Luftflotte I in Berlin at Kurt's specific request, despite some initial opposition from the Brigadeführer. As soon as they were alone he enveloped Kurt in a bear hug that showed that he had lost little of his strength; then he held him by the shoulders in those great hands and seemed to examine every line of Kurt's face.

"It's all right, it is me," said Kurt, smiling.

"You've changed. Something different. In the eyes,

perhaps? Never mind, we've all changed, isn't that so? It's a miracle! I heard you were dead, I heard you'd been killed by the Fascists in Spain!"

"The report was premature," said Kurt.

"But now it's worse," said Wolf solemnly. "Out of the frying pan into the fire. How the hell did you let yourself be caught by these bastards?"

"A long story," Kurt said. "Tell me about you."

"It's a comedy," said Wolf. "After you disappeared, I sort of dropped out of things, kept my head down. I made a living, I still had my connections—you know what I mean. I thought of getting out, but then I thought—what the hell, this is my country too, I'll survive the same as I've always done. Then one night, I got stupid. There were these Brownshirts swaggering along the pavement, shoving everybody out of their way, and I had a rush of blood to the head. The truth is—I'd had enough. So I shoved them into the gutter. Next thing I know I'm on my way to Sachsenhausen."

He sat down at the table and lit one of Kurt's cigarettes. "It was bad at first: they really took it out on me. But then like always, they got bored with beating the same back all the time and they more or less left me alone. One of the senior guards turned out to be someone I used to know in the old days—in the same line of business, you understand. We'd often worked together on various little jobs."

"Like what, for instance."

"Ah, come on, Kurt!" Wolf looked pained. "In all the time we knew each other before you never once asked such a question. That's what I liked about you."

"Sorry."

"Anyway, this fellow—Linge, that's his name—he's working a nice racket at Sachsenhausen. He hires out groups of prisoners for outside work, gives the camp commandant a cut, then pockets the rest. The work gangs have better food to keep them fit. Not good, you understand, but better than the swill dished out to the others. And there are other little privileges."

"And you got onto a work gang?"

"My name's not Wolfie Goldberg for nothing, is it?" The big man laughed and drew on the cigarette, then suddenly his eyes darkened and he added bitterly, "Why am I laughing? I should be ashamed. So I'm one of the lucky ones. In that place, I tell you, Kurt, in that place things are happening that should make God ashamed he made the world."

"Wolf," said Kurt, "do you trust me?"

"If you don't mind my saying so, that is a stupid question. Look, all of a sudden, they take me from the camp, and bring me here, all this way. I am driven in a Luftwaffe car, like I am somebody important. When I arrive, they bring me to this room, and who do I find? My old friend Kurt Reiss. You are sitting here, large as life, in a warm room, with coffee, cigarettes. The Major talks to you politely then leaves us alone together. What am I to think? That you are their friend, that somehow you've turned your coat and gone over to them? Impossible! I know you. You are Kurt Reiss. You have something up your sleeve, there must be a reason. Do you still want to know if I trust you?"

"Wolf, listen," said Kurt. "In a way, I am working for them."

"If any other Jewish boy was sitting here and he told me that, I would break his neck. Don't joke on such matters, Kurt, don't play such games."

"Sit tight, keep quiet, and listen."

For the next few minutes Kurt explained the whole bizarre situation while Wolf sat with his brow wrinkled in thought. When Kurt had finished he shook his head in wonder. "It was you! You killed Stutz, that bastard from Dachau!"

"Yes."

"We heard he'd been done for, even in Sachsenhausen we heard it. And you tried to kill the Reichsmarschall also! For this alone they should make you a medal!"

"I failed."

"Never mind. Even to fall from a fine horse is worthwhile. You see, you have changed. You wouldn't believe me when I told you that to kill them was the only way. Now it's already too late, they have both the whip and the reins." He shook his head again and lit another cigarette. "Do you know what they want you to do?"

"No. I can only guess."

"And?"

"My guess is that they want somebody killed."

"Who?"

"God knows and he won't tell."

"And you're prepared to do it?"

"For ten thousand Jewish lives? Next question."

"They are bastards, but they are not fools. How can you be sure that when you've done what they ask they will release the ten thousand?"

"I don't know—yet. But when the time comes, I will find a way. I have to." Kurt paused. "Wolf, will you join me—take a chance?"

"I thought you were never going to ask!" The big man smiled. "Anyway, how could you manage without me?"

"The same thought crossed my own mind. I couldn't. And now, another problem. We need two more volunteers—good men."

"I'll get them."

"Where from?"

"The camp. Where else? From Sachsenhausen I could bring you a hundred." Wolf caught the look of doubt that hovered on Kurt's face. "Listen," he said, "I know what you're thinking. You're thinking you don't want a couple of villains like me, correct?"

"There aren't any villains like you, Wolf; you're unique." Kurt paused. "I just want to be sure—"

"Will you leave it to me? Say I bring you six men and you take your pick?"

"No," Kurt said, shaking his head quickly. "If you bring six, four will have to go back to the camp. That would be a diabolical thing to do. I would like to select from a dozen, two dozen, but it would be a cruelty to those we rejected. No, I will have to leave it to you. Tell me the sort of men you have in mind."

They talked for a while of various people, with Wolf supplying a brief background to each man and answering Kurt's questions. In the end, they settled on two names. Kurt was uneasy about it, but he could see no other alternative.

"You're sure they will agree?" he asked.

"To get out of Sachsenhausen they would walk barefoot over hot ashes."

"No!" said Kurt sharply. "That is not what I asked, and it's not what I want. I don't want you to fill their minds with the idea of freedom. I don't want men who want to get out of Sachsenhausen simply to save their own skins, because they see it as a means of escape. Do you understand?"

"No problem," said Wolf calmly.

"They call us scum, subhuman vermin," said Kurt. "They think Jews have no guts, that we can't and won't fight."

"Then we'll give them something to open their eyes, eh?" said Wolf.

Two days later, with three days to go before the week was up, Kurt was able to tell the Major not only that he had recruited his combat team but that all the arrangements had been made for the evacuation to Sweden of the Jewish orphans at Wittenberg.

6

The children were unusually quiet at first, for they had been woken from sleep early, while it was still dark. They had been told only that they were going on a journey, for Frau Meysel, the head of the orphanage, was afraid that even at this late stage something might go wrong and that they would be turned back or diverted elsewhere. Although she had done her best to protect the children from a full knowledge of what was happening to the Jewish people, she knew that the older ones in particular understood the course of events and were frightened; this sense of insecurity naturally communicated itself to the younger children.

However, once the train had actually moved out of the station and Wittenberg was behind them, her charges began to brighten up, and the three coaches that had been allocated to them became alive with their chirruping voices and the shrill inevitable sounds of laughter and argument. She moved from coach to coach, checking with members of her staff, and she could feel that they too had snatched a little hope from the air. When they looked at her the apprehension was still there in their eyes, but she could see relief also. She did not have the heart to warn them that it was a little too early for optimism. For her part, she would not relax or allow herself to hope until the boat docked at Trelleborg in Sweden and she knew, without a shadow of a doubt, that they were free.

"Wish for a miracle," she kept telling herself, "but don't expect one."

But even her reserve broke when the train pulled in

at Sassnitz, and she saw the freezing, gray waters of the Baltic and the ship in the harbor flying the flags of Sweden and of the Red Cross. Farther out in the channel she could see an icebreaker, tossing aside the loose ice floes, keeping the passage to freedom open. It seemed to her to have a special significance, and she sniffed back the tears.

Kurt stood on the quay with the Major, watching the lines of children as, clutching their cases and bundles and shepherded by the nervous teachers, they made their way to the customs shed. He heard their chatter as if it were an echo from a distant land and another time; he felt suddenly old, as though his own childhood were centuries away.

A car flying the pennant of the SS drew up nearby, and the driver hurried to open the door for the Brigade-führer. He strode across to Kurt and the Major, his boots clicking on the smooth stones.

"The Gelders. Father and daughter. Delivered as arranged." He spoke curtly, as if he were confirming the transfer of livestock.

Emmy and her father came slowly toward them from the car. As soon as she saw Kurt she ran to him and embraced him, but almost immediately she drew back, feeling no response in him.

"Is everything all right?" she asked, a little edge of apprehension in her voice.

"Yes." He nodded. "It is all arranged. In a few hours you will be in Sweden."

Her eyes brightened. "I still can't believe it!"

Gelder came up to them and grasped Kurt's hand. He was still a shade of his former self, but on this day his mind seemed to have grasped what was happening. "I have to thank you, Kurt—for Emmy and me both."

"Take care of each other," Kurt said. They were the only words he could think of.

"And you—what about you?" Emmy said. Her dark eyes searched his face.

"As you see," he said.

"You should be proud," she said.

"For what? For a handful of children?" And he added bitterly, raising his voice so that the Major and the Brigadeführer would hear: "Why should they have to go at all, why should they have to leave their own land?"

"Sh-sh." She hushed him as a mother might hush a child. "If you do nothing else, you have done this. It is a great deal, believe me."

"We shall speak for you in our prayers," said her father.

"Do that," said Kurt.

He insisted on waiting until all the passengers were aboard and the ship had pulled out of the harbor. Up to the last moment Emmy stood at the rail watching him. Neither of them waved; it did not seem appropriate.

"You see," said the Brigadeführer, "we are men of our word."

Kurt turned on the man then, with murder flaring in his heart, but the Major stepped between them quickly. He laid a restraining hand on Kurt's arm.

"Come," he said gruffly.

EIGHT

1

Each morning at Sachsenhausen concentration camp the day began with the tolling of a bell. This was the signal for the prisoners to scramble from their bunks, fold their blankets in regulation style, and stand rigidly to attention. There was no need to dress, for each man slept in his coarse striped uniform. Many prisoners, especially the older ones, woke early and had their blankets in place before the bell sounded, for they were terrified of being even one second late.

An SS man then inspected each hut, walking round with measured tread, not simply checking each bunk, but searching every face for the slightest hint of defiance or even hope, for to reveal any such feeling was the worst offense of all. It was quite common for prisoners, out of fear, to wet themselves or worse as they faced this morning scrutiny.

As part of his basic training, each man in the Tötenkopfverbaende, the so-called Death's Head units of the SS, whose main task was to provide guards for the camps, was required to attend indoctrination classes at which he was taught to squeeze out of his heart all feelings of pity toward prisoners. He was trained to understand that ruthless, naked terror and cruelty were necessary not merely to reduce the inhabitants of the camps to unthinking, obedient robots, but for a wider political reason. National Socialism could only be protected if the entire German people understood that even the slightest act or expression of hostility toward the regime would bring down upon the head of the offender the most terrifying punishment. In this way, acts of inhumanity that would be unthinkable in any other context could be given a philosophical justification and even elevated to the status of honorable duty in the service of the fatherland.

The bell tolled again, and now the prisoners hurried from the huts and lined up in the freezing wind, for what the camp commandant, who had once been a headmaster and had a highly developed sense of duty, was pleased to call "Morning Assembly." First, the guard hoisted the swastika flag on the big pole near the central watchtower, and the entire company was required to spring to attention, make the Nazi salute, and shout in unison:

"Heil Hitler! Sieg Heil Hitler!"

Then the camp band struck up the national song, "Deutschland Über Alles," and the non-Jewish prisoners were granted the privilege of singing. (It was not considered proper for the anthem to be sullied by Jewish lips.) The commandant was particular in this matter and insisted always that there should be adequate display of enthusiasm; anyone who did not respond to the full capacity of his lungs was dragged from the ranks and hauled before him. The procedure seldom varied and always ended with the unlucky prisoner receiving twenty-five strokes of the cat-o'-nine-tails.

There followed what the commandant proudly referred to as his litany, which was reserved exclusively for the Jewish inmates. This composition, based largely on the Führer's own words, was posted up in all the barracks, and the first task of every newly arrived Jewish prisoner was to learn it by heart, in preparation for the Morning Assembly. The Jews, who were assembled in front of the other prisoners, were ordered to kneel and to chant in unison:

I am a Jew and therefore I am a plague carrier, the ferment of all social decomposition. I am a Jew and therefore I am evil, the enemy of all humanity. I am a Jew and therefore I am a Christ killer, a murderer. I am a Jew and therefore I am scum, I stink in the nostrils of the world. I am a Jew and therefore I am beyond mercy or redemption. Jews pollute the earth and therefore it is fitting that we should be exterminated. Amen.

Visiting celebrities were often treated to this display; indeed the so-called litany became quite famous and was even taken up by that ardent anti-Semite, Julius Streicher and printed in his paper, *Der Stürmer*.

When the chanting had finished, there was a long pause, during which the commandant surveyed the parade. This was the time when each prisoner held his breath for fear that he would be called forth and singled out for punishment. They had long since learned that it was not necessary to have committed an offense; it was simply a question of whether the commandant's eyes stopped at your face; it was a matter of luck. He always prolonged this moment because he could sense their fear, and it gratified him to know that he was so successfully fulfilling his duty.

On this particular morning, however, there was no random selection, at least to begin with. Instead the commandant consulted a slip of paper and called out a number.

"S/349/40/37—come here!"

A man stepped from the ranks of the Jewish prisoners and stood to attention before the commandant, his head bowed, eyes on the ground. His face and hands were blue with cold, but he forced himself to stand rigid, for he knew that even to shiver without permission could lead to punishment.

"Who are you?" asked the commandant.

"With respect, Herr Obersturmbannführer, I beg to report that I am Prisoner Number S/349/40/37." This was the formula all prisoners had to use when replying to a question.

"What is your name?"

Name? It had been so long since the man had used his own name, that he hesitated. And for a Jew even to suggest that he was anything other than a number meant a certain beating.

"Speak up, scum! Your name!"

"With respect, Herr Obersturmbannführer, Prisoner Number S/349/40/37 begs to report that I am a Jew and therefore I have no name." He stammered as he answered, partly from cold and partly from fear.

"Tell me your name, Jew! The name you were given when you had the misfortune to be born!" The commandant's voice cracked like a whip.

"With respect, Herr Obersturmbannführer," said the man hurriedly, "Prisoner Number S/349/40/37 begs to report that my name is Moshe Kahn."

"Moshe Kahn, eh? A good Jewish name." He consulted the slip of paper again. "Number S/451/39/37—step forward!" Another prisoner stepped from the ranks. "Give me your name," said the commandant, "and I mean, your name!"

"With respect, Herr Obersturmbannführer, Prisoner Number S/451/39/37 begs to report that my name is Max Meyer."

"How nice!" said the commandant. "Well, Herr Moshe Kahn and Herr Max Meyer, I trust you have enjoyed your stay at my little health resort. Perhaps one day we will be able to welcome you back." He clicked his fingers, and an SS man took the two prisoners away.

The commandant turned his attention to the parade.

His eyes moved along the row of prisoners and stopped; he pointed his stick at one of them.

"That one," he said. "He looks insolent. The bastinado. Twenty-five strokes. Assembly dismissed. Heil Hitler!" He stepped down from the small mobile platform and strode toward his quarters, with an aide flapping at either side.

2

Neither of the two prisoners, Moshe Kahn and Max Meyer, could understand what was happening. They had been taken to washrooms normally reserved for the SS and told to shower; they were then issued with fresh warm underwear, blue overalls, new boots, and service overcoats from which the insignia had been removed. Then, to compound their bewilderment, they were taken to a detention room where a breakfast of fried eggs, hot rolls, cheese, and real coffee was set before them. They fell on the food ravenously, saving their questions for later.

"Well, they're not going to kill us, Moshe, that's for certain," said Max as he laid down his knife and fork.

"How can you be sure?"

"And waste all that good food?"

"Perhaps they're fattening us up for the kill."

Max ran a hand along the edge of the table. "Do you know," he said wistfully, "I'd begun to think that I would never again eat from a real table."

"Or use a knife and fork!"

"Or taste real hot coffee!"

Moshe smiled. "With respect, Herr Shithouse Obersturmbannführer, Prisoner Number S/349/40/37 begs to report that I have enjoyed my breakfast and that you can stuff the crockery."

They began to laugh, hesitantly at first for they had

not laughed in a long time, but eventually it burst out of them, as though longing for release, and the shrill note of hysteria crept in. Then, as a bolt grated in the door, they both stopped suddenly, fearfully, as if a line had been cut, and sprang to their feet.

The SS man stood aside and the great bulk of Wolf Goldberg filled the doorway. They stared at him in astonishment as he moved toward them and embraced each one in turn.

"What's going on? What's going on?" muttered Moshe, tears glittering in his eyes.

"Sit down, and I'll tell you," said Wolf.

Fifteen minutes later they were taken before the commandant. Two officers they had not seen before, a brigadeführer of the SS and a major in Luftwaffe uniform were standing together at one side of the room. The commandant's aide handed each prisoner a pen and pointed to some documents that were spread out on the desk before them.

"You will sign here. The documents testify that you have received strict but fair treatment during your stay at Sachsenhausen, that you have no cause for complaint concerning the food or the general conditions, and that you wish to place on record your appreciation of the humane attitude of the camp administration and of Obersturmbannführer Streibeck."

The two prisoners hesitated for only a fraction of a second, signed the document, and stepped back.

"They're all yours, Herr Brigadeführer," said the commandant smoothly. "I don't think they'll be any trouble. You'll find that they have been well broken."

3

"Ah, Erich," said the Reichsmarschall casually, as if it were an afterthought, "I understand that you have

been making inquiries about a certain Herr Engelhardt."

So that's it, thought the Major. He had been with the
Reichsmarschall for an hour, going over a series of
routine documents, and during the time, it had seemed
to him that the other man's mind was largely on other
things; moreover, there had been moments, looks,
glances that for some unknown reason, had filled him
with an odd sense of foreboding. Now it was out in the
open, and he felt a sense of relief for that. At the same
time, he tried to order his thoughts, stiffening himself
mentally for whatever was to come.

"Yes, sir," he said, with as much calmness as he
could muster, "I took the liberty of asking the Brigadeführer to find out where the man was being held and
why."

"Why didn't you come to me?" asked the Reichsmarschall pleasantly.

"With respect, sir, it is a small matter and I did not
wish to bother you."

"You know the man?"

"No, sir."

"No?" There was a note of surprise in the voice.

"I have never met him."

"Then why your interest?"

"It is not really even an interest, sir. I happened to
hear about his case and thought it would do no harm to
inquire."

"You were asked to intervene?"

"Not to intervene, sir. I simply said I would get what
information I could. He has a wife, naturally she is concerned."

"Naturally. You know the wife then, is that it?"

"No, sir."

"Extraordinary! You know neither the man nor his
wife, yet you allow yourself to become involved. Your
interest is—what?"

"As I said—"

"Political? Is that it?"

"I know very little of political matters, sir." The Major was beginning to curse the impulse that had exposed him in this way.

"Yes, yes, so you've told me. Many times." The Reichsmarschall, without taking his eyes off the Major, without for one second relaxing the steady stare, took a thick envelope from a drawer. He laid it on the desk, smoothing it with his soft fingers in what was almost a caress. "So, if your interest is not political it can only be sentimental. And that, my friend, is even more dangerous."

"It is not important, sir," said the Major awkwardly.

"That is where you are wrong. You must allow me to know better. The strength of National Socialism lies precisely in the fact that we have turned our back on sentimentality. Let me give you but one example. In 1934, the Führer and I had to make a bitter decision. We had to take action against Ernst Röhm and the leadership of the SA. They were old party comrades, but they had taken the wrong path and were threatening our revolution. Old comrades or not, we did not hesitate, we did not give way to sentiment. They were liquidated. I tell you, Erich, I tell you quite solemnly that if I had cause to believe that my own wife—my own wife—was behaving in a way that threatened National Socialism in the slightest degree, I would myself hand her over for punishment. Do you understand what I am telling you?"

"Yes, sir."

"I hope so. And do you understand why I speak to you in this manner?" The Major could find no answer to this, and as he remained silent, the Reichsmarschall continued, speaking in a slow, measured tone: "It is because I am about to impose the greatest trust in you, Major. I speak not only for myself, but on behalf of the

Führer also. We want you to undertake a task of the highest importance to the future of the Reich."

"I am honored by your confidence," muttered the Major, stunned by this abrupt turn in the discussion and by its implications.

"However, when I heard about your interest in this man Engelhardt, I confess I began to have my very first doubts." The Major opened his mouth as if to protest, but the Reichsmarschall waved him down. "No, no, not of your loyalty, I am not speaking of that, nor of your ability and courage. But it is this germ of sentiment in your soul that concerns me. Unless you take it in hand, suppress it ruthlessly, it could destroy you as a man, as an officer of the Reich. Do you get the message?"

"Yes, sir."

"Good. Enough of this then. Now to come down to brass tacks. The four Jews. They represent the spearhead of a mission to which we have given the code name of 'Thunderbird.' You have been itching to get back into action, I know that. Well, this is your chance. Not flying—something vastly more important. For the next four weeks I want you to train those Jews, I want you to forge them into a combat team of the highest class. The Reichswehr will provide one of their best instructors, who will work to your orders. At the end of one month, no longer, I want a combat team that is capable of taking on all comers. Do you accept?"

"Naturally, sir, of course." He tried to keep the disappointment from his voice. It was not the assignment he'd wanted or expected, but there seemed no choice but to agree.

"Excellent. I expect nothing less. I'm putting you on this, Erich, for two reasons. First, because I trust you. And second, because I don't want the blasted SS to take over the operation. I intend to keep it in our hands. Clear?"

"Yes, sir."

"From time to time I will give you additional instructions. And you will report direct to me at regular intervals, keep me fully informed."

"Very good, sir."

The Reichsmarschall rose, picked up the envelope, and removed from it a typed letter, which he handed to the Major. "Here is all the authorization you will require. Note that it has been signed by the Führer himself—and others."

The Major glanced at the paper, but the words swam before his eyes. He felt a great surge of pride. "I am honored, sir," he said, conscious that he was repeating himself.

"So you should be, Erich, so you should be." The Reichsmarschall's eyes glowed with boyish enthusiasm. "If Thunderbird succeeds—and we must make damn sure that it does—it could be worth twenty or even thirty divisions to us when war comes. Think of that! It could mark the difference between victory and defeat. I hope you realize that you have been given a unique opportunity to serve the fatherland—a chance that comes to few men. Grab it, my lad, grab it with both hands! Come back successful—bring me success— and I'll see that you're so weighed down with medals and crosses that you'll be hard put to it to walk! And you can go back to your unit—back to flying. I know that's what you want."

He moved round the desk and clapped the Major on the shoulder. "Now perhaps you understand why I went on at such length about this business of sentiment. When you work closely with a group of men, a certain bond springs up between you, isn't that so? Mutual respect and all that. That is what you will have to watch. Don't allow yourself to become too fond of your Jews, Erich. They are a weapon in our hands—no more, no less. When they have served their purpose ..." He shrugged. "They are dead men on leave anyway."

"I understand, sir," said the Major, though he was far from sure that he did.

"Right. Get on with it. Good luck. Heil Hitler!"

"Thank you, sir. Heil Hitler!"

As he reached the door, the Reichsmarschall said: "Ah, one more thing."

"Sir?" The Major turned.

"This man Engelhardt. You can put him out of your mind." He went back to the desk, reached for a pipe, and added inconsequentially: "He's dead. As a matter of fact they've hanged him."

"Hanged?" The Major frowned, as if this thought, on top of everything else, was too much to take.

"Oh, yes," said the Reichsmarschall, reaming the pipe with a knife. "I signed the authorization myself." He smiled and looked directly at the Major, as though challenging him. "The only thing to do in the circumstances, don't you agree? Don't want to clutter up your head with details of that sort. Now you'll be able to concentrate all your attention on the job in hand—right?"

4

On the journey from the Air Ministry building back to Luftflotte I, the Major saw and heard nothing. He sat in the back of the car as it splashed through the wet gray streets listening only to the questions that hammered in his head like messages clicked out by some giant typewriter.

The mission—Operation Thunderbird? A combat team? A combat team of Jews—"dead men on leave," the Reichsmarschall had called them. Did this mean a suicide mission? And if so, against whom or what was it to be directed? And why a team of Jews? Was it simply that they were expendable?

No, that could not be the whole answer. If the mission was so vital to the Reich, so vital that it had the support of the Führer himself, then surely it would have been possible to draw a hundred, a thousand volunteers from the ranks of dedicated Nazis in the SS, or even from the army. So there had to be a special reason for using the Jews; a special and important reason, for why else would the Reichsmarschall have gone to such elaborate lengths to ensure the cooperation of Kurt Reiss and the others?

And then again, why had he selected Reiss of all people—the man who had attempted to assassinate him? Assassinate? The Major's mind closed on the word like a trap. Assassination? Was this then the purpose of the operation? Reiss had proved himself to be skilled and courageous and he'd had military experience in Spain, he knew how to use a rifle. There surely could be no other answer. *Assassination!*

He drew in his breath sharply, awed by the thought. Something else the Reichsmarschall had said came into his head, and he pounced on it, pinning down the words. *Come back successful—bring me success—and I'll see that you're loaded down with medals and crosses.* Something like that. But what had he meant by the words *come back?* Was the operation to take place outside the borders of the Reich? Was he to be involved in it at that stage also? And if its aim was assassination, who was the target?

It was warm in the back of the car, but he shivered nevertheless. That morning, only a few hours before, he had woken as Major Erich Koller, an insignificant Luftwaffe officer whose only wish was to get back to his squadron. His ambition had soared no higher than the reasonable hope that one day he might make his way up the ladder to the rank of Generalmajor and have command of his own *Fliegerkorps*. And now, from on high, the hands of the mighty had reached down and plucked him—him of all people!—from obscurity and honored him with this awesome responsibility!

The letter rustled in his pocket. He took it out for the third time and, as before, he felt that strange mixture of bewilderment and pride tingle in his blood as he read the brief message.

From the Office of the Führer.

TOP SECRET. January 16, 1939.

The bearer of this letter, Major Erich Koller is engaged on a mission of vital national importance. All organizations of the party and the state, and all military, naval, Luftwaffe, and civil personnel are hereby ordered to extend him the fullest cooperation. This order is valid from the date printed above until March 31, 1939.

And there, below the words, were the signatures of the three most powerful men in the Reich: Adolf Hitler, the Reichsmarschall, and Heinrich Himmler.

He replaced it carefully in the envelope. The dates rang in his head. It was now January 17; in a few weeks it would be all over, the piece of paper would be worth only the value of those weighty signatures. And before then, in a month perhaps, he would be told more, he would learn the objective.

Then, as he sat back, relaxing a little, he remembered Leni, and with her, inevitably, that unknown man who was now dead, the man called Engelhardt. He had been a fool to speak to the Brigadeführer, stupid to involve himself in any way. It was the first time he had ever abandoned his natural caution over matters of that sort, and it would be the last! In all probability, when it came down to it, Leni and he could count themselves responsible for the poor devil's death; if they had done nothing, not even mentioned his name, the chances were that he would be alive still, that he would have served a sentence in the camp and then been returned home. It had happened like that to hundreds of others. But merely by making an offhand inquiry he had put a cross against Engelhardt's name, marked him down for execution.

All the same, the calculating ruthlessness of the killing shocked him. Engelhardt had been hanged simply as a warning, to drive home to the Major the lesson that, in a soldier, sentiment could be a dangerous weakness.

Don't allow yourself to become too fond of your Jews, Erich. They are a weapon in our hands—no more, no less. When they have served their purpose ... They are dead men on leave anyway.

He stiffened as the car drew up at the barracks, gathering himself mentally. Right, he told himself, that was the way it would be from now on. He had learned his lesson; there would be no sentiment, no more rubbish of that sort!

The Reichsmarschall wanted a combat squad capable of taking on all comers, and, by God, that was what he would get!

5

Unteroffizier Hermann Lugert had spent his entire adult life in the army and knew no other God; his bible was the *Reichswehr Manual of Regulations,* his church, the parade ground and the assault course. In his eyes, all recruits were sinners to be converted to the true faith—that was his task, his vocation, his joy. Converted they had to be, whether willing or no, but conversion could not be cheaply purchased. The recruit had to buy his place among the chosen of the Reichswehr by work, sweat, blood, pain, and obedience. The Unteroffizier had never failed—that would be unthinkable. At regular intervals they handed him the raw human material and, as if by some miracle, he transmuted that base metal into hardened steel.

This was the man who now stood, stiff as a ramrod, before the Major. He was not actually a big man, but he gave the impression of size and seemed somehow to fill the room. His face was brick red perhaps from constant exposure to the wind or from too much shouting, and his eyes, bright, sharp, and hard as glass marbles, kept swiveling from side to side in their anxiety to miss nothing. With those eyes he could spot a speck of mud at ten paces and an unfastened button at twenty; it was the view of most recruits who passed through his hands that he could also see out of the back of his head. Below the large nose, which was twisted slightly to the left, there nestled an elegant, waxed moustache; the false teeth gleamed in his mouth, white as new gravestones. The uniform was immaculate; the boots shone like black glass.

Why is it, thought the Major, that all training sergeants look the same? Did the job attract a certain type of man, or did the job itself change the man until he conformed to the regulation image?

"Herr Major, sir, Unteroffizier Lugert reporting for special duty, as ordered. Sir!" He kept his voice down out of respect, but even so, the windows rattled out a gentle protest.

The Major winced slightly, acknowledged the salute, and rising from the desk, held out a friendly hand. "Welcome to Luftflotte One, Herr Unteroffizier."

Lugert hesitated a moment, looking at the out-stretched hand as though it were an unwelcome in-truder. From his expression it was clear that this sort of thing wouldn't be allowed to happen where he came from; but since the other man was an officer, and since this was the Luftwaffe, where all sorts of peculiar things were reputed to happen (like NCOs drinking with officers when off duty and calling them by their first names), he accepted the hand and gave it what he hoped was a soldierly but respectful shake. He then re-sumed his former rigidity.

"At ease, Herr Unteroffizier," said the Major. The other man made a token gesture of relaxation, but it was hardly noticeable. The Major sighed and contin-ued: "Have you been told the nature of your assign-ment?"

"Sir! I was instructed to report to the Herr Major for special duty, unspecified. Sir!"

"I see. Well, briefly, this is it. We have four men here. As it happens, they are all Jews." He paused, ex-pecting a reaction, but the other man's face registered nothing. "They are untrained, though one has had some irregular military experience. None of them could be described as fit. In one month, you and I have to weld them into a disciplined fighting unit. I am not, you understand, speaking simply of parade-ground drill, though that may be important. They must also be-come as proficient as is possible in the time in un-armed combat and in the use of arms and explosives. Any questions?"

"Sir, with respect. The Herr Major said four men?" He emphasized the number in such a way as to suggest that they had brought in a sledgehammer to crack a nut.

"I did. Four men."

"Yes, sir!"

There was a short silence while the Major wondered what he could do to break down the man's iron front. He took the Führer's letter from his pocket. "Before we go any further, you'd better take a look at this."

"Sir!" The Unteroffizier's expression changed not one whit as he read the document; for all the impression it made upon him, he might have been looking at an army requisition for sausages. He handed it back with the air of a man for whom Hitlers and Reichsmarschalls meant little; they could come and go, but the army would be there forever.

"Right!" said the Major curtly, trying not to show his irritation. "Two things. First, you now know that the assignment you've been given is of supreme national importance. Second, you must realize that it is top secret. Top, top secret. Tomorrow, at first light, we move off to a camp about ten miles from Kyritz. It is the main training center for our penal battalions; all the men there have committed some offense against regulations. We shall, of course, train separately. But if you are asked any questions you will reply that these four men are special prisoners who are being given basic training before joining a bomb-disposal unit. Is that clear, Herr Unteroffizier?"

"Sir!" Once again, the window rattled.

The Major, taking this response as an affirmative, put the letter back into his pocket and stood up. "Very well. Let's go and look at the stuff we have to work with." And he added, with a touch of malice, "Be warned. Don't expect too much."

He led the way to the guardroom, with Unteroffizier Lugert crashing along behind at a respectful distance. A guard unlocked the door of the main cell and flung it open.

Two of the men inside, Moshe Kahn and Max Meyer, sprung instantly to their feet and stood at attention.

Wolf Goldberg responded in the same fashion, but more slowly. Kurt remained seated, his legs straddled across a chair, and looked up calmly.

"On your feet! You, you lump of frog spawn! On your feet and stand to attention in front of the officer!" The voice roared and echoed in the enclosed space, the face went a deeper shade of red, and the eyes glared with such concentrated malevolence that Kurt, almost as a reflex action, jumped up and joined the others.

"Gentlemen," the Major said quietly, "allow me to introduce Herr Unteroffizier Lugert. For the next month, he is to be your instructor. You will, in accordance with our understanding, obey his orders in every respect, without question. From this moment you are, to all intents and purposes, recruits under his command, and he is responsible only to me. Understand?"

There was a pause, then Kurt nodded. "Understood."

"Sir!" shouted Lugert.

"Sir," said Kurt, without any great enthusiasm. "But I must insist on one condition," and he added wryly, "Sir."

"You will shut your mouth until you are told to open it!" snapped Lugert.

"That's all right, Unteroffizier," said the Major. He looked at Kurt with a cold eye: "Conditions? And we have hardly begun!"

"We are not to be insulted," Kurt said. "We have had enough of that. We will work, we will obey orders. But we are to be treated with respect."

It gave the Major a certain satisfaction to note that a look of something akin to shock was showing in the Unteroffizier's eyes, but he did not allow his mind to dwell on it. To Kurt he said: "You will be treated as any other ordinary recruits, no better, no worse." He turned to leave. "Carry on, Unteroffizier."

Lugert moved forward as soon as the Major had

gone, and stood before each of the four men in turn, surveying them from head to foot, staring into their eyes as if he were trying to read their minds.

Then he stepped back and pointed his swagger stick at Moshe.

"Name!"

Moshe answered without hesitation. "With respect, Herr Unteroffizier, I beg to report that my name is Moshe Kahn."

Wolf and Max responded in a similar manner but Kurt replied in less formal fashion.

"Kurt Reiss, sir."

The Unteroffizier looked him over for a long, cold moment. "Right!" he said. "You heard the Herr Major. I don't know where you come from, but I can tell you where you're going. You're going to hell and back. I'm going to work you until you drop, until every muscle in your lousy bodies aches, and then, when you think I've finished, we'll start all over again. For the next four weeks I'm going to make you wish you'd never been born! At the end of those four weeks, you'll either begin to look like soldiers or you'll be dead!"

He paused and moved a step closer to Kurt. "You," he said, "you want respect. Well, where I come from that's not something we give away as a free gift. You have to earn it. Until then, as far as I'm concerned, you're the lowest of the low—you're just scum." He drew a breath and pushed his stick into Kurt's chest. "And you—you are the lowest of all. A maggot. I've seen better things than you crawl out of rotten cheese!"

It was a deliberate challenge. Kurt pressed forward, the stick jabbing into his flesh, struggling to control himself. And then the Unteroffizier said something that surprised and checked him.

"Don't get me wrong. Don't run away with any funny ideas, just because you happen to have the bad luck to be Jews. It doesn't matter a cuss to me whether a man is a Jew, a Hindu, or a Hottentot with one ball and a black prick. I fought alongside Jews in the last lot and never had any cause to complain. So when I call you pigshit or a poxy pimp it's not because some rabbi trimmed your bloody wick. It's because that is exactly what you are. Do we understand each other?"

He lowered his stick. Kurt thought he detected a tiny gleam in the other man's eye; it was the first sign that there was a human being under the rock-hard exterior, and he smiled.

"Understood, Herr Unteroffizier!"

"Take that grin off your face when you address me, pigshit, or I'll knock it off with my fist!"

Lugert turned abruptly and left the cell, the door clanging behind him.

"Oi vey," said Wolf, "what a bastard."

"He's what we need," said Kurt.

"Are you out of your mind? Have you gone *meshuge*?"

"Look at us," Kurt said. "We're a load of rubbish, no doubt about it. And in a month—one month—he has to turn us into a combat team. Right. We'll surprise him. We'll obey orders, we'll work twice as hard, we'll swallow all his insults. And at the end of the month we'll make him do the swallowing: we're going to be the finest squad he's ever turned out."

"Or kill ourselves in the process," said Moshe sadly. He was a poet of sorts, and had an inclination toward pessimism.

"Or kill ourselves in the process," said Kurt.

6

That evening, the Major drove out to Wriezen to see Leni, to say good-bye to her. He had convinced himself that it would be better for her if he ended their irregular relationship, but on a deeper level he knew that he was, in fact, running for cover, and he was aware of an undertow of guilt and shame. Within the Luftwaffe he felt safe, secure; it was not necessary to concern oneself with awkward political or social matters, to allow one's conscience to become involved. This was one of the reasons why he had never been entirely happy working with the Reichsmarschall. There had been too many occasions when he had felt ill at ease, exposed, vulnerable, when the course of events had troubled him. Soon, when this strange mission had been completed, he would be able to rejoin his squadron, immerse himself once more in that enclosed world of men and machines, feel again the pure, uncomplicated freedom of flying.

He did not know about love; he had never allowed his mind to dwell upon the subject at any length. He held his parents in deep respect, felt affection for his mother in particular, but he would have considered love an unsuitable word with which to describe their relationship. When they met, there was always a certain decent reserve between them, and this was considered to be proper.

With Leni also, he had carefully avoided the question of love. He was deeply fond of her, that could not be denied; he felt closer to her than to any other human being, and she had drawn from him a degree of warmth and tenderness that had surprised him. But such was his nature that the more his emotions were released, the more uneasy he felt; and at such times he immediately applied the brake, so to speak, and retreated once more behind his customary wall of reserve.

For reasons that he could not explain even to himself, he sensed danger in his relationship with Leni. The business with Engelhardt was a case in point.

Against all his instincts he had allowed himself to become involved, with disastrous results. In this new Germany it was unwise to ask questions, to lift one's head. Perhaps it would not always be so; but until it changed it was best to keep one's deeper feelings under lock and key. All he wanted to do, after all, was to live his own quiet life, follow his career, keep his own counsel. He was only thirty-four; marriage, children, and all that were issues he could face later.

It would be painful to break with Leni; he could feel the pain already, even before it happened. But if he continued to see her, sooner or later she would breach his defenses and bring him face to face with questions that, in these times, were best left unasked. . . .

When he let himself into the apartment he found that Leni was out. She had left a letter on the table for him.

Erich, darling.

A terrible thing has happened. This afternoon the Gestapo brought Mr. Engelhardt's body to the house in a sealed coffin. They told Mrs. Engelhardt that he had died of a heart attack but that on no account was the coffin to be opened. You can imagine what must have happened! They threatened her with terrible things if their orders were disobeyed. I have taken her to her sister in Eberswalde—she can't possibly stay in the apartment. I will be back soon. How is it possible that people can be guilty of such cruelty?

Love, Leni.

He poured himself a drink and sat down. He thought of the coffin in the apartment below, a coffin containing the body of a man he had never known. He put down the glass and looked at his hands, as if they were in some way responsible.

After waiting a half hour he wrote Leni a brief note in which he told her that he could not wait, that he had to get back to Berlin. In the morning, he told her, he would be leaving on a special mission and would not be back for at least three months. He would write to her. And he added an expression of sympathy for Mrs. Engelhardt.

He put his key to the apartment in the envelope with the note and left quickly. He reached the car with a sense of relief, glad that he had not met Leni on her way back. It was, he told himself, the best way. No scenes, no tears, no sentiment.

All the same, when he got back to his quarters he locked the door, and then, in solitude, he drank a whole bottle of brandy. It did not entirely achieve its purpose.

When he went to bed at last he could not sleep for a long time; despite all efforts, his mind would not free itself of the heavy burden of unwelcome thoughts.

NINE

1

Unteroffizier Lugert knew his trade, and, within the limits of that trade, he could measure with amazing precision the nature of the human material with which he had to work. He had seen the telltale signs of malnutrition and deprivation in Kurt and, to a greater extent, in the others, and for the first few days, to their surprise, he drove them on a light rein. With the Major's backing and on the advice of a doctor, he arranged that they should receive double rations and a course of vitamin treatment.

Within a week it was possible actually to see the improvement in their condition. The strained gaunt look, which was so marked in Moshe and Max, fled from their faces, and their shoulders shook off the stoop that had seemed fixed for all time; the eyes were wary still, but the dullness was replaced by the sharp gleam of health. Above all, they lost the distant musty smell of slow decay and the sense of constant weariness that had nagged in their bones and made a burden of their bodies. They moved with a new confidence and vitality, and, as the human beings emerged from the gray numbered units that had left Sachsenhausen, Kurt began to understand why Wolf had suggested Moshe and Max as members of the team.

Moshe Kahn was a journalist with a sharp mind, a caustic tongue, and a cautious, not to say cynical, nature. He was, to some extent, a loner. For over a year he had both written and circulated a small underground paper that savagely lampooned Hitler and his New Order and exposed, in hilarious detail, the private lives and rackets of the leading Nazis. On a more serious level, Moshe had realized almost from the beginning that Nazi policy was directed toward the extermination of the Jewish people, and in the paper he had repeatedly warned the Jews that their choice lay between resistance or death. To ram home the point, he had published articles on the subject of street fighting and such associated themes as the manufacture of the homemade petrol bomb, which had found fame in the Spanish Civil War as the Molotov cocktail.

In typically thorough fashion he tested the product before putting the idea to the public. Following the sacking of a synagogue and the lynching of a rabbi by a bunch of Brownshirts, he tracked some of the vandals to a local beer cellar and, at an appropriate moment, tossed a "cocktail" in through an open window. He found the results impressive and felt able to recommend the recipe to his readers, although to his disappointment there was no apparent response.

Because Moshe worked cautiously and alone, the Gestapo had never been able to track him down. It was his misfortune to be arrested almost by accident in a random roundup of Jews on Crystal Night, and it was thus that he landed in Sachsenhausen concentration camp.

Max Meyer was a different kettle of fish entirely. Whereas Moshe was short and shaped somewhat like a cube, with a sallow skin and a prematurely balding head that made him look much older than his twenty-six years, Max, who was about thirty, looked handsome and boyish; his broad open face and twinkling brown eyes seemed to reflect a mixture of innocence and impudence. This, as various people had discovered to their pain and discomfort, was strangely deceptive. As a youth he had been an amateur boxer of some distinction, and, in the ring, his ruthlessness and lethal approach had prompted one of the more florid sportswriters to dub him "The Smiler with the Knife." This label, crude though it was, had stuck.

Until his arrest, he had worked as a cab driver in Berlin and was reputed to be a mechanic of exceptional skill. He was not politically motivated, but in 1929, driven more by an urge for adventure than by conviction, he had joined the left-wing paramilitary organization, the Reichsbanner. He wanted to fight the Brownshirts, and on the streets of the city in those days he was presented with ample opportunities. Before long he became a section commander.

When Hitler took over, he considered it prudent to remove himself from an area where he had become so well known and went to relatives in Vienna. There, disillusioned by the inability of the Left in Germany to unite against the Nazis and by the passivity of his own people, he became an ardent Zionist. He now believed, with a complete and single-minded passion, that the Jews would never recover their soul or dignity until they entered and possessed their own homeland.

He had helped organize the illegal entry into Palestine of a large number of Jews and was on the point of going there himself when the German army moved in and annexed Austria to the Reich. Within six weeks he was on his way to Sachsenhausen.

It was there that he met Wolf Goldberg and Moshe Kahn, and perhaps because, beneath the superficial humility imposed by the camp, each man saw in the others that some spark of spirit remained, they had struck up an unlikely friendship. Before this new and bizarre turn of events, the three men had been planning an escape bid.

Even now they found it almost impossible to believe

what was happening. They contented themselves with living for each day, eating while they could, and accepting the orders they were given. Compared to the commandant of Sachsenhausen, Unteroffizier Lugert seemed like a blessed angel from heaven!

2

But as they moved into the final weeks of their training, they began to revise this opinion. They were housed in temporary hutments away from the main camp and saw no outsiders. Thus there was no distraction for them and none for Lugert, either. He had only four men on whom to concentrate his formidable energies, and as time passed he began to turn the screw, working them almost round the clock. When he rested, which was not often, the Major took over and drove them just as relentlessly. No sooner had they collapsed into their bunks for the night than they were summoned forth again for yet another exercise. They were shouted at until their heads reeled, and they longed for the ecstasy of rest and silence.

At night, even in their sleep, they heard the voices of the Major or Lugert pounding instructions into their head:

"Both eyes open ... look along the line of sight.... Relax, relax, relax your body.... Point the gun.... Keep the arm straight.... Point, point ... don't aim.... Try it again.... Relax ... relax.... Hold the knife this way ... thumb on top.... Relax.... Keep the wrist loose.... Move the blade ... keep moving it.... Relax ... don't tense.... Go for the kidneys, throat, or heart.... Try again.... Relax, relax...."

All this and Lugert's Prussian fanaticism also! How could they relax?

They had been issued with full German army kit and were expected to fall in each morning in steel helmet, tunic, pack, ammunition pouches filled with sand, rifle, bayonet, trenching tool, and greatcoat. Formal drill was kept to a minimum, but Lugert was a spit-and-polish fanatic, and he insisted on regulation cleanliness. Any breach of his standards meant extra drill, extra work. Those swiveling eyes caught every unwarranted movement, noted every spot of dust.

What amazed the others was that Kurt made no further protest. Indeed, on the rare occasions when they were alone, he drove them as relentlessly as Lugert, criticizing any slackness or casual behavior, insisting on the most rigid discipline.

When they protested he told them: "We're Jews. Therefore we have a point to prove. We have to work harder and fight better."

Lugert insisted also that everything should be done at the double. In full marching order they ran to the range and back; they ran over the huge assault course with its spiked walls, bridges, wire entanglements, chasm, sand hills, bogs, and swaying ropes and then turned and staggered back, still running; they ran for their rations and back, and to hell with the fact that by the time they'd finished, all the coffee had splashed from the mugs. At one point, Moshe muttered that he was in danger of forgetting how to walk. Lugert could hear a whisper at fifty paces, and he heard this. He apologized to the squad for his thoughtlessness.

"I am sorry, gentlemen. I didn't realize that you liked walking. Right! Atten-shun! You shall have a little walk. Forty times round that field! By the left, quick march!"

It was, Moshe estimated, a total distance of about sixteen miles. He did not complain again.

3

The final four days and nights of training were spent on an exercise in the countryside beyond the camp. It was a grueling ordeal in which they were pitted both against geography and the elements, the ultimate test of stamina. They crawled across frozen fields, waded through icy rivers, scaled clifflike hills, hurled themselves into ditches thick with putrid mud that thawed under the heat of their sweating bodies. They fought each other in unarmed combat and did so ferociously, ruthlessly, as though they were releasing some deep frustration. And if Lugert wasn't satisfied, he would take them on himself, yelling instructions and fighting at the same time. It was the fact that both he and the Major were prepared and able to do any exercise themselves that made the fanaticism and discipline bearable and even induced a certain respect.

On the afternoon of the last day, Lugert sent them to a nearby wood to collect timber for a fire. They were weary and dispirited, and in all their minds there lay like a weight the thought that soon the mission itself would begin. For the past month they had been like men living in a vacuum, cut off from any sense of time or reality. Tomorrow they would emerge into the world again. But into what world? And what would they be asked to do?

As they dragged a large branch across a clearing, Max said to Kurt: "I have an idea."

"What?"

"Those two bastards, the Major and Herr Unteroffizier—Pigshit Lugert. Why don't we slit their throats, bury them in a ditch, and make a run for it?" He smiled engagingly as he spoke, like a boy suggesting a minor prank.

Kurt seized him by the collar of his tunic. "Listen!" he said savagely. "Listen! We're not here to try to save our own necks. Get that into your head, once and for all, or I'll drive it in with my fist!"

Max shook himself free. "You want to try that—you want to try?" He almost crooned the words as he moved onto the balls of his feet, crouching forward, arms on guard, fists clenched.

Wolf put his huge bulk between them. "Hold it! Hold it! Haven't we got enough enemies already? Is it necessary for us to fight each other?"

"He's a maniac," said Max. "A joke—I was making a joke, and he flies at me like a tiger!"

"There are jokes and jokes," said Kurt.

"Easy. Easy," said Moshe. "It's this place. We're all worn down to our nerve ends. But what's the point of fighting? Quarrels solve nothing. A quarrel is like an itch—the more you scratch the more it itches."

"Praise God," said Wolf. "He has sent a sage among us!" He checked suddenly and lifted his head as though sniffing the air. "Listen," he whispered, and put a finger to his lips.

The noise of a twig snapping underfoot somewhere among the trees cracked the strained silence. They turned toward the sound expecting to see Lugert or the Major, but no one appeared.

"It's nothing," said Moshe.

"No?" said Wolf. "Look behind you."

A man had emerged from the belt of trees and stood facing them, hands on hips, as if in challenge. He was dressed entirely in black, from the woolen hat on his head to his soft rubber-soled shoes. A knife hung in a sheath on the belt at his waist.

More movement. Three other men, dressed in the

same way, stepped out of the wood one by one, forming the corners of a square in which Kurt and the others were enclosed. They moved forward slowly, shrinking the area between them.

"What the hell—" began Kurt.

"Shut your mouth, Jew-boy!" snapped the man nearest to him. And then he shouted: "Right! Let 'em have it!"

The men drew their knives and moved forward in a weaving motion, one arm held against the stomach, the other thrusting the blade backward and forward, like the flickering tongue of a snake. Kurt mentally cursed himself for allowing his group to break the most elementary rule of all: they had left the temporary camp without arms of any sort.

Wolf had the ax that they had been using to fell the timber, and he swung it loosely, menacingly, in his huge hands, standing his ground.

Kurt stumbled as he backed warily away and recovered just in time to avoid his opponent's vicious lunge. He felt a needle thrust of pain as the knife cut into the cloth of the tunic on his left arm and pricked the flesh, but this gave him fresh impetus. He picked up a long freshly cut branch and, as the man made another dart forward, swung it at him. The man dodged easily and laughed.

Moshe had gone down with another man on top of him and was struggling desperately to hold back the hand that held the knife. Kurt sidestepped and, in one swift movement, swung the branch like a club at the man's head; he grunted, dropped the knife, and rolled over. In an instant, Moshe rolled free, took up the knife and straddled his opponent, holding the point of the blade against the shuddering throat.

Wolf had his man by the throat also, but in a different manner. He had him pressed back against a tree, with the haft of the ax forced against the larynx. The man's eyes were buttons of fear, and his face was crimson, as though all the blood was being squeezed into his head. Suddenly Wolf relaxed the pressure, and as the gasping man sagged forward he crashed his knee into the crutch; the man wrenched and fell to the ground, writhing in agony. Wolf, with brutal calm, kicked him twice in the ribs. He rolled over and lay still.

Max, as light on his feet as a matador, taunted his opponent, who was becoming flustered by his inability to make contact with this man who twirled on his feet and seemed, indeed, to be playing him like a bull. Each time he rushed, it was into empty space, as Max sidestepped and then turned to face him again.

"Come on, come on?" Max urged. "It's only a little Jew-boy. You're not frightened of a little Jew-boy, are you?" And as Wolf moved in to help, he shouted: "No! Keep out of it—this one's mine!"

"Then finish him, you stupid bastard!"

Max sidestepped again as the man made another lunge, and gripped the wrist holding the knife. In the same movement he pulled him round and let fly with his right fist, burying it in the man's guts. His opponent gave him a look of startled surprise, and his head jerked back; he did not so much fall as collapse, slowly, like a sack being emptied of its contents.

Kurt's opposition had proved to be the more durable. He had avoided the flailing branch with some success and was gradually forcing Kurt back toward a small hollow filled with water on which there lay a thin coating of ice. But he was aware that Wolf and Max had advanced, and though they were not intervening, he tried to keep them in his sight also. He was less sure of himself now; the mocking smile had vanished.

Kurt felt the earth sloping beneath his feet. He moved forward again to firmer ground, and the other man, in an incredibly swift movement, sheathed his knife and grasped the end of the branch with both hands. He pulled suddenly, surprising Kurt, who lost his grip. The man threw the branch aside, drew his knife again, and, as Kurt backed off, rushed him. Kurt waited until his opponent was nearly upon him, then sidestepped and kicked at the man's shin. All the weight of a heavy service boot was behind the kick; the man screamed, lost his footing, and plunged backward into the water.

"Took you long enough," said Max dryly.

Kurt went across to Moshe, who still held the point of the knife against the throat of his terrified opponent.

"You want me to kill him?" said Moshe in a matter-of-fact tone.

"Wait!" He bent over the man. "Are you SS?"

"No!"

"Where are you from?"

"Second Squadron, First Company, Second Penal Regiment."

"Christ!" Kurt pulled off the woolen cap. The man's head had been shaved, and suddenly, seen like this, he seemed like them, like a victim rather than an enemy. Kurt waved Moshe away. The man watched the retreating knife with uneasy, flickering eyes.

"Who sent you?" asked Kurt.

"Our company commander. We were told to wait in the woods for four escaped Jews masquerading as soldiers."

"And?"

"I don't—"

"What were you told to do?"

"They said it would be easy—"

"What were you told to do?" Kurt grasped the man's throat.

"We were promised—they promised us extra privileges, shorter sentences if we brought you in alive."

"And if that wasn't possible?"

"Only to kill if necessary."

"It was a sodding set-up!" said Wolf. "A set-up!"

"Let's cut their throats and be done with it," said Max.

"Trouble?" said the Major. They turned and saw him standing at the edge of the clearing with Lugert at his side. As the two men moved forward, the Major repeated the question. "Had some trouble, have you, Reiss?"

"Not so you'd notice," said Kurt, omitting the salute or the formal mode of address. "Next time you want to try us out you'd better find something better than this garbage!"

"Watch that tongue!" bawled Lugert.

Kurt ignored him. "Suppose we had killed them?" he asked the Major.

"They are criminals, felons, deserters."

Kurt shook his head. "You wanted us to kill them—you wanted us to—Christ, they were just guinea pigs! They were expendable."

"If you want to put it like that."

"And if the boot had been on the other foot—if they'd killed us?"

"That possibility never occurred to me," said the Major.

Kurt drew a deep breath. "You bastard!" he whispered. "You bastard!"

The Major went white; a muscle twitched in his cheek. He made an involuntary movement with his arm, as though to strike Kurt, but the movement was not completed. Instead, he turned on his heel and strode away.

4

To their relief, they returned to camp before dark that day, but they were given no respite. Lugert surveyed them with his beady eyes. "My God, what a load of pigshit! You look like shit and you smell like shit! Well, we're going to change that—right, Reiss?"

"Yes, Herr Unteroffizier!" said Kurt correctly.

"You have one hour! Sixty minutes! Then I want you out on parade in full marching order—and clean. Clean! You understand what that means, Goldberg?"

"Yes, Herr Unteroffizier!" answered Wolf smartly.

"Clean!" roared Lugert, his face reddening. "If I see one speck of mud, by God, I'll keep you at it all night! Dismiss!"

They spent the next hour in a feverish rush to keep up with the clock. By this time they had worked out a system to cope with this sort of situation, dividing the work among themselves. They stripped down to their underclothes and then, while Wolf and Moshe scraped and washed the clinging mud from boots, greatcoats and tunics, Max and Kurt cleaned and oiled all four rifles. Wolf then pressed each tunic and greatcoat in turn, Moshe polished the boots, and the others turned their attention to the rest of the equipment. As each man finished, he showered and shaved, put on clean underwear, and dressed. It was a team job, carried out at great speed but with enormous thoroughness.

They were on parade outside the hut with one minute to spare. Lugert arrived on the stroke of the hour.

"Right!" he said grimly. "Everything in order, is it?"

"Everything in order, Herr Unteroffizier," they replied in unison.

"Speak up! What are you—men or a choir of sodding sopranos? Let's hear it again!"

"Everything in order, Herr Unteroffizier!" they shouted.

"Clean?"

"Clean, Herr Unteroffizier!"

"Well, well. We shall see!"

Lugert circled each man in turn, not once but two or three times. There were agonizing moments when he paused or grunted or stared directly and accusingly into their eyes, sniffing noisily as he did so. They remained rigid, hypnotized by his presence. Even Wolf was sweating; he could feel the dampness under his armpits and in the small of his back. A bead of sweat swung from the tip of his big beaked nose, but he dared not make the slightest movement of his head to shake it away; by ill chance, as Lugert faced him for the third time, the droplet fell, splashing onto the immaculately polished toe of Wolf's boot.

An eternity of waiting. Lugert looked from boot to face, lowering and raising his eyes in an elaborate movement. Wolf tensed himself for the wrath to come as the Unteroffizier stepped back and faced the squad once more.

"It's not good," he barked. A pause, and then he added in what for him was a milder tone. "But it isn't bad." As they relaxed, he yelled again: "Stand steady in the ranks!"

Another long pause while he surveyed them. "Don't get bigheaded just because you beat the shit out of four of that scum from the other side of the camp! I saw it all. They were useless, and you weren't much better." He turned his sharp eyes on Moshe. "You—Kahn! You shouldn't be alive, you know that? Do you know that?"

"Yes, Herr Unteroffizier," said Moshe shamefacedly.

"Why?"

"I was too slow, Herr Unteroffizier. I allowed myself to be taken by surprise."

"Slow as a cart horse! And about as useless as a whore at a wedding. All of you! I'm talking to all of you! Meyer, what's the first thing you do when a man is coming at you with a knife? What have I told you? Get your coat off—or get something—and wrap it round one arm as a guard—right?"

"There wasn't time, Herr Unteroffizier!"

"Time! You had time enough to strip and take a shower! But no, not you, Meyer—you know better. You start dancing and prancing around like a tart in a ballet! As for you, Goldberg, what the hell were you playing at?"

"With respect, Herr Unteroffizier I don't—"

"You don't understand!" Lugert took the words from Wolf's mouth. "He doesn't understand. No wonder—he's got a brick in his head where his brain should be. You finished your man first, correct? So why did you stand around while the others were still at it? War isn't a game, Goldberg, fair combat, one against one. When you've won an advantage, exploit it!"

"Yes, Herr Unteroffizier."

"And now your commander, Herr Pigshit Reiss! Christ, were you lucky! The way that idiot charged at you, it was a gift! And what was your left arm doing at the time? Nothing! Swinging loose like a sodding bell rope! And you were standing full front on, offering him the maximum target. Side on, man, side on! Coat wrapped round the free arm, arm held across the stomach for protection! What did I say?"

"Side on, Herr Unteroffizier, to cut down target area. Coat round free arm, arm held across the stomach for maximum protection."

"Correct. Remember it next time—or there won't be a time after that. Next time you may come up against some real opposition." He paused and whacked his leg two or three times with his swagger stick. "Now, before we leave the subject. I have one more question. Reiss, you will answer. When those men jumped you, what did you think they were after?"

"Herr Unteroffizier?" Kurt's bewilderment showed in his voice.

"Come on, for Christ's sake!" said Lugert. "They weren't after your virtue, were they? Or did you think they were out to bugger the lot of you?"

"No, Herr Unteroffizier."

"Then what?"

"I wasn't sure, Herr Unteroffizier. I assumed they wanted to kill us."

"Marvelous! Four villainous bastards come at you out of the woods with dirty great knives and you assume—you assume!—that they are out to kill you. Now, listen! When anybody—anybody outside of training— when anybody springs out of cover and flashes a knife in my face, I don't make assumptions. I *know*. I know he is out to kill me. So what do I do? I kill him first. You understand? No half measures! You let that pigshit get up and walk away. You had them down and you let them get up. Crazy! You should have stuck the lot of them. Clear? Clear?"

"Clear, Herr Unteroffizier," they replied in chorus.

"All right," said Lugert wearily, as though he had written them off. "You will be ready to leave here at first light. The Major knows where you're going. I don't, and I don't sodding-well care. You will travel in the clothes you brought with you. Your uniforms and all equipment will be left on your bunks—clean and in good order."

He dismissed them, and they moved, in relief, toward the hut. As they reached it, Lugert called Kurt back.

"Reiss!"

Kurt hurried to him and came to attention.

"Reiss," said Lugert, "there's one other thing I have to say to you. If I had my way you'd be up the other end of this camp, doing three years with the other pigshit. Do you know why?"

"No, Herr Unteroffizier."

"No? Then I will tell you. I don't know about the Major's parents, I don't know whether he is a bastard or not. Either way it's none of my business." His voice sharpened. "But one thing I do know. No one under my command—but no one—calls an officer a bastard to his face and gets away with it. Clear?"

"Clear, Herr Unteroffizier," said Kurt.

"Rifle!" snapped Lugert. Kurt handed it to him. "Hands above your head!" Kurt lifted his arms as directed, and Lugert jammed the rifle into his hands. "Now, keep it there. Ten times round the field. I'll be watching. And if you drop your arms as much as a centimeter, I'll double the dose! Move! At the double!"

Forty agonizing minutes later, Kurt stood once more before the Unteroffizier, who had remained rigidly in place, watching his movements round the field like a hawk. Every inch of Kurt's body was bubbling with sweat; his arms felt like dead weights that at any moment might drop from his shoulders. The heavy boots held his swollen feet as if in a grip of iron, dragging at his legs.

"Well?" said Lugert.

Kurt licked his cracked lips and eyed the other man with pure hatred.

"Nothing to say?" asked Lugert.

"With respect, Herr Unteroffizier—"

"Yes?"

"You are a bastard also."

There was a long heavy silence. And then Lugert's face twisted itself into something like a smile. "That's different," he said. "I know about my parents. It's the truth. I am a bastard."

He clicked his heels, swiveled round, and marched away. They did not see him again.

TEN

1

The Reichsmarschall poured the gentle-looking rose-colored wine into two glasses, held one of them up to the light for a moment, and then handed it to the Major. He raised the other glass to his lips and nodded in appreciation.

"Congratulations," he said. "I hear your Jews did well."

"Thank you, sir," said the Major.

Both men sipped the wine. "What do you think of it?" asked the Reichsmarschall.

"Excellent, sir."

"Do you know anything about wine?"

"No, sir," said the Major with a smile.

"Then how do you know it is excellent?"

"I don't, sir. I know that I like it. And I also know that Your Excellency only drinks the best."

"My God!" The Reichsmarschall laughed. "You're on the way to becoming a diplomat, Erich."

"God forbid!" said the Major.

The Reichsmarschall settled his bulk into a chair and loosened the top button of his white uniform. He wagged a finger at the Major, indicating that he should be seated. "They gave no trouble? Your Jews, I mean?"

"No, sir. None at all."

"And you're satisfied that they are fit?"

Fit for what? thought the Major. He wanted the man to come to the point. And when that moment arrived he knew already what he was going to try to say. Aloud, he said: "In very good shape, sir."

"Good. They'll need to be." The Reichsmarschall sipped his wine, looking over the glass thoughtfully at the Major. "Now, Erich, while you've been away on vacation enjoying yourself, we have been busy. A great deal has been done." He waved a hand. "I'm not going to bother you with the details now: Himmler's pet Brigadeführer will fill you in. He's been doing most of the legwork. But I gather that everything is more or less ready for you."

"Ready, sir?"

"For Thunderbird—the mission. We've not been training Reiss and his crew up for nothing!"

"Yes, sir. I understand that, sir. But it wasn't clear to me that I was to be further involved."

"Who else?" The Reichsmarschall wrinkled his brow, as though puzzled by the other man's attitude. "I thought I'd explained everything when we discussed the subject a month ago."

"With respect, sir—I understood then that my task was to train these four men, weld them into a combat unit."

"Which you've done. And very well indeed, from all accounts. But you surely didn't imagine that your responsibility would stop there? You can't load a gun and not fire it, man! No, no, you know them and they know you. You're the logical person to see this thing through."

Come back successful—bring me success—and I'll see that you're weighed down with medals and crosses.

These earlier words paced their way through the Major's mind. And another word—*assassination*—dogged their footsteps and would not be shaken off. He had agonized over the whole business for the past four weeks, gone over those words again and again, hoping that they did not mean what he thought they meant. He knew now that it had been a forlorn hope.

The Reichsmarschall smiled. "Don't look so concerned, Erich. I'm giving you a holiday—a beautiful trip! I only wish I could go along."

"A trip? Where to, sir?"

"Where would you like to go?"

The Major hesitated. He stood up, gathering his courage. "With respect, Your Excellency, I would like to go back to my Gruppe, back to flying."

"Oh, no, Major Koller," said the Reichsmarschall. "That is not possible."

"With respect, sir—"

"Damn your respect!" The Reichsmarschall thumped the table, sending his wine glass crashing to the carpet. It fell unbroken and rolled under his chair. As the Major stooped to retrieve it, the other man dropped a hand on his shoulder, forcing him down on one knee.

"Major," said the Reichsmarschall quietly. "I am not in the mood for discussion, still less for argument." He sighed wearily, like a man with the weight of the world on his back. "Haven't I got enough problems? What the hell's wrong with you, man?"

"With respect, sir, I am an officer in the Luftwaffe. I am not an assassin." The words came from his lips, but they seemed somehow to have been spoken by another person; and it all sounded absurd and melodramatic, like a speech by the handsome hero in some old-fashioned play. Absurd, melodramatic, and above all, inadequate. How could he convince this man, express his revulsion? In his heart, he knew that the struggle was already lost. He would be borne along, as always, on the tide of the Reichsmarschall's will.

As he rose to his feet, he heard, from somewhere beyond these heavy thoughts, the sound of laughter. The Reichsmarschall was laughing, his belly dancing beneath the uniform.

"I like it, oh yes, I like it. It's good. Your honor at stake and all that, eh?" The laughter stopped suddenly, characteristically, as if controlled by some inner level. And the bland face tensed. "So you worked it out, eh? Worked out what it all meant. Well, it wasn't difficult, I suppose. And you've come to the conclusion that you don't like the idea, eh? Don't want to dirty your hands— it offends your beautiful code of honor. Damn your honor, Major! Where would Germany be now if we had stuck to your namby-pamby notions? Still in the gutter, governed by effete democrats and controlled by Jews— that's where Germany would be! We have only one concept of honor now, man—National Socialist honor! And it is very simple. Anything, any action that serves the Führer and the fatherland—that is honorable." He waved an impatient hand. "Enough of philosophy. It bores me. Get me some more wine."

The Major took a fresh glass, filled it, and carried it back, conscious all the time of those eyes following him, weighing him up.

"After all that," said the Reichsmarschall, "why do I persevere with you? A good question. And what is the answer? Because I know you, Erich. I have studied you, watched you. And I know that, despite everything, if you are given an order you will carry it out faithfully and well. That's how your life has been—ordered—isn't that so? And you need that order—it's a kind of faith. Without it, you'd be nothing. You may have certain doubts, scruples—haven't we all?—but whatever happens you will do your duty. Correct?"

"Correct," said the Major, smiling faintly. He knew he had lost; not that he had nursed any real hope of winning. What a mess he had made of it: his resistance had crumpled at the first touch! He felt the shame twist in his guts like a snake. Yet he told himself defensively, the Reichsmarschall was right after all. It was true: a man had to have some solid ground beneath his feet, an ordered pattern to his life. For him it was summed up in the one word—*duty*. Without that to brace him, there would be no foundation, no strength to his life. An image of Leni, the blonde hair spread across the white pillow like threads of gold, flickered in his mind, and he felt a stab of pain, as from an old wound.

"Go to the desk, Erich," said the Reichsmarschall. "Sit down." And as the Major hesitated, he added, "In my chair, man. It won't bite you. Now, in front of you is the Blue Paper for last December. Do you remember it?"

"Yes, sir."

"Did you read it?"

"No, sir. The Blue Papers are listed documents, with a limited circulation."

"Quite correct. However, this particular paper has a special relevance to your new assignment. You might even say that it inspired the idea of the mission." The Reichsmarschall sat back and linked his hands across his chest, like a man preparing to hear a favorite symphony. "Tell me, Erich, do you believe in auguries?"

"I don't think I do, sir," said the Major, wondering down which new path the older man was going to lead this strange conversation.

"Then you are wrong. I believe that there are secret voices that speak to us at certain times and in various ways. They give us a hint, no more, of the future and nudge us forward, so to speak. I wouldn't want to exaggerate the point; if we ignore the signs, little is lost. But if we read them correctly and act upon them, then the gain may be immense."

"Aren't you really speaking of instinct, sir?" asked the Major.

"Perhaps." The Reichsmarschall put a match to a pipe and began to puff out smoke. "Perhaps," he said again. "But I have a feeling that what I mean goes beyond instinct. Consider the following sequence of events. First, a couple of weeks or so before Christmas, an attempt is made on my life by a man named Reiss. The morning after that attempt, the latest Blue Paper lands on my desk."

"I don't see the connection, sir."

"Neither did I, at the time. At least, not clearly. But somehow the two events did form a relationship in my mind. Normally, as you know, I would have handed Reiss over to the Gestapo for punishment and execution. But I didn't do so. I couldn't have told you why, at the time. Now I know that I held back because an idea was forming in my mind. Reiss is a determined man: he came within a few seconds of bringing me down. He has courage, he hates us to the point of obsession, and, though he is a Jew, some inner voice told me that his entry into my life had not been entirely accidental. More practically, I wondered whether it would not be possible to use him in some way to our advantage."

He paused, fiddling with the pipe, loosening the tobacco with the blade of a knife. "You don't smoke, Erich?"

"An occasional cigarette, sir. But I can take it or leave it."

"You're lucky. I enjoy a pipe, but they are messy, temperamental things." He sucked the stem noisily, nodded, and relit the pipe. "I'll be quite frank with you; there were a couple of occasions when I was on the point of chucking the whole thing, telling the Gestapo that they could have Reiss. Then came New Year's Eve. I went through the old Teutonic ceremony of the molten lead. It was quite remarkable, Erich. The signs were good. And part of the lead formed a very distinct letter—the letter *R*. I don't believe entirely in these old superstitions, but nevertheless the coincidence—if one can call it that—was remarkable, don't you agree?"

The Major looked blank. "I'm not sure that I'm following you, sir. The significance of the letter _R_ ..."

"R for Reiss, man!"

"Oh, of course." The Major responded with as much enthusiasm as he could muster, but he felt utterly lost.

"R for Reiss. It was more than coincidence—it had to be. And then a day or so later, it all fell into place. I met Himmler and one of his top agents. What they had to tell me put the seal on the entire project. It was incredible, Erich! Years ago, I found my way—more by accident than design—to a meeting at which a man named Adolf Hitler was the speaker. But the moment I saw and heard him, I knew that my presence there was no accident. Fate had led me to his side. And I feel the same way now, as if fate has once more taken me by the hand and directed me toward a certain goal."

It occurred to the Major—not for the first time—that the Reichsmarschall was mad, or at least that there was a streak of madness in him. It showed in the eyes and the voice most of all: when he was in this sort of mood his irises seemed to contract and grow darker and his voice trembled on the edge of breathlessness.

And then, quite suddenly, as if he had read the Major's thoughts, the Reichsmarschall relaxed and smiled. "It's all right, Erich," he said. "All this business of fate and auguries—it offends your practical mind, I can see that. You think I'm a little mad. Well, you're probably right. No point in false modesty. All truly great men have a touch of madness in their makeup, isn't that so? An extra charge of imagination or a single-mindedness that makes them different. Next time you hear the Führer speak, watch his eyes. There's madness there, a sort of divine madness. Really. I am quite serious. Which leads me on very nicely to the next point on the agenda. The Blue Paper. Open it and study the last page—the paragraphs I've marked. And tell me if you think that is crazy."

The thin, closely typed pages crackled as the Major turned them, and in the sudden silence even this small sound took on a dramatic quality. He found some passages at the end that had been marked off in the margin by bold red strokes and that bore the general heading: SUMMARY OF CONCLUSIONS. He began to read, steadily at first, not knowing what to expect, but as he went on he was gripped by a rising sense of excitement, and the dry, matter-of-fact words seemed to whirl and dance before his eyes.

1. It is now clear that the splitting of the atom is no longer a theoretical question. Experiments conducted at the Kaiser Wilhelm Institut (and in other countries), in which uranium was bombarded with neutrons, have confirmed this.

2. It has been estimated and confirmed by experimentation that the splitting of one atom will release approximately 200 million volts of electricity. It follows, therefore, that the first nation to harness this new source of power will lead the world in energy resources.

3. Apart from its conventional use, what we have called nuclear energy will have a profound effect on the outcome of a new war. We estimate that within 3 to 5 years it should be possible for an industrially developed nation to produce a new type of bomb that would be *20 million* times as powerful as the same weight of TNT. To put it into perspective, we could say that a single atomic bomb would have the capacity to destroy the entire area of Greater London and its population, or New York and its environs.

4. Apart from the very important work done by German physicists at the Kaiser Wilhelm Institut, significant progress has also been made by scientists in Italy, Sweden, Denmark, France, the USA,

and especially in Britain. However, this remains a very specialized field. We estimate that there are probably not more than 15–20 top nuclear specialists in the world today. We do not think it an exaggeration to suggest that the outcome of the next war lies in the minds and hands of this small group of people. Recent information indicates that a significant proportion of this group of specialists has decided to continue their work in the United States and, to a lesser extent, in Britain. This should be a matter of concern.

5. We are confident that, guided by the genius of the Führer, the physicists of National Socialism will once again prove their superiority and be the first to place in our hands the ultimate weapon—a weapon that will ensure German world hegemony for all time.

The Major sat in silence for a long time, staring at the typed pages, trying to reduce what they contained to terms that his mind could grasp, but it did not seem possible. It was like a piece of science fiction—exciting and imaginative but too incredible for belief; but on the other hand, this was an official document prepared, as he knew, by some of the most eminent thinkers in the Reich.

"Well?" The Reichsmarschall's voice startled him, and he looked up quickly.

"Is it true, sir? Is it really true?" The Major shook his head as if to answer his own question.

"True? Oh, it's true—have no doubts on that score, Erich. I tell you, we are on the threshold of a new age, compared to which the Industrial Revolution will seem like a hiccup. In five years, perhaps four, all that you've read there will be a reality. Or rather, it could be, it could be."

The Reichsmarschall got up and began to pace the

room. Outside a sudden gust of wind rattled the windows and drops of rain began to patter against the glass. The Major had the strange feeling that he was imprisoned in this moment of time, that when it passed neither he nor his life would ever be the same again.

"War is coming, Erich," said the Reichsmarschall. "You know it, I know it. In a year, perhaps two, war will come. If Britain resists, and if she is joined by the United States, then it could be a long war—and one that will be fought to the death. As it goes on, both sides will become exhausted, desperate. And at that point, whoever is in possession of this ultimate weapon—this atom bomb—will use it. And win the victory."

"But our scientists have a head start over the others. According to the Blue Paper—"

"We did have!" interrupted the Reichsmarschall savagely. "We had a world lead until a few months ago. And we have thrown it away! Oh, the Blue Paper wraps it up nicely, in polite words, but the plain truth is there for those with eyes to see!"

He picked up the Blue Paper and began to quote from it, stabbing the page with his finger. "'... not more than 15–20 top nuclear specialists in the world today.... the outcome of the next war lies in the minds and hands of this small group of people. Recent information indicates that a significant proportion of this group of specialists has decided to continue their work in the United States and, to a lesser extent, in Britain. This should be a matter of concern.'" He threw the document down on the desk. "A matter of concern! What they are trying to say is that we have cut our own throats. At least four of the top specialists who have gone to America are our own people, Erich! Our own people! And we let them go, with all their notes, their knowledge! We let them walk out, find their way to a country that is a potential enemy! Have you ever heard of a greater stupidity? Do you realize what it means?"

"That the United States will—"

"Exactly. There is every chance that they will win the race. They have the material resources and now they have the experts." He stopped his restless pacing and favored the Major with a grim smile. "However, we can console ourselves with the thought that the stupidity is not all on one side. There is every reason to believe that the Americans do not realize the richness of the treasure that has fallen into their hands. The United States government has not yet allocated any real resources. The work of the physicists has not been classified, and their findings are more or less published openly. This state of affairs won't last much longer, of course, but it means we have some time in hand. Time to correct the balance. Which is where you come in, Erich. You—and Reiss."

"I don't see the connection, sir."

"You will, man, you will. I told you that I met Himmler and one of his top agents. What I learned from them confirmed that what you prefer to call my instinct had been right all along. The next day I went to the Führer and obtained his full support for your mission. Reiss and his little band of Jews are going to perform a signal service for the Fatherland. They are going to kill a few scientists for us, Erich, a few very important scientists."

The Major ran a finger over his forehead and it came away greasy with sweat. And as if some dam had broken in his head, the thoughts roared and tumbled like a torrent, bearing him along with them on a current of excitement that was electric in its intensity. He heard the Reichsmarschall's voice as from a long way off.

"They have made us a present of them, Erich. An absolute gift. Himmler's man told me that in early April there is to be a meeting of the World Association of Physicists in Montreal, Canada. We know that about eight, possibly ten of the leading nuclear scientists from Europe and America will be there. Thus with one blow—one blow—we shall regain our lead and put their work back by ten years at least."

"It doesn't seem possible."

"Everything is possible to those who have the will. And consider the neatness of the whole concept. We couldn't kill these people ourselves—that would be tantamount to a declaration of war. But by using these Jews, we cover ourselves completely. Win or lose, the Jews will be blamed."

"Suppose Reiss reveals that we were behind the plan?"

"We shall dismiss the suggestion with contempt, as yet another Jewish fabrication."

"And if he refuses to carry out the assassinations?"

"Why should he?"

"To kill ten people—"

"He has no love for the Americans or the British. What have they done for him and his people? I've watched him, Erich. He is fueled by bitterness and hatred, not only against us, but also against those hypocrites who support the Jews with fine words and nothing else. He believes that the only people who can help the Jews are the Jews themselves. I have offered him ten thousand Jewish lives. For that price, he would kill a hundred scientists."

"When will you tell him the target?"

"I won't. That will be your job. But not yet, not yet. You will put him in the picture at the appropriate moment. Now you see why I want you on this, Erich. You will travel out ahead of Reiss and his team and set everything up as far as possible. Buttmann, Himmler's agent in New York, has been ordered to give you every assistance. You alone will have contact with Reiss, although naturally you will remain discreetly in the background with no direct or obvious involvement. You leave on the Bremen for New York in three days. Reiss and the others will follow later."

"I can tell them that much?"

"Tell them as little as possible at this stage. Tell them only that they will be leaving Berlin in a few days—but not where they are going."

The Major stood up. He felt slightly unsteady on his feet and gripped the edge of the desk. "I'd better see the Brigadeführer, sir, and get a full briefing."

"Do that," said the Reichsmarschall. He smiled and added: "Well, if I've done nothing else, I've succeeded in breaking through that iron control of yours, Erich. You actually seem excited, animated."

"Hard not to be, sir. It's an incredible project."

"Make it credible—that's your job." As the Major went to the door, the Reichsmarschall checked him. "Erich, one more thing."

"Sir?"

"I understand that the Jewish Council here has already drawn up a list of one thousand Jews who will be the first to leave under the arrangement with Reiss."

"I wasn't aware of that, sir."

"Check it. You'll find it's true." The Reichsmarschall's voice hardened. "We shall be providing Reiss and the others with new identities and the necessary passports and so forth to go with them. It is possible, of course, that once they embrace Canadian or American hospitality, they may decide to abandon our little project. You might tell them, at some appropriate point, that if anything like that happens, we shall kill every Jew whose name appears on the list. Every man, woman, and child."

2

Kurt and the others had been taken back to their old cell at the HQ of Luftflotte I. Their bodies were hungry for rest, and they slept from the moment of their arrival in the morning until the late afternoon. That evening, the Major and the Brigadeführer came to brief them.

"You leave here in three days," said the Major.

"Where are we going?" said Kurt.

"You will be told in due course."

"Do you know?"

"You will be told in due course," said the Major stubbornly.

"And the purpose of the mission?"

"That also. In due course."

"In due course, in due course!" Kurt's hand spanned his forehead, thumb and fingers pressing into the temples, like a man in despair. He had waited a month for this moment, four long bitter weeks during which he had forced himself to think only of the day, to free his mind of the question that haunted his mind like a specter: What did they want him to do?

The question roared and echoed in his head, but there was still not even the whisper of an answer.

The cold, controlled voice of the Major broke in on him. "I understood that we had an agreement. A bargain. So far we've kept our part of it. We expect you to keep yours."

"I am not trying to back down!" Kurt cut the space between them with his hands, desperate to make this man understand. "I simply want to know where we are going—and the ultimate purpose of the operation. Is that so much to ask?"

"Too much. I can only repeat—you will be fully

briefed at the appropriate time." As Kurt hesitated, shaking his head, the Major continued, "If you refuse to cooperate further, my orders are explicit."

"Sachsenhausen?" said Kurt bitterly.

"The Brigadeführer can have a truck here in ten minutes."

"It'll be like going home," said the Brigadeführer. "I'm sure the commandant will lay on a real welcome." He tittered, enjoying his little joke, but he was the only one in the room who did.

"Please God," whispered Moshe, "please God, not that!" It sounded like a prayer.

"I'd like five minutes with my friends," said Kurt.

"I'd like five minutes with you!" said the Brigadeführer, in the same irresistibly jocular tone as before.

The Major nodded. "All right, Reiss. You shall have your five minutes."

"While we're waiting, I'll order that truck. Just in case it should be needed," said the Brigadeführer.

As soon as the door closed, Wolf and Max rounded on Kurt. "What are you doing to us?" said Wolf. "For God's sake, what does it matter where we go?"

"Anything—anything is better than Sachsenhausen!" Max said.

"Anything is better than being dead," said Moshe, who was sitting on a bunk, looking mournful. Then he added reflectively: "Or is it? On this question I'm no longer sure."

"We've talked it over a dozen times," said Wolf. "You went into it blind—so did we. So what's the difference now?"

"Nothing," said Kurt. "Look, I'm not proposing we chuck it in. I'm not crazy. They'd send you to the camp and hang me with piano wire. But I want to be sure, I've got to be sure that you know what you're doing, that you understand why we are here."

"Because we've got no bloody choice!" said Max.

"No!" said Kurt, shaking his head. "No! We're doing it because we have a chance to save ten thousand people. Not many. A handful. But something. Isn't that the reason?"

"That's what I meant," said Max.

"Did you? Listen, a month ago things looked different. You were different. You were offered a chance to get out of that camp and you jumped at it. You would have said anything, promised anything. Well, you did make a promise. We all did. We agreed to carry through this mission in exchange for the lives of ten thousand of our people. *Carry it through.* Remember that. OK—now you've had a month to think it over. You've got food in your guts, you're as fit as fleas. Do you still feel the same way?"

"What's the point?" said Max, spreading his hands. "Even if we didn't feel the same, what choice have we got?"

"Back at the camp," said Kurt, "you suggested that we kill the Major and the Unteroffizier and make a run for it."

"I told you," protested Max, "I told you, I was making a joke."

"I hope so," said Kurt. "I hope you were. Because you know what would have happened if we'd taken you seriously? We might have got clear away but they would have killed a thousand Jews in revenge for the Major and five hundred for Lugert. They would have marched thousands of others off to the camps. That's what would have happened, Max, my friend. Maybe another Crystal Night."

"He's right," said Moshe. "He's not wrong, he's right."

"It was a joke," said Max uneasily. "Sometimes I think you have no sense of humor."

"All right," said Kurt. "I just wanted to make the point. If any one of you—of us—gets the notion to quit, to make a break for it, just remember the thousands of poor buggers out there who will have to pay the price."

"I personally make a promise," said Wolf. "I will break the legs of anyone who tries to quit. Or even talks about it." He flexed his hands. "Understood?"

"God of our fathers!" said Max. "A man makes a joke and suddenly he's a villain!"

"There are problems," said Moshe. "I can see problems looming ahead."

"Problems!" said Wolf. "When didn't we have problems? Problems come more often than chicken soup."

"No, listen," said Moshe, "I've been giving the subject a lot of thought. Listen." He held up a hand and began to tick off the fingers. "Number one: They want us to carry out a mission, correct? Number two: They won't tell us what it is—not yet. Number three: In their eyes, this mission is so important that they have already released one hundred Jews and promised that another ten thousand may also go. Number four: They don't choose their own men for this very important mission, they choose a bunch of Jews. Number five: They feed us up and train us like we're special soldiers. So what conclusions must one draw from this?" He began again. "Number one—"

"Talk faster," said Wolf. "Who needs the fingers?"

"First," said Moshe, partly conceding the point by lowering his hand. "First, there can be no credit in this mission, or they'd do it themselves. Second, it must be a dirty job, a very dirty job. Otherwise why choose Jews to carry it out? Third, it must mean violence, maybe killing, or why waste time training us? So let us assume they want us to kill someone. Who? Not anyone, that's for sure. Not a nobody—a somebody. An important somebody. What conclusion must one draw from this, I ask you?"

"Don't ask. Tell!" said Wolf. "And get on with it!"

"So if we succeed, we kill an important somebody.

What happens, who is blamed? The Jews, naturally. Goebbels will trumpet it to the whole world. I can hear him saying it. Look, he'll say, weren't we right all along about these terrible Jews? Murderers! Cutthroats! That's what he'll say."

"And if we don't kill this somebody?"

"The same thing. Goebbels will say the same thing. Murderers, cutthroats, Jews. They tried to kill this important man—they should be punished."

"So we lose whatever happens!" wailed Max.

"And maybe get ourselves bumped off in the bargain!" cried Wolf.

"When a Jew loses, he loses twice," said Moshe, with a sweep of his hands.

"Shut up, Moshe," shouted Kurt. "All of you. Shut up! Look at you, a bunch of *nebekhs*. We haven't started yet, and already you're talking as if we're finished!" He shook his head and sighed then continued in a quieter, more reasoned tone. "Look. Don't you think I've considered all that, gone over and over it in my mind? Of course, they're up to something. Of course, they're using us for some dirty game. Of course, whatever we do, they'll try and turn it against the Jews. Is that something new for us, a novelty perhaps?"

"But what can we do about it?" asked Max.

"I don't know," said Kurt. "That's the truth. At this minute, I don't know. But there must be a way. Listen, we've saved a hundred people already. Because of us, a hundred people, mostly kids, are safe in Sweden. Isn't that something? A little bit of victory? All right, the bastards think they've got us by the balls. Maybe they have for the moment. All we can do is to go along with them. But perhaps the time will come when we can turn the situation to our advantage. When you must, you can, isn't that so?"

There was a small, prickly silence. Then a slow smile spread from face to face, and Wolf clapped Kurt on the shoulder with such power that he staggered under the blow.

"He's right!" Wolf said. "If you want to beat a dog, you can always find a stick. He's got brains this one— he'll think of something."

I hope so, thought Kurt inwardly, though without any great conviction. But he was relieved that he had been able to revive their flagging spirits and made a mental resolve to keep a closer eye on them in the future. Not because of any lack of trust, but simply because the experience of the past few weeks had, to a certain extent, disoriented them; they had been subject to so many abrupt changes, there had been so many ups and downs, highs and lows that there was no certainty in their minds. They could descend from extreme and exaggerated optimism to the depths of depression in the space of a few minutes. He had felt the same pendulum swing of feeling in himself, and he knew that it was dangerous. They were physically fit; now it was his task to bring some balance and strength to their morale.

The door opened and the Major came in with the Brigadeführer. "Well?" he asked.

"A unanimous decision, Herr Major," said Kurt cheerfully. "We have decided that we prefer not to go to Sachsenhausen."

"Good," said the Major. "Now perhaps we can get down to business." He spoke without relief or enthusiasm.

3

The following evening, Kurt went to the café to see Joseph Zellner of the Jewish Council. The other customers greeted his appearance with curious looks; some muttered half-audible cynical comments and others with more cautious minds drank up their coffees and slipped away.

Kurt could feel their unease and shared it. Earlier in the day, as part of the preparations, he and the others had been taken through the staff entrance of a large store and, in the privacy of a stockroom, fitted out with new clothes. They had then been conducted to an apartment, maintained by the Luftwaffe for the use of its high-ranking officers on their visits to Berlin, and told that this was where they would stay for the next two days and nights. Two men from the Luftwaffe Polizei, the equivalent of the military police, mounted a discreet guard over them. It was another abrupt change of circumstances, and it gave Kurt no pleasure. The contrast between this luxury and the conditions at the penal camp was too much; it could only unsettle his team. But there was nothing he could do about it. There had already been talk among the men at Luftflotte I about the four Jews in the guardroom who were being given such special treatment, and the Major had insisted that their continued presence there would be unwise. The guards had been allowed to believe that the Jews were being removed to a concentration camp.

Since his other clothes had been taken away, Kurt had no choice but to wear the new suit and raincoat, which had been tailored in a fashionable American style. In the dingy café, facing the shabby Zellner, he felt like an intruder, like someone from that other world beyond the Jewish quarter.

Zellner raised a quizzical eyebrow. "A transformation already! You know, I didn't expect to see you again. This crazy business—I didn't think they'd go on with it."

"What's the news?" said Kurt abruptly.

"Not good," said Zellner. "I told you before—nobody wants to take in Jews. Mention ten thousand to them and they throw a fit. However, we have been working on the Cuban angle. It is possible that the Cubans will accept one thousand at a price."

"Price?"

"Nothing is for nothing. We can buy entry visas for Cuba at six hundred marks per head. At least, that was the price yesterday. It goes up every day. But the World Council of Jews is helping—it will find the money in Britain, Canada, the U.S."

"For only one thousand people?"

"It's a beginning."

"Children?"

"As many as possible. But you must understand that we cannot send a thousand children alone. It would not be possible. As far as we can, we are selecting families—parents with children."

"How will they get to Cuba?"

"We think it may be possible to charter a Norwegian ship. The Scandinavians, they are the best, the most helpful. But they are small nations; their resources are limited. Whereas the United States—" He checked and shook his head. "They still refuse to increase the quota."

Kurt nodded. "How about the rest? The other nine thousand?"

"We're doing what we can." Zellner sighed. "There are others who still have money. But it is not easy, you understand. To raise false hopes would be a cruelty. And even if we manage to find a country that will take ten thousand Jews, do you believe the Nazis will let them leave?"

"I don't know," said Kurt. "Maybe we can find a way to make them."

"You have a plan in mind?" asked Zellner.

"No," said Kurt wryly. "I wish I had."

Later, as he was about to leave, he remembered something else, and he turned back to Zellner. "The Jews who are to be allowed to leave. You said you were selecting families—parents and children—for the first thousand."

"Correct."

"Have you made a list?"

"Naturally."

"And has this list gone to the Nazi authorities?"

"Of course. It went to Heydrich's office. There was no choice: they must give the necessary clearance. Why do you ask?"

"Not important. Just checking," Kurt said, wondering whether the lie showed in his eyes. He mumbled a farewell and left the café.

As he walked back to the apartment to join the others he felt like an old man weighed down with despair. Now, through his own stupidity, he had presented them with a thousand hostages! If he failed to complete the mission, the Major had warned him that the people on the list—men, women, children—would pay the price. They were in his hands.

As he turned the corner into Bismarckstrasse, head down, he collided with a man and woman going the other way. The woman almost lost her footing, and the man said angrily: "Why the hell don't you look where you're going!"

"Sorry, sorry," Kurt mumbled automatically.

"Clumsy bastard!" the man said. "Do you own the sidewalk? Who do you think you are!"

"I am a Jew," said Kurt.

"What?"

"I am a Jew," said Kurt, his voice rising. "A Jew, a Jew!"

The man stared at his white face for a moment, then grasping the woman's arm, he hurried away.

"I am a Jew!" shouted Kurt.

The man's voice came back to him on the raw night wind.

"Drunk! Had a skinful from the look of him!"

ELEVEN

1

By the morning of April 4, the German submarine U-826 had almost completed the long journey from Kiel. To the west lay the hazy outline of the American coast, and to the east, the darker and more distant blur of Nova Scotia. The commander of the U-boat, surveying the scene through the periscope, had the feeling that he was sailing his vessel into the arms of a giant nutcracker. From time to time he checked and rechecked their position, and it seemed that the arms of the nutcracker were closing in on them.

In the late afternoon the U-boat slipped past Grand Manan Island into the Bay of Fundy. The operator took radio bearings on the Canadian cities of Fredericton and Moncton in New Brunswick, and Halifax in Nova Scotia and reported that they had crossed the invisible sea border between the U.S. and Canada and were within two or three hours of their objective. The commander ordered the speed to be reduced to three knots and set a course that would take them nearer to the New Brunswick coast. An hour or so later, in the darkness, the U-boat surfaced without lights, and the commander was able to make a further visual check on their position. There was a full moon, and along the coastline the lights hung in little golden clusters, interspersed by stretches of darkness, like lanterns on a black rope. About two miles away, a lighthouse winked brazenly at the night, cutting it into segments of light and dark.

He sucked in the sharp night air, filling his lungs

with its freshness, then went below and gave the First Officer the order to submerge to periscope depth. Again the vessel edged forward, closer to the coast, until the water depth reached 150 feet. The commander set the U-boat on the bottom and stopped engines. He checked with the Navigation Officer, who confirmed that they were bang on target.

In the wardroom he opened a bottle of North German rum, known by the intimidating name of Flensburg Fire, and toasted the occasion. It was reasonable that they should feel a certain pride in their achievements: the journey had taken six weeks, and they were exactly on course and on time. Moreover, the experience would be invaluable for any similar expeditions in the future. The U-826 was one of the newer long-range submarines, and the German Admiralty had seized this opportunity to test its capabilities. It had a displacement of nearly one thousand tons, a speed of sixteen to seventeen knots on the surface and of seven knots when submerged, and could travel a distance of twelve thousand miles on one load of fuel. The master of the U-826 was Leutnant Eugen Pashke; at twenty-six, it was his first command, and he was delighted with his new vessel. Apart from one or two minor problems, she had more than come up to expectations.

As the rum tingled in his blood, he thought of Flensburg and Germany. Within an hour or so, he would be able to land his human cargo and turn his head toward home.

2

Down below, in a section of the torpedo store that had been temporarily partitioned off for their use, the four men changed out of the working overalls they had worn throughout the long journey into outfits that, it was hoped, would enable them to pass as lumberjacks. It was hot and stuffy in the confined space, and they laid their heavy topcoats aside until the moment came to go on deck. Each man carried a case containing a civilian suit, spare underwear, shoes, and personal articles; each item had been carefully checked so that there were no incriminating labels or marks. They also had passports, papers, photographs, and letters that confirmed their new Canadian identities, plus about one hundred dollars each. A good deal of time during the long tedious voyage had been spent rehearsing their background stories.

Wolf and Max spoke scarcely any English, but Kurt had coached them to a point where they could speak and understand a few essential phrases. If they ran into any trouble, they were to pass themselves off as Polish immigrants.

They said little as they made their preparations to land, and when these had been completed to Kurt's satisfaction, they sat in silence in the cramped quarters, which had been both home and prison for the past six weeks. It seemed that they had exhausted all conversation; their minds and tongues were frozen, set only on what lay ahead.

An hour after their embarkation at Kiel, the Brigadeführer had come aboard and briefed Kurt, telling him the destination and the final objective of the mission. Kurt had braced himself for this moment, but even so, he was shattered by the enormity of the task and by the calculated ruthlessness with which it had been put forward. To kill one person, to get one man's body in your sights and squeeze the trigger on him, that was difficult enough, but it was possible. What they were asking now bordered on the fantastic. To kill eight, perhaps ten people—they were asking him to organize a massacre!

Yet there was no going back. He had walked like an innocent into their trap. He had made a deal with the devil, and he was being pressed for a devil's payment. The Brigadeführer had tersely reminded him of the penalty of failure, of the one thousand Jews on the list who were virtual hostages.

On the first night at sea he had revealed the plan to the others, and for the first week they had argued and debated the subject until they were sick of it. In the end, it was agreed that they had no choice but to go ahead. It was a simple matter of arithmetic—the lives of eight or ten unknown scientists against those of a thousand Jews and possible freedom for nine thousand more.

Wolf put it into words for them all. "Do you see a queue of people waiting to help the Jews? Does anyone see such a queue? Look with a telescope, you won't find it. So we have to help ourselves. We're four people only, but maybe we can start something. So let's stop the argument and get on with it!"

Kurt thought of all this as they waited for the next sign of movement from the submarine. In his heart, he knew that the solution was not likely to be as simple as they thought. In his experience, two and two made four at school, but never in real life. But for the moment he had no alternative to offer. The thing was in motion now, in full flood, and he had no choice but to allow himself to be carried along on its tide.

The minutes dragged by. Each time Kurt checked his watch the hands seemed scarcely to have moved. At last, he heard the motors start up again and felt the U-boat lift from the seabed.

Leutnant Pashke ordered the First Officer to stand by and went up to the bridge. From there he gave orders for the U-boat to move closer to the shore. They were still in good water, but within a few minutes it began to lose depth, dropping rapidly from 150 feet to 100 and then to 80. He stopped the engines and studied the shoreline, which was about 600 yards distant. There were no lights, no sign of habitation. The wind had freshened, and the waves bounced angrily against the sleek sides of the submarine.

What concerned the Leutnant most of all was the moonlight, which seemed to have intensified. At its brightest, it illuminated a great swathe of water, and he mentally cursed the people who had arranged the time of the rendezvous for choosing this particular night. He felt vulnerable, exposed, as if he were caught in some giant searchlight. Checking his watch, he decided that he would wait fifteen minutes. He ordered two seamen to lower a rubber boat and attach it to the U-boat with a long, stout line, so that everything would be in readiness, then sent a message to Kurt to tell him and his companions to stand by.

Fifteen minutes passed. By this time the moon had momentarily hidden itself behind a bank of clouds, and Pashke decided to wait a little longer. Three more minutes and then, at last, he saw what he had been waiting for—three short and two long flashes of light from the shore. He replied with three short flashes, which were acknowledged in the same way.

The four men emerged from below, pulling on their jackets. Now that the moment had come, the young Leutnant was embarrassed, feeling that he ought to say something. These men were soldiers of the Reich, after all, who were about to go ashore on a strange continent. No doubt they were on an important mission for the fatherland, and while they were risking their necks he would be making his way back home. They were brave, he thought, but at the same time they puzzled him. It was not something one could put into words; it was simply a question of attitudes.

When, for example, he had gone to them with the joyous news that the Führer had won yet another bloodless victory, and that the whole of Czechoslovakia was now in German hands, they had shown no enthusiasm. Their reaction had been one of moody silence, as if he had brought word of a setback rather than a great triumph! In the end he had left them to themselves, assuming that this strange behavior arose from their training as spies, and from the inner tensions created by the nature of their secret work.

Kurt was the last one to drop into the rubber boat, and just as he was about to do so, the moon evaded its escort of clouds and flooded the scene with clear, mellow light. The Leutnant stiffened to attention and raised an arm.

"Heil Hitler!" He spoke in little more than a whisper and he intended the words more as a tribute, or a farewell, then as a salute. Kurt turned stiffly making no response and the Leutnant dropped his arm in embarrassment.

"I mean—good luck," he stammered, and held out a hand.

Kurt stared at him coldly for an instant. But the Leutnant's face was so boyish, the look so innocent and devoid of malice, that he smiled and shook the proffered hand.

"Shalom," he said, with a teasing smile.

It was not a word the Leutnant had ever heard before, and he was still thinking about it when a tug on the line told the seamen that the boat had reached the shore. He stood on the bridge peering at the beach as they hauled the dinghy back to the U-boat, and later, when they had cleared the coast and were safely submerged in deep water, the strange word echoed in his head.

He mentioned it to the First Officer who smiled and said: "Shalom? It's a Jewish word."

"What does it mean?"

"Peace. Peace be with you. Something like that. You mean you've never heard it?"

"Not until tonight," said the Leutnant, half apologetically. "I've never really met any Jews, not to talk to, that is. You don't suppose that fellow was a Jew, do you?"

"Of course not."

"Then why did he use that word?"

"It was a joke. He was pulling your leg. It was a joke." And he added seriously, because he was a good Nazi who had been trained in the Hitler Youth: "Not a very good joke. I should forget it if I were you, Eugen. A word like that, used in the wrong place, could get you into all sorts of trouble."

3

Three half-second flashes of light showed in the shadows above the beach, and the four men stumbled toward the signal, the sea baying at their heels. It was the first time in weeks that they had set foot on land, and they found themselves slithering and sliding like drunks on the loose shingle. Their labored breathing formed into little clouds in the clear, frosty air as they clambered up the steeply shelved shore. At last, at the top of the incline, they reached a narrow belt of soft sand and, beyond that, a dirt track, where they paused. The track was patterned with patches of snow that having partially melted during the day, had now frozen hard again, and it splintered under their feet like broken glass.

The moon had hidden its face again, but there was sufficient light for them to make out the dark outline of a small parked truck. A slim figure in a hooded coat came forward out of the darkness, and to their surprise, they heard a woman's voice. "You are out late tonight. Have you lost your way?"

She spoke in English with a strong North American accent, and it was a moment or two before Kurt remembered that this was the prearranged password. In spite of the circumstances, he felt a sense of absurdity of the situation, as if he were involved in some childish game. In truth, the last time he had used or responded to passwords was at school, when he had been initiated into some juvenile society.

And so, with a slight edge of mockery in his tone, he replied according to instructions. "I am afraid that we have missed the road. I should be grateful if you could help us."

"I shall be happy to give you a lift." This time she spoke in German.

He replied in the same tongue. "Thank you. That is most kind. We are pleased to accept."

She moved nearer. The hood framed an attractive oval face and clear blue eyes. "My name is Greta Frank. And you are—?"

"Richard Lloyd," he replied. They had decided that he should keep and use the English name he had adopted on his return to Germany.

"You will come in the front with me. The others, in the back. Quickly, quickly!" She could not keep the nervousness from showing in her voice.

They drove for about three miles, climbing slowly upward from the shoreline until they reached a made-up road. Plows had cleared the track, and on either side there were great banks of frozen snow, which glittered like crystal in the moonlight. As the truck picked up speed on the firmer surface, the girl seemed visibly to relax.

"Where are we exactly?" asked Kurt.

"In New Brunswick, Canada. About eight miles north from a town called Saint John."

"Are we going there?"

"Tonight we stop in a cabin outside the town, near the lake. In the morning I will drive you to Saint John, where you take the train to Montreal. Those are my instructions."

They lapsed into silence for a few minutes and then he ventured another question. "Are you German?"

"Didn't they teach you not to ask such questions?" she countered.

"It's simply that you speak English like an American."

"Like a Canadian, you mean. There is a difference. It is not surprising. I was born here, in New Brunswick, in Fredericton, the provincial capital. My parents came from Esslingen, near Stuttgart. Do you know it?"

"I am afraid I don't."

"I was there two years ago on a long visit. It was wonderful—I mean, the whole atmosphere, everything. I felt truly German for the first time, really for the first time. I heard the Führer speak in Munich—that was an experience, a revelation. I wanted to stay on in Germany, but they asked me to—" she stopped suddenly, as if aware that she was chattering too much, and smiled. "I don't need to tell you, after all. There are many ways of serving the fatherland, isn't that right?"

"No question about it," he said. She did not catch the dryness in his tone. At least, he thought, she knows nothing about us, and probably no more than we do about the mission. They had left the road now and were bumping over an uneven frozen track. The truck gave a sudden lurch, throwing him against her. He was conscious for a moment of her closeness, of an inviting warmth, of a body scent that stirred his blood, as if her flesh were sending out signals.

"Whoops! Sorry," she said.

"Any time," he answered.

He levered himself up, his fingers pressing into her

thigh. She gave him a quick, smiling, almost flirtatious glance.

"Nearly there," she said.

4

The cabin stood in a clearing among slender pine and sturdy maple trees. From the front there was a view of the lake, and beyond it a pattern of intermittent lights that marked the outskirts of the town. After the stuffiness of the U-boat, the air had an icy sharpness that stabbed at their lungs with a force that made them gasp for breath.

But inside the cabin it was snug and warm, with a great log fire crackling in an open hearth. Greta had laid in stores, and they wolfed down a meal of soup, beans and meat, and great slabs of fresh bread and butter, washed down with what they regarded as some rather inferior beer. She watched them with a furtive curiosity, which amused Kurt, and he wondered what thoughts were going through her head. Max with his casual, open good looks, and Kurt, who had bleached his hair again, could both have passed as what the SS would define as males of good Aryan stock; but, by the same token, Wolf and Moshe looked so aggressively Jewish that they might almost have modeled their appearance on some Nazi anti-Semitic cartoon.

Since his release from Sachsenhausen, Wolf's hair had not so much grown as flourished, as if it were determined to make up for all those wasted months. Black as jet, it covered his head in great curling waves; below this dark foliate his huge beaked nose thrust forward like the prow of a ship, and his brown luminous eyes surveyed the world with cautious humor. The impression of shagginess was enhanced by his heavy body, which seemed to exude a sort of bearlike strength.

By contrast, Moshe appeared pathetically small and almost yellow, like the dried-up kernel of a nut. His hair had grown also, but in a perfunctory, wispy way, so that it clung to his balding head like a fringe; his thin, hooked nose looked as if it had been stuck on as an afterthought by some careless plasterer. Kurt knew from experience that within that lean, bony body there lay great reserves of stamina and a strength, which was the more effective for being unsuspected, but there were times when he wondered how the man managed to keep going.

After the meal and before they put their heads down for the night, Kurt pulled on his jacket and went outside. A freshening wind blew a thin, powdery snow into his face. He circled the cabin twice, when he heard a footfall behind him, and turning, he saw the girl.

"What are you doing?" she asked.

"Just checking the layout," he said.

"There is no need. You are safe here. No one will come."

"We must have left tracks."

"They will be covered by the morning."

"What about that?" He pointed to the plume of smoke that billowed out from the chimney.

"We are not fools," she said sharply. "The cabin belongs to my uncle, and I have been staying here for the past two weeks. People know it is occupied. They would be surprised not to see smoke."

"And tomorrow, when you drive into Saint John with four strange men—that won't surprise them?"

"You will travel in the rear of the truck, under cover. You will get out when I give the signal." She laughed. "You worry too much. The people here are simple folk. They know me and my parents. For them,

Europe is another planet. They do not think in terms of spies or agents or things of that sort. Believe me, they make it very easy for us."

"They make it easy for you everywhere," he said, and turned to go inside.

"Wait," she said, touching his arm. He saw the question in the blue eyes before she asked it. "Listen. I don't understand. The big man and the small, pale one. Are they ... are they ... *Jews?*" She whispered the last word, screwing up her face as if she had caught the whiff of an unpleasant odor.

"Why? Does it matter?" he asked, half mockingly.

She gave him a look in which perplexity warred with disbelief. "But surely they wouldn't send—" She stopped in surprise as he pulled her toward him and pressed his mouth against hers. She tried to turn her head away at first, but he held her firmly. His skin felt rough and cold, and there was a faint saltiness on his lips as he kissed her. A ripple of excitement ran through her body growing stronger as his kissing grew more urgent.

"Is that what six weeks on a submarine does for you?" she said, as he drew away at last.

It had been Kurt's intention to ask her whether she had appreciated the non-Aryan flavor of the kiss, but he held back the words. As she stood there smiling, her cheeks glowing, she seemed like a sister to the U-boat commander: she had the same clean, fresh, eager, almost naïve look; it was hard to see any depth of malice or evil in her. And then he told himself sternly that such thoughts were dangerous. She was a Nazi, and a dedicated one at that, or she would not have been chosen for the job she was doing. His hatred was his strength; it was all he had left, and he dare not allow it to be weakened. And yet ...

"Is anything wrong?" she asked, puzzled by his silence.

He shook his head. "No."

This time she came to him, offering up her lips, and he asked no more questions of himself. Later, when the others were asleep, stretched out in front of the fire on the floor of the main room of the cabin, he went through to the small bedroom, where she was waiting for him, naked under the heavy covering of sheets, blankets, and furs. She was already moist with expectation, and the first lovemaking was desperate and almost brutal as their quivering bodies clashed and locked together. It was all over quickly, but then, with the fever gone, they made love more gently, tenderly exploring each other, crooning incoherent words until, much later, he entered her again, and it was beautiful.

5

It seemed that Greta had been right on all counts. When they went out the following morning the land was covered by a fresh sheet of snow, effectively obscuring their earlier tracks. And when they arrived at Saint John and the railroad station, there were no problems. They had changed into their suits for the journey, and they looked like a group of young Canadian businessmen. Kurt was nervous, for this was their first public exposure, but it soon became obvious that, apart from the odd, curious, amused glances at Wolf, who seemed to be bursting out of his clothes, no one was interested in them, and they began to relax. Kurt was concerned because the railroad to Montreal ran across the state of Maine, and this meant that they would have to enter and leave United States territory, but Greta reassured him on this point also.

"They rarely check," she said, "especially if you've got a through ticket to Montreal." She smiled as if she were commenting on the foolishness of such people.

"It's an open frontier, you see, an open border."

Kurt thought how good it would be if there were open borders all over the world, but he did not say so. Up to this point she had been brisk and matter-of-fact, making no mention of their night together, but just as he was about to board the train with Wolf, she drew him aside.

"I don't suppose we shall meet again," she said.

"I doubt it."

"It was good," she said.

"Very good."

"I am glad that I was able to make you happy," she said. There was a hint of pride in the blue eyes, and he realized suddenly that she saw herself as some kind of Brunhilde and that she had cast him as the Nordic hero who was off to perform deeds of danger and daring for the Führer. By her reckoning, it was an honor and a privilege to have given love and succor to such a man. His feelings veered between outrage and pity, and, remembering the sweetness of her body, pity won.

"Greta," he said gently, "do you hate the Jews?"

"Of course." She looked at him as though bewildered by this sudden turn in conversation. "The Führer has said—"

"No, no. Not the Führer. I am not asking what the Führer thinks. You. What do you feel? Truly feel?"

"What a question!" she said, still with the same puzzled look. "We all know what the Jews have done, what they are. Why are you asking?" And then she looked beyond him toward Wolf and back again, searching his face for the answer to her own question, until understanding dawned on her face.

"He is a Jew!" she whispered. "And the other one."

"All of us," he said. "All four."

"You? You can't be!" There was horror in her voice; her full lower lip trembled.

"Why not?"

"Because—"

"Because they wouldn't send Jews here—at least, not by submarine?" he said mockingly. "Your Führer moves in mysterious ways."

"Not that," she said. "I didn't mean that."

"Ah," he said. "I see. I can't be a Jew because I look like a human being and even perform like one in bed, is that it?"

She stiffened, and for a moment he thought she was going to strike him. Then she said coldly: "You have your instructions. In Montreal you are to go to the Windsor Hotel on Peel Street. Rooms have been reserved for you. You will be contacted there by a friend."

"A friend? I doubt it," he said dryly.

She turned and strode briskly away. He watched for a moment and joined Wolf.

"A beautiful piece!" said Wolf.

"Shut up!" said Kurt savagely.

"We all heard you go to her last night. We weren't asleep. We lay there, sweating with envy."

"Shut up!" Kurt said again.

"So what's wrong?" said Wolf genially. "You didn't enjoy it perhaps? Stop snarling! You have so much luck that you can afford to spit in its face?"

During the journey, Moshe picked up an American magazine, and after studying it with furrowed brow, he handed it to Kurt. "It's like a sickness," he said shaking his head. "Like a sickness. Now it has swum the Atlantic Ocean."

The magazine contained an article in the form of a profile of a man named Father Coughlin, known as the Radio Priest. It was estimated that he had a listening audience in America of forty million people. One picture showed him giving the Nazi salute at a rally in New York and quoted him as saying: "When we get through with the Jews in America, they'll think the treatment they received in Germany was nothing!"

The strange thing was that in the picture, Father Coughlin looked a little like Kurt's father, and this odd resemblance brought a resurgence of all his old hatred. Here, too, in this so-called new world, it seemed that there was to be no mercy, no sanctuary. Only a few hours before his body had been that of an ordinary man lying with a woman, but now, again, it was suspect, less than human, a Jewish body for which there was no home in the entire world.

Kurt tore out the photograph with the quote and put it in his pocket. He would keep it, he thought bitterly, as a talisman against any further weakness of the sort he had shown toward the U-boat Leutnant and Greta. Henceforth he would find no room for feelings of pity toward anyone but his own persecuted people. And that, at least, would make what he had to do more bearable.

6

They checked into the Windsor Hotel late that evening, and an hour later Kurt had a visitor. It took him a moment or two to recognize the sturdy figure in the civilian suit.

"May I come in?" said the Major dryly. "These bags are heavy."

He moved into the room and dropped two large cases onto the bed. Kurt closed the door and turned to him. "I didn't expect you," he said.

"That makes the thought mutual," said the Major. "I half expected that you would all disappear once you reached Montreal."

"We have a job to do first," said Kurt.

"Which is why I am here. Do you want a briefing to-night, or would you rather have it in the morning?"

"Now," said Kurt. "The sooner we know what we have to do, the better." He spoke coldly, giving nothing. This man seemed to have brought with him the smell of the Reichsmarschall, to have transformed this hotel room in Canada into a little part of Hitler's Germany.

"I take it that you were given a general briefing before you left? You know the target and so forth?"

"Yes. Targets would be more accurate."

"The latest information we have is as follows." The Major, responding to the other man's tone and manner, spoke brusquely. "Seven of the European scientists are traveling to New York on the *Queen Mary* and will arrive tomorrow. They are staying there for two days as guests of various American colleagues. Then, on Friday, they take the train from New York to Montreal. There will be about fifteen in the party, Americans and Europeans. The actual conference starts next Tuesday."

"Where?"

"Here. In the main conference room of this hotel."

"How many will be there?"

"We're not certain. About a hundred, we think. Some have already arrived. But you understand, we are really only interested in the people named on this list."

He handed Kurt a sheet of paper. Ten names were typed on it: Chadwick, Craig, Hahn, Strassman, Bohr, Manasse, Taylor, Planchonnet, Einarsson, Pastori. Kurt recognized none of them; they meant nothing. Since he had to kill them, it was better that way.

"Is that all?" he asked.

"That's all," said the Major. "The rest is up to you."

"Thank you!" said Kurt savagely. "Thank you for nothing! What do you expect us to do? Go into the conference, ask these people to identify themselves, and then shoot them? Or do we mow down the lot, all one hundred of them? Perhaps blow up the hotel? What would you suggest, Major?"

"I am not here to make suggestions. You're in command. And it might be better if you kept your voice down."

"I want to make sure you hear me! Why wasn't I brought out earlier, to carry out a proper reconnaissance? I've been cooped up on that damned U-boat for six weeks, and now you pop up and tell me that we've got three, maybe four days to work out some plan of operation! God, it's incredible!"

The Major shrugged. "I was not responsible for your travel arrangements."

"We should be in New York, not here! That would have given us a chance to study the targets. It might have been easier to take them there. We should have photographs of these people, so that we can recognize them. We should have—oh, a dozen things! Do you want us to fail, Major, is that the idea? Because if you do, you've gone the right way about it."

"My instructions are that your mission is still top priority and that I am to give you every support to make it successful."

"Well, I'll tell you one thing, Major," said Kurt. "For the first time in months I feel a little hope. Because if this is an example of Nazi organization, when the war does come, you'll lose it."

He went to the bed and sprung the locks on the cases. They contained two rifles, two hand machine guns, four handguns, ammunition, and a half-dozen grenades. "Wonders will never cease," said Kurt. "You actually thought of weapons. For a moment I thought you expected us to do the job with our bare hands!"

"Is there anything else you need?" asked the Major, ignoring this new outburst.

"Yes," said Kurt. "First, I want to know about our deal." He tapped the list. "Remember? We liquidate this lot, and you release ten thousand Jews. I hope you've organized it a bit better at that end than you have at this!"

"I understand that a Norwegian vessel has been chartered and that it is standing by in the harbor at Hamburg. One thousand of your people have been granted exit permits, and they will be allowed aboard the moment we send a signal to the effect that your mission has been completed successfully."

"And the remainder, the other nine thousand?"

"They will be allowed to leave within one month. There are certain difficulties, as you know."

"You mean, no one will take them?"

"Exactly."

"Let us meet in the morning, Major," said Kurt wearily. He felt suddenly as though all the spirit had drained out of him. "I need to think, to talk this over with the others."

"Very well." The Major moved to the door. "I will come back at eight in the morning." And then, for no reason that he could think of, he paused and added: "I am sorry, Reiss."

"Sorry?" Kurt lifted his head.

"You're quite right about the planning. It's been abysmal. They've given you an impossible task."

"What would you do in my place, Major? Cut your losses? After all, we're in Canada, we've got papers, new identities—we could simply disappear. And a thousand poor bastards back in Germany, waiting to board that boat, would have their throats cut."

"I—I understand how you must feel," said the Major stiffly.

"Do you? Do you really?"

The Major hesitated, then spread his hands. "No. I

am an officer in the Luftwaffe, that's all. There are many things I don't understand."

"What is an officer in the Luftwaffe doing here?"

"I did not ask to come."

"You are merely obeying orders, doing your duty?"

"Exactly."

"And you can't imagine a situation in which you would refuse to obey an order?"

"If it came from my properly constituted superiors—no."

"And they are properly constituted—the gang of murderers who now rule your fatherland?"

The Major stiffened. "I will see you in the morning, Herr Reiss."

"You are the worst," said Kurt quietly.

"I beg your pardon?"

"You are the worst," said Kurt, raising his voice. "Because you are a decent man. And you accept indecent, obscene orders." The Major swung round toward the door, but Kurt checked him. "Wait! Major, wait!" The other man stood with his back to him. "We're in the same boat, you and I. Think about that. Both caught in the same current. I am not a murderer by nature or inclination but I have been forced to become one. Isn't it the same for you? And is there no alternative? No other way?"

There was a long moment of silence, then the Major opened the door and went out. The lock clicked behind him.

Neither man slept well that night. The Major dreamed that he was in a plane, flying over an unknown city. For some reason, the Reichsmarschall was at his side, and the only other passenger was Leni. She sat in a black nightdress in the body of the plane, staring at a coffin on which there was a brass plate bearing the name ENGELHARDT. The city was clearly visible from the plane, but the Major could not find a place to land and could get no guidance from the radio. The fuel gauge was almost at zero, the engine beginning to cough. . . .

Kurt was untroubled by dreams. He lay awake, spreading the problem out in his mind, seeking a solution. After a while he dozed off, and, as so often happens, when he awoke an hour later, the answer was clear in his mind.

TWELVE

1

When the Major returned the next morning he found Kurt and the others poring over a map that they had spread out on the bed. Kurt greeted him brusquely and came quickly to the point. He seemed to have changed; they had all noticed it. On the U-boat, perhaps inevitably, he had been quiet, subdued, brooding silently for long periods. But now his spirit seemed to have reasserted itself. His movements were brisk, his manner confident, his eyes burned with a new intensity.

"There's a train leaving for New York in ninety minutes, Major." Kurt thrust a thumb in Wolf's direction. "Goldberg and I need to be on it."

"For what reason?"

"We got this map from the hotel bookstore. It doesn't give enough detail. I want to take the trip as far as the border—at Lacolle, just here." He pointed to a spot on the map. "I need to know exactly where the train stops, the nature of the terrain, the actual layout of the train itself."

The Major stared down at the map for a moment. "Why do you need this sort of information?"

"Because," said Kurt patiently, "because you and your lot have left us up the creek without a paddle. No plan, nothing. Last night you said it was up to me to work something out. Well, I have. Sort of. It's just an outline at the moment, needs a lot of filling in. But it could work. I don't have to explain it to you, but I will if you want to hear it."

"I'm listening," said the Major.

"We have to choose a time and a place when our target group can be defined. If we wait until they reach Montreal, they'll be lost among the other delegates. If we try to take them in New York, we'll have the same problem. But there is one time and one place when they will be together in a group—on the train to Montreal on Friday. They'll probably travel in a reserved compartment—you can check that out for me with your connections in New York. If that isn't too much to ask."

"I think we might manage it," said the Major dryly.

"The general idea is that we board the Friday train at the point on this side of the frontier," said Kurt. "Where, when, and how depends on a hell of a lot of things. When Wolf and I have been down the line and taken stock, we might be able to come up with some answers. If we can't, we'll have to think of something else."

"If you decide that the train idea is feasible, you'll come back here to pick up the others?"

"Of course. The job will take all four of us—and even then we could be shorthanded. But I reckon we can just about manage with four. Max and Moshe will remain here, as a kind of insurance. No point in putting all the eggs in one basket. I don't expect there'll be any problems, but if Wolf and I do get into any sort of trouble, they'll be able to carry on with the operation. With luck, we'll be back here tonight. If not, sometime tomorrow morning."

"That seems to make sense," said the Major. "Is there anything else you want from me?"

"Three things. First, all the information you can get about the traveling arrangements of the target group. And I want to be informed at once of any change in the arrangements."

"That will be done."

"Second, you can inform Berlin that we are making progress, and ask them to clear the Norwegian ship and the first one thousand Jews."

"I will inform them, but I doubt if any action will be taken until I can give them more positive news about the outcome of the mission. What was the third thing?"

"Explosives."

The Major's eyebrows went up. The others looked at Kurt in astonishment. "God of our fathers!" said Max. "You're not thinking of blowing up the train?"

"Part of it," said Kurt calmly. "The part that matters."

"It's crazy," said Max. "Crazy."

"We made a contract." Kurt's voice was even, cold. "Major, I want blasting-gelatine cartridges, fuses, detonators." He held out an envelope that bore the insignia of the hotel. "I've made a note. I need the stuff in twenty-four hours." He might have been handing over a list of groceries.

"You know about explosives—how to handle them?" asked the Major warily.

"Oh, yes," said Kurt. "I got my experience in Spain. Bridges, viaducts, trains—we became quite good at it."

The Major shook his head over the words that Kurt had scribbled on the back of the envelope. "I can't give any guarantee about this."

"I've indicated the alternatives."

"I'll do my best." The Major was uncomfortably aware that the roles had been reversed, that Kurt was very much in command now. In a strange way, he was reminded of the Reichsmarschall. Kurt seemed to be revealing the same sort of clinical, cold-blooded ruthlessness; he was talking about the killing of ten or more people as if it were simply a question of logistics, supplies, timing. This attitude puzzled him, and somewhere at the back of his mind he heard a warning bell.

Kurt cut across these thoughts. "There is one more thing, Major. We shall need some money."

"Money?"

"We started with a hundred dollars each, and some of that has gone. I suppose they thought that if they gave us any more we might be tempted to take off. Well, now we need some real money."

"For what?"

"Transport, for a start. We may have to cover quite an area of countryside before we find the right spot. And, of course, when it's all over, when the job's done, there is the question of escape. We'll need transport for that—and cash."

As the Major hesitated, Wolf said: "Come on, come on. It's not your money we're asking for."

The Major opened his case and took out a bundle of notes, which he handed to Kurt. "Five thousand dollars. That's the limit of my authorization."

"Do you want a receipt?" asked Kurt dryly.

And to his astonishment, the Major replied: "Please. As Herr Goldberg pointed out, it is not my money. These are official, public funds. I shall have to account for every mark." He tore a sheet of paper from a small pad, wrote out a receipt, and offered it to Kurt for his signature.

"Cost of assassinating ten people—five thousand dollars. About five hundred dollars a head. You know something? It's cheap. Sweated labor, that's what we are!" said Wolf.

Kurt shook his head and signed, and the Major folded the paper carefully and put it away in his wallet.

"Tell me," said Moshe sadly, "when we have carried out the mission, you will give us a receipt for the bodies, perhaps?"

2

It was the first time that Dr. Alma Manasse had crossed the Atlantic, and the view from the foredeck of the *Queen Mary* was her first sight of New York and America. She told herself for the twentieth time that this was one of the greatest moments in her life. She told herself that she was free, that she was about to set foot in a land where millions before her had sought and found liberty. She told herself that the skyline of Manhattan was beautiful, incredible, a testimony to the energy and power of this young, restless country. She put a hand in the pocket of her coat and touched the letter from Columbia University and told herself that she was a privileged person; they had actually asked her to come and smoothed her path of all difficulties. She told herself that she should feel happiness, exhilaration, relief, and that, like the Pilgrim Fathers of old, when she set foot on American soil, she should kneel and kiss the earth and give thanks to God.

She told herself all these things, but to no avail. She could not lift her spirits; she was saddened by thoughts of the homeland she had left and might never see again. And besides the homesickness, there was this terrible trembling fear of the future, which lay like a shadow across her days, and from which there was no escape. The sense of urgency that had so oppressed her during the voyage had only been heightened by the arrival in New York. Would the Americans understand what she had to tell them, would they take the necessary action, and take it in time? What if they could not be convinced?

It was no idle fear. One of her British colleagues, who was with the group on the voyage, had told her of his efforts to persuade his own military establishment and some leading politicians of the importance of a nuclear program. His prophetic warnings had been received with the sort of tolerant skepticism that practical men normally display toward those whom they regard as "boffins or long-haired cranks." In a way, as her colleague had said, you could not altogether blame them. War was coming, and it was taking them all their time and resources simply to produce an adequate supply of conventional weapons. They needed Spitfires, Hurricanes, ships, and guns now; how could they be persuaded to divert enormous resources into a shadowy, uncertain project that only a few people could understand? Yet Alma knew it was, literally, a matter of life or death, and because of her background, the sense of urgency, of desperation, was greater.

On the pier below, a pack of photographers and reporters was awaiting the arrival of the great ship. They were not interested in the little group of scientists who had come to attend some obscure conference in Montreal. There were film stars like Olivia De Havilland and Fred Astaire aboard and a Russian princess and a famous heiress, whose dog had been housed in a special kennel on the voyage, attended by his own private veterinary surgeon. There was nothing wrong with the animal, but its wealthy owner was not sure how it would take to the Atlantic crossing and decided that it would be better to be safe than sorry. It had been stated, and not denied, that the kennel had cost five hundred dollars to build, that the vet had been paid two thousand dollars plus expenses for his trouble, and that each evening the dog enjoyed a cocktail made of raw eggs, champagne, and goat's milk.

It was quite a story, certainly more newsworthy than the one Dr. Alma Manasse and her colleagues had to tell.

They simply wanted to inform someone in authority, anyone who would be prepared to listen, that Germany had decided to ban the export of uranium ore from Czechoslovakia, and to explain the terrifying implications of this decision. They wanted them to know what was going on at 69 Unter den Linden in Berlin, where "Operation U," directed by Germany's top nuclear scientists, had been given the go-ahead by Hitler.

The purpose of Operation U was to produce an atomic bomb. It was possible, almost certain, that within a few years, Hitler, the madman of Europe, would have in his hands a weapon that could destroy whole armies and desolate entire cities.

__3__

"It's a madness," said Max for the tenth time. "The whole thing—a madness. Crazy."

"When there is no meat, you have to pick the bones," said Moshe, stirring his coffee. "We're in it now, and we have to do the best we can."

They were sitting in a small bar near the hotel, talking in low voices; Kurt and Wolf were already on the train, on the first stage of their reconnaissance. Since the early-morning conference in the hotel room, Max had been in a somber mood.

"I wouldn't mind," he said, "I wouldn't mind if there was a real chance. A reasonable gamble—that would be worth taking. But it's not even that."

"What do you suggest—we do nothing?"

"We could go to the authorities, we could tell them the whole story. Or go to one of the newspapers maybe."

"That's crazy talk, Max!" said Moshe in a shocked voice. "Headlines in the paper! What do you think would happen back home? That ship would never leave Hamburg, a thousand Jews would be dead. Do you want such a thing on your conscience?"

"Do you think that ship will sail? Listen, don't fool yourself. It'll never leave harbor. Once those Nazi bastards have got what they want, they'll forget their end of the bargain."

"You can't be sure."

"I'm certain. Are you telling me that you trust them?"

"No."

"Exactly. And there's nothing we can do to make them keep their word. Can you think of anything? No, of course you can't."

"Maybe Kurt will find a way," said Moshe.

"We've been saying that for weeks! What has he come up with? Nothing. There is no way. Face it, Moshe. They've been stringing us along, Kurt most of all. They've made a fool of him, taken him for a *schlemiel*."

"Maybe a miracle will occur. It's been known."

"You can believe in miracles if you like—I gave up that foolishness years ago. Look, while we were in Germany and even on the U-boat, we had to go along with this crazy scheme. What else could we do? But here in Canada, it's different. Here they can't touch us."

"Please," said Moshe uneasily, "please, do me a favor, Maxie. Don't speak such things, don't even think them."

A man and a girl came in and sat down at a table on the opposite side of the room. The man had smooth, silver hair, and the girl was young enough to be his daughter, but they clasped hands across the table like lovers, and she looked into his face with shining eyes. From a radio behind the bar came the sound of a man singing "There's a Small Hotel."

Max watched the couple reflectively for a moment.

"That's right," said Moshe encouragingly. "Think of something else."

But Max was not to be diverted. "Listen, Moshe," he said. "You know what they do with murderers in this country? So all right, I wouldn't mind having a noose around my neck if I'd achieved something. But to be hung for nothing—that's a different question already."

"Why didn't you say all this to Kurt this morning? You didn't open your lips. Not a word."

"I wanted to. But that *schmuck* the Major came in. And listen, there's another thing."

"Something else? You'll wear out your tongue!"

"Just listen a minute!"

"A minute! You've been talking for fifteen already."

"Answer me this question. Who are these people we are supposed to murder?"

"Please, don't use such a word."

"How else would you describe it? So tell me, who are they?"

"All I know is what you know. They're scientists."

"They must be important, correct? So we do the Führer a big favor—we kill off the whole bunch. He's laughing—he actually got a bunch of stupid Jews to do his dirty work. Of course, he denies that he had anything to do with it. He blames the Jews and turns the screws on them even harder. So what's the end result? Hitler gets what he wants, the Jews get it in the neck as usual, and we finish up at the end of a rope! Or blow ourselves up! Now, tell me, tell me the truth, does that make sense to you?"

"Look," said Moshe, "maybe you got a point, maybe not. When Kurt comes back, we'll talk it out with him. All right?"

Max sighed. "We have to make him listen. That's not an easy thing. Did you see the look in his eyes this morning? Like a fanatic. Sometimes I think he's a little crazy in the head."

"This crazy man got us out of Sachsenhausen concentration camp!" said Moshe sternly. "And he got a hundred Jewish kids to Sweden. Maybe you should remember that! And maybe you should remember that we all made a promise—a promise to see this thing through. We'll talk to Kurt, yes. But if he decides to go ahead, that's what we do. All four of us."

"If I could see just a little gleam of hope," said Max.

"Even hope can't be trusted," Moshe replied. "Do you know what Sholem Aleichem said? He said, 'Hope is a liar.' And I'll tell you something. He was right."

They returned to the hotel a few minutes later. Max went to his room and spread himself out on the bed, staring at the ceiling. He stayed like this for a long time, and then, jumping up suddenly, he picked up the telephone. He gave the operator a name and address in New York and asked her to find the number and put through a call.

Ten minutes later the telephone rang. He paced the room for a full half minute, listening to the harsh, insistent ringing tone, staring at the black instrument as though it were some hostile intruder, then he picked up with sweating, trembling hands.

The operator said, "Your New York number is on the line, sir."

A woman's voice, sounding slightly irritated, as if she had been interrupted: "Hello. Rose Meyer speaking."

"Auntie Rose?" His voice was little more than a squeak, and, clearing his throat, he said again: "Auntie Rose?"

"Who is that?" The woman sounded suspicious, puzzled.

"Auntie Rose. This is Max. Maxie. From Germany."

"Maxie? Maxie?" There was a pause, and then she said in a strangely formal tone: "From where are you speaking?"

"Auntie Rose," he said, "it's Maxie speaking. Maxie Meyer, your nephew, son of your brother-in-law, Morris." It sounded foolish, inadequate, but he could find no other words.

"Maxie!" Her voice screamed down the telephone. "Maxie! Where are you? Where are you?"

"I'm here. I mean, I'm in Canada." He felt a movement on his cheeks, and brushing his eyes, was surprised to find that they were brimming with tears.

"Canada! You mean, you got out! You got out!" He heard her voice recede, yelling to someone in the background. "Alex! It's Maxie. *Maxie!* Morrie's boy! He's here, he got out, he's here! He's in Canada!" Then her voice came back again. "Maxie! Don't go! Don't go! Here's your uncle Alex."

A man came on the line, the voice cautious, unbelieving. "Maxie?"

"Uncle Alex?"

"My God! Maxie! Where are you, where are you?"

He heard his aunt scolding in the background and his uncle shout an aside. "Shut up, woman!"

"I'm in Canada, Uncle."

"Canada! That godforsaken place! Why didn't you come here?"

Before he could answer, his aunt came back on the line. "Maxie? How did you get out? It's a miracle! How did you do it?"

Then the man again. "What about your parents? Esther, Morrie. We hear such terrible things. Never mind, never mind. What's good is that you are here." The voice faded again. "Give me a chance, will you, woman!" Then, louder again, booming down the line. "Maxie, are you still there?"

"Yes, Uncle. I'm here."

He stood there, muttering an occasional response, listening to their excited voices as each grabbed the telephone from the other. "You can't stay in Canada! What are you doing in Canada? Nobody stays in Canada. What are you doing there anyway? Maxie, are you there, are you listening?"

Yes, he thought, I'm here. And I'm listening.

4

The reception given to Dr. Alma Manasse and her colleagues in New York was cordial, but the news was not encouraging. In the whole of America, nobody in authority seemed to be interested in the new discoveries of the nuclear scientists; nobody wanted to listen. Enrico Fermi, the Nobel Prize winner, had been turned away politely but firmly by the State Department, as had others. When the little group from England and Europe met with some expatriate and American friends at the Biltmore Hotel that evening, the atmosphere was one of despair. If Fermi, with his record, had failed to get a hearing, what chance had they?

And then Pastori, a small gnomelike man, said almost apologetically: "What about Einstein? It's only a thought. An idea. The President would perhaps listen to such a man, you think?"

There was a long silence as they considered this— Albert Einstein! Alma had seen him once only, at a lecture in Brussels years before. She had felt then that she was sitting at the feet of the master, and even now, the simple mention of his name induced in her a feeling of awe.

"Would it be possible?" she asked.

"We could try" said Einarsson, whose experiments

in Copenhagen had done much to confirm that the construction of an atomic bomb was theoretically possible. "At least he would understand what we are talking about. And with his prestige . . ."

"It's one hell of an idea!" said Taylor, an American physicist, a tall, gangling man who reminded Alma of the film star James Stewart. "What have we got to lose? We'll appoint a delegation to go down to Princeton and see the old man."

"He is not at Princeton at this time," said Pastori with the same deference as before. He stroked his broad forehead as if looking for the hair that had abandoned it years before. "I took the liberty of making a checkup. Einstein is taking a spring holiday on Long Island at a place called . . ." He consulted a notebook and continued with a questioning look, "Patchnik? Patchogue."

"Peconic?" Taylor corrected him politely.

"Yes. Perhaps that is it." Pastori blushed. "Peconic."

Within a few minutes it was agreed that Taylor, Pastori, and Alma Manasse should go to Peconic the following day, seek out Einstein, and enlist his help. They would propose that he lead a delegation to see the President; if this was not possible, then they would ask him to write a personal letter to Roosevelt, which would be handed directly to him by Alexander Sachs, a White House adviser whom Taylor knew.

The fact of taking a decision cheered them, and they spent the next hour in a more relaxed mood. But after this, one of the American guests, a journalist, unwittingly jarred their spirits yet again. He tried to amuse them with the story of the panic that had set in after Orson Welles, the actor, had broadcast a play about an invasion of the earth by Martians. It had been done in such a realistic way that thousands of families, thinking that the end of the world was really at hand, had fled their homes, storming rail and bus stations, sheltering in churches, driving west in convoys of cars to escape the monsters from Mars who were said to have landed in the Jersey farmlands armed with death rays and to be advancing on New York.

After a little while, Alma excused herself and left the table. She remembered Europe and those great columns of marching Stormtroopers too vividly. And, on a deeper level than this, there lay her own throbbing nightmare doubts about the nature of the work on which she and her colleagues were engaged.

They had the knowledge, if not as yet the means, to create a weapon that would make the fictional death rays of the Martian invaders seem like toys for little children. When such a weapon became a reality, would mankind be able to control it? Would he be able to control himself? In this respect, she thought wryly, the record was not good.

Which meant that the end of the world was no longer a subject to be debated only in terms of science fiction.

5

Kurt and Wolf caught the last train back into Montreal, and by the time they arrived at the Windsor terminal, Kurt had the main outline of the operation clear in his mind. The day had gone well: he had discovered what he needed to know, and though he would have preferred more time to plan and prepare, he was satisfied that his scheme stood a fighting chance of success. And it seemed that fate had, at last, decided to tip the scales in his favor and throw in an extra bonus. From an obliging porter on the train he had learned that the coming Friday was, in fact, Good Friday, the opening day of the Easter holiday. This meant that there would only be one train from New York that day, fewer coaches and fewer passengers.

It occurred to him that there was a certain grim irony in the idea that they would be making their strike on the first day of a Christian festival, though the thought gave him no satisfaction and he did not dwell on it. His mind was too occupied with other matters; he had the outline clear now, but he kept going over it again and again, mentally filling in the details, trying to work out where, if at all, he might have miscalculated.

On the journey back, Wolf said little. He watched Kurt carefully, wondering what was going on in his mind. There were moments when, catching the look in Kurt's eyes, he felt that the other man was like someone in the grip of a fever.

Wolf's own thoughts were dominated by one question. He was almost ashamed to think it, because it inferred a certain lack of faith in Kurt whom he trusted to the point of idolatry, but he could not make it go away. He did not regard himself as a political creature, and he certainly did not pretend fully to understand the bizarre situation in which they now found themselves. In that respect, he was content to leave the thinking and the decisions to Kurt and to follow where he led.

Nevertheless, he could not escape the thought that they had somehow allowed themselves to be blackmailed into an impossible position. And at the back of his mind there lurked, like a small, dark, unpleasant animal, the idea that perhaps, after all, it would be better for them to cut their losses and simply run for cover. The very existence of the thought gave him a feeling of guilt, and this was the reason for his silence on the journey. He did not want to betray his feelings by so much as a word or even a look.

When they arrived at the hotel, all this came back to

him like a bad dream, heightening his sense of shame. An anxious, angry Moshe was waiting for them with a piece of shattering news.

"Max has gone!"

"Gone?" Kurt stared at the pale face.

"Disappeared. His room is empty, all his things are gone. He checked out of the hotel at about eleven-thirty this morning."

"No message?"

"Not a word."

"When did you see him last?"

"This morning, after you left. We had a *schmooze* over coffee. He was in a sort of funny mood. Kept on about what we are doing, said the whole thing was crazy, that there was no way we could win. Anyway, he said he was going back to the hotel. I went to the art gallery."

"You went to the bloody art gallery!"

"Don't shout! What did you expect—I should sit in the room, twiddling my thumbs? I got back about twelve-thirty and went to see Max. No sign. Room empty. When I couldn't find him, I remembered that he told me once about some relatives in New York. An uncle, I think, runs a delicatessen."

"For God's sake—"

"I went down to the station—a train left for New York at noon. In my opinion, he was on it."

"The bastard!" said Wolf.

"What about the money?" asked Kurt. He had left two thousand of the five thousand dollars behind as a precaution, splitting it between Moshe and Max.

"What do you think?" said Moshe with a shrug of his thin shoulders. "He wasn't going to leave that, was he?"

There was a tap on the door, and at a nod from Kurt, Wolf opened it to admit the Major.

"I've organized the explosives," he said. "I have to

collect them tomorrow." And then, sensing the tension: "What's gone wrong?" He looked round. "Where's Meyer?"

Moshe told him. The Major shook his head, as if he had expected something like this to happen, but he made no comment. Instead, he asked: "How was your trip?"

"It can be done," Kurt said. "The trouble is I'd reckoned on having a team of four, and that was going to be tight. Maybe we can still work it out—I'm not sure. It'll be chancey."

"You can still have four," said the Major quietly.

"How?"

"Include me. I'll take Meyer's place."

Kurt looked at him, frowning. "Don't make jokes."

"I'm serious."

"He is serious!" said Moshe. "He's not joking, he's serious!"

"The success of this mission is more important than anything else—those are my instructions," said the Major. There was a long pause during which the two men studied each other, as if each was trying to read the other's mind. The Major thought that he detected a hint of mockery in Kurt's eyes.

"What's the matter? Is there any reason why you wouldn't want me to be on that train?" he continued, and made it sound like a challenge.

"There's the question of odds. I calculate that the chances of our getting away after the operation are—"

"That doesn't concern me," said the Major, interrupting him. "My concern is to reduce the chance of failure."

"I don't like it," said Kurt.

"You said we need four people," said Wolf. "So what's wrong? Why not take him?"

"If it means we stand a better chance ..." said Moshe.

"We seem to be in a majority," said the Major. "A democratic decision."

"What would you know about that?" said Kurt. He sighed and shrugged. "All right. But we do it my way. You'll take my orders."

"Naturally."

"Very well. Be here tomorrow at noon. We'll have a full briefing then. And don't forget those explosives."

"My connections were rather worried. They could not understand why you needed explosives in addition to the weapons they have already supplied."

"Tell your connections," said Kurt, "tell them that I'm doing this job, not them. I know what I need."

6

The Major made his regular report by telephone later that evening to the secret New York number that he had memorized. He told Buttmann, the SS agent, that the Thunderbird party would take place on Friday, and asked him to inform his superiors in Germany accordingly.

"Can you rely on our friends?" asked Buttmann. His tone was not cordial. He resented having the Major on his patch and was annoyed that such a mission should be handled by an amateur. And he was quite sure that, win or lose, the backlash from the operation would make the position of his own network more difficult.

"I think so," said the Major. "They have had one defection, but the remaining three seem determined to see it through."

"A defection? Which one?"

"Meyer. Max Meyer."

Buttmann made a note of the name. "Only one defection. Not bad. I expected that we'd lose the lot. Will they be able to make it with three people?"

The Major hesitated for a moment, but in the end he reassured the other man and said nothing about his own participation. It would have been difficult to explain anyway. To Kurt he had tried to make it sound like a spur-of-the-moment decision, but in fact he had been considering some way of becoming involved ever since the hit team had arrived in Canada. He wasn't clear what had prompted the feeling, but he had come to know Kurt and to understand what this man was capable of. With him, it was necessary to expect the unexpected. It was his duty, the Major told himself, to see this thing through to the finish. The mission was of vital importance to the Reich, and that was the chief, indeed, the only consideration. The voice of the Reichsmarschall echoed in his head.

... *I know that, despite everything, if you are given an order you will carry it out faithfully and well. That's how your life has been—ordered.... And you need that order—it's a kind of faith. Without it, you'd be nothing.... Whatever happens you will do your duty.*

After the Major had rung off, Buttmann consulted a dossier he had brought from Germany. Kurt and the others would have been surprised at the amount of detail it contained. For example, it took Buttmann only a few seconds to confirm that Max Meyer had an uncle in New York; what was more, the dossier also provided the address of the delicatessen store that he owned and over which he lived.

Buttmann lost no time. He had two men on whom he could call for assignments of a special nature, and he ordered one of them to report to him. The agent was shown a photograph and given the address of the store.

Max Meyer arrived at Grand Central Station in the early hours of the morning and took a cab to his uncle's address in Queens. He rang the doorbell, and as he waited for an answer, a car came cruising past. He was hit by a volley of bullets and died almost instantly.

7

At the Windsor Hotel in Montreal, Wolf and Moshe at last heard the answer to the questions that had been haunting their minds, as Kurt briefed them on his plan. When he had finished, neither man spoke for a long time. Then Wolf nodded, and his face expanded into a huge grin.

Moshe was more circumspect. "On the whole, I like it," he said, "but I foresee one problem."

"Problems, always problems," said Wolf. "What's the matter—it hurts you to smile? It's a fantastic idea!"

"Did I say it wasn't?"

"So what's the problem?" said Kurt.

"The Major. I was watching him earlier on. He knows you are up to something. He doesn't trust you. That is why he was so eager to step into Maxie's shoes."

"So why did you agree that he should come along?" asked Wolf.

"Better we should have him where we can see him."

"You think so? I think so too," said Kurt. "So Wolf, you have a special task. To watch the Major."

"And if he creates trouble?"

"Kill him," said Kurt.

"I hoped you would say that," said Wolf.

"Now," said Moshe, "I am not a drinking man as a rule. But I suggest we spend some of the Führer's money on a little celebration. Agreed?"

"I'm not opposed to the idea," said Wolf, "but wouldn't it be better to celebrate afterward?"

"Wolfie," said Moshe quietly. "Let's celebrate now. While we can."

THIRTEEN

1

George Hatch had lost count of the number of times he had done the New York–Montreal run. He had been with the New York Central Railroad Company for thirty-four years, thirteen as a stoker-fireman and the rest as an engineer. So when he bothered to count, which wasn't often, he reckoned that he must have made the trip, either there or back, about five thousand times. And that was a conservative estimate. Since the total distance was around four hundred miles, that meant that he had traveled something like two million miles during his career with the company, not counting the periods when he had driven on other routes.

He used to say that he knew the line as well as he knew his wife's face. Out of Grand Central to Albany, following the east bank of the Hudson all the way; then through Saratoga Springs, Whitehall, Port Henry, Westport, and Port Kent, skirting the edge of Lake Champlain to Rouses Point, over the border to Lacolle, the Canadian customs post, on to Delson and Verdun, and finally, across the St. Lawrence River into the terminal at Montreal. The timetable allowed nine hours for the journey, but there were times, in the worst of the winter, when it took a good deal longer. George could remember one occasion when eleven inches of snow had fallen and they had been bogged down between Fort Ticonderoga and Westport for over twelve hours.

Nothing like that was likely to happen today, he reflected, though you could never be sure. He had known the weather to play some freakish tricks, and only the week before there had been a seven-inch fall of snow on the middle section of the route. But now it seemed that spring had definitely decided to make its presence felt; the snow on the lower ground had already melted, and he had seen welcome patches of green and brown on the approaches to the Catskills and the Adirondack Mountains.

At Rouses Point he stepped down from the cab for a few minutes to stretch his legs and found the air softer and warmer than it had been for months. When he climbed back in and set the big Hudson 5200 locomotive moving toward Lacolle and Canada, he checked his watch. It was three-thirty in the afternoon; they were dead on time, and in just under the hour they would be steaming into Montreal.

He would spend the night, as usual, at the hostel run by the railroad company; in the evening, after dinner, he might take in a movie, see that new Spencer Tracy film. He was a regular cinema goer; it was his chief relaxation. But then he remembered that it was Good Friday and that the cinemas would be closed, and the bars too. He would have to content himself with a beer and a game of pool at the hostel. Sometimes he wondered why the company bothered to operate on holidays such as this; there were probably less than a hundred people on the train. Still, he told himself sternly, they were in the railroad business and service was the name of the game.

A brief stop at Lacolle. Three passengers joined the train, two young men who looked like lumberjacks, and an old lady. A few parcels and a bicycle were loaded into the luggage van. The Canadian authorities sometimes made random checks on the passengers, but today no one was interested, and he didn't blame them. He smiled and lifted a hand as the depot guard flagged him on.

He glanced at Bailey, the young fireman. He was

turning the handle that regulated the flow of coal to the automatic stoker, and his eyes were on the steam gauge. They had it easier these days, thought George. When he'd started, the coal had to be shoveled in manually; the job was all muscle, sweat, and grit. Still, Bailey wasn't a bad kid. He was going steady with one of the train maids, the young hostesses who looked after the passengers, serving them coffee and doughnuts, keeping an eye on the children, generally making people feel relaxed and comfortable. Bailey's girl, Sue, was on the train today. George guessed that she had volunteered to take the unpopular holiday trip because her boyfriend was aboard. They won't be wondering what to do tonight, he thought, smiling inwardly.

He slowed the speed of the train, easing the brakes on gently. A mile ahead, around the bend, they would stop at a water tower to fill the boiler for the last time before reaching Montreal. At this point the track had been cut through thickly wooded remote country; on either side the land, heavy with spruce and balsam fir, sloped steeply upward, and pockets of snow still clung to parts of the hillside.

As they rounded the curve, George saw a man standing beside the tower. For a moment he assumed that it was one of the track maintenance engineers, but then he thought that it was unlikely that he would be out at this isolated spot on a holiday. Unless, of course, there was some sort of emergency. He judged the distance with a perfection born of long practice and brought the huge engine to a halt by the water tower.

He did not recognize the man, who was dressed in a heavy corduroy coat over dark overalls, which were tucked into calf-length boots. He moved toward George, not hurrying, smiling a little.

"Anything wrong?" George asked, leaning out of the cab.

"Landslide, six hundred yards ahead," said the man. "The track's blocked." He spoke English with a slight accent, which George couldn't place.

"Is it impassable?"

"Not too bad. I think we can clear it. Better come and take a look for yourself."

George hesitated and then turned to Bailey. "Take on the water," he said. "I'll go check."

He climbed down from the cab and dropped onto the track. And then, to his utter astonishment, he saw the man's hand come out of his pocket holding an automatic.

"Just do as you're told and you won't get hurt," said Kurt.

"Bailey!" shouted George, and gasped as the automatic thudded into his body, jarring the ribs.

"I won't warn you again!" said Kurt.

As he straightened up, George saw that another man had appeared and that he was covering Bailey.

"You. You get down too!" said Kurt. As the fireman clambered down, his descent covered by the Major, Kurt raised his automatic and fired a single shot into the air.

2

"Nobody move!" shouted Moshe. He covered the group of passengers in the end coach, moving the submachine gun menacingly. A woman screamed and a man rose angrily from his seat. Moshe lifted the gun, squeezed the trigger, and fired a volley into the roof; fragments of glass from the light fittings and splinters of wood fell to the floor. The woman stopped screaming and the man sat down. There was a stunned silence.

"I'll kill the next person who moves!" said Moshe,

and he spoke as if he meant it. Someone banged on the door behind him; he stepped aside, watching the passengers, and slid the door open. The conductor and a train maid came through, their hands clasped above their heads, and behind them, also armed with a submachine gun, was Wolf.

"Over there!" ordered Moshe. "Sit down!" The conductor and the girl squeezed into a seat near the other passengers. There were about twenty of them altogether.

"Anybody else back there?" asked Moshe, speaking in German.

"No. All clear," said Wolf.

"Keep this lot covered," said Moshe. He reverted to English as he turned to the passengers: "No talking. No movement. If you disobey, you will be shot."

He slipped behind Wolf and went through the door.

3

Some of the passengers in the other coaches were hanging out of the open doors, peering down the track, trying to make out what had happened. Others had their faces pressed against the sealed windows.

Four men were coming down the track. The engineer and the fireman came first, and behind them, very close, were the other two. As they passed the passengers, moving toward the rear, Kurt said cheerfully: "Don't worry. Get back to your seats. We'll be on our way again in a few minutes." At intervals, he prodded George with the automatic, which he held in the pocket of his coat.

"What were those shots?"

"We heard shooting—"

"What's going on?"

To all the shouted questions, Kurt replied in the same way: "Nothing to worry about. Sit down, close the doors. We'll be moving in a few minutes."

They stopped by the end coach, where Moshe waited by the open door.

"All right?" asked Kurt.

"Everything in hand," said Moshe, smiling.

Kurt turned to George and Bailey. "Right—you two. Uncouple this coach from the rest of the train. Move! The quicker you do it, the quicker you can be on your way!"

"Do you know the penalty for train holdups?" asked George.

"Do you know what it is like to be shot in the kneecap? They have to fit an artificial kneecap, and you will limp for the rest of your life," said Kurt. He gave the man a shove. "Get on with it!"

He climbed up into the coach, leaving Moshe and the Major to cover the two railroad men. Wolf greeted him with a grin.

"Quiet as a lamb," he said.

Kurt moved up the coach, studying the faces of the frightened passengers. He stopped by the old lady who had joined the train at Lacolle. "We don't need you, mother," he said. "Go and sit with those two." He indicated the conductor and the train maid.

"Thank you, sir," she said gratefully, and snatching up a bag, hurried to the other seat.

A thick-set man with close-cropped hair rose from his seat, spreading his hands in a sort of apology, and smiling tentatively. He spoke quickly, in German.

"Excuse me. I heard you speak in German. I am an Austrian. Well, a German citizen now naturally. I am on a visit to this country. My name is Lieneweg—"

"Shut up!" said Kurt savagely.

"You don't understand. I am here on important business for the Reich. Whatever your motives, I am sure that—"

The words choked in his throat as Kurt hit him on the side of the head with the automatic. He fell back into the seat, still conscious but stunned; blood began to trickle down his cheek. No one spoke: their eyes, liquid with shock and fear, watched Kurt.

"That's a warning," he said. "No talking. Not a word! Now, you will all take out your travel documents, passports, and so forth and hold them up so that I can see them."

They fumbled in pockets and purses and, like obedient children, held up passports and rail tickets. He passed among them, checking the documents against a list of names he had taken from his pocket. He paused as he studied the Czech passport that bore the name: Dr. Alma Manasse. As he handed it back, their eyes met for a moment. He ordered ten of the passengers to remain in their seats. To each of the others he said: "Move to the other end of the coach and wait."

They joined the conductor, the train maid, and the old lady. It was only at this moment that Alma realized the significance of what was happening. She had imagined, at first, that this was an ordinary train hold-up by criminals intent on robbery, if such an event could ever be described as ordinary. Now she saw that her own group, the group of nuclear physicists, had been separated from the others. The man clearly had a list of their names and knew just who to look for. And two of the men had spoken to each other in German. A new kind of fear clutched at her stomach as she considered the meaning of this. Were they, perhaps, agents of the Nazis? And even as this thought hammered at her mind, she was aware of something else, something that made immediate nonsense of such a theory. She was almost certain that of the three men she had seen so far, at least two were Jewish.

The coach lurched slightly, and they heard the harsh clanging complaint of metal. Kurt turned to the conductor and to the passengers clustered round him and waved the automatic at them. "Right. You, all of you, outside."

"What are you going to do?" The conductor's face was gray, his voice trembled.

"Outside!" said Kurt sharply.

He left Wolf to guard the others, went through the door, and dropped down onto the track. The coach had now been separated from the rest of the train; George and Bailey were standing to one side, watched by Moshe and the Major. The conductor, the train maid, and a little group of silent, terrified passengers left the train and joined them. Lieneweg, holding a bloodied handkerchief to his temple, stumbled and almost fell. Kurt caught his arm and pushed him to one side. The train maid gave a little cry when she saw Bailey and, ignoring the guns, ran to him. He put a protective arm around her and stared at Kurt with dark, hostile eyes.

"Listen carefully," said Kurt, "because I don't intend to repeat myself." He spoke directly to George. "When I give the word, you'll go back to the engine with your stoker and take the train on to your next stop."

"I'm not leaving without her," said Bailey belligerently, tightening his grip on the girl.

"She can go with you." Kurt looked at the conductor. "You will take these passengers and put them in one of the other coaches."

"What about the ones in this coach?" asked George. "What happens to them?"

Kurt ignored him, but his eyes locked with the Major's for an instant. Then he continued to address the conductor. "When you reach Delson, you will go straight to the police post there. You will give them our exact location, and hand three letters to the officer on duty. Tell him that I want an answer by eight A.M. tomorrow. If there is no reply by then, I will blow up this coach and everybody in it. Understand?"

The conductor gulped and nodded quickly. Kurt drew three sealed envelopes from his pocket and handed them to him. "Now, get moving. Walk, don't run. Act calmly. Moshe—cover them all the way."

Lieneweg moved at that moment. Lowering his head, charging like an enraged bull, he hurled himself at Moshe, taking him by surprise. Moshe crashed to the track, and as the Austrian's hands closed on the submachine gun, Kurt fired twice.

The roar of the explosions hung in the air for an instant and then faded into the distance like a roll of thunder. The black shapes of protesting birds flew up from the nearby trees.

And then a silence that was heavier than before.

"Christ!" whispered George.

"Tell them," Kurt said, "tell them that we are not bluffing." He waved the automatic at Bailey. "Pick him up. Take him with you."

Bailey hesitated, then with casual ease, he shouldered the heavy body. George led them along the track, watched from the windows by rows of white faces. Willing hands pulled the conductor and his frightened group into one of the other coaches. George climbed aboard the locomotive and helped Bailey up with the body. They laid it on the tender, and Bailey covered the shattered face with his coat.

George wasted no time. A sharp hiss of steam, three defiant blasts on the whistle, and the train began to move forward. He checked his watch. To his astonishment, they had lost only fifteen minutes.

Kurt watched the train disappear into the distance, then looked down at the automatic in his hand. His body trembled and his skin felt raw and dry, as though it had been scrubbed with salt.

"I'm sorry, Kurt," said Moshe. His voice was almost inaudible.

"Get the explosives," said Kurt. He looked at the Major. "You. Give him a hand."

"First, you will tell me what is going on?"

"Look," Kurt said wearily. "We've got the target group. Isn't that enough for a start?"

"Those letters. This business of waiting till morning. I don't understand. We can set the explosives, blow this lot, and then make a run for it. Why the delay?"

"Look, Major," said Kurt, "we agreed to do it my way—right? We'll finish the job when I say so."

"And when will that be?"

"When I've received an assurance—more than that, some kind of proof—that the Norwegian ship has sailed from Hamburg and is well outside German territorial waters. Until then, I'm holding these people as hostages." He smiled. "Don't look so grim, Major. Your Nazi boss is a man of honor, isn't that right? You trust him. I don't quite share your faith, that's all."

The two men measured each other for a moment. Then the Major said quietly: "You do realize that in a few hours they'll have this place surrounded by a regiment of police. There'll be no escape for any of us."

"You can leave now if you wish, Major. We can handle it from here on."

"No," said the Major. "I'll stay." Almost before the words were out he realized the significance of what he had said: there was no longer any way out for him, there would be no escape. He stood for a moment, wondering after all whether to change his mind. The truck on which they had brought the supplies and explosives was hidden only a few hundred yards from the track. There was still a chance.

He put the thought aside instantly. His orders were to see the mission through to a successful conclusion, and if that meant staying, he must stay, whatever the consequences. If Kurt was bluffing—and he might well be—then he would have to find a way to do the job himself. The idea sickened him, but there was no choice. It had to be done. Perhaps the Reichsmarschall had intended it to be like this all along; perhaps this was his way of eliminating a man who, by his standards, was too sentimental?

He emptied his pockets of all his papers, anything that might identify him. There wasn't much, but what there was he screwed up and laid in a little heap beside the track. Then he bent down, and cradling a lighted match with his hands, he made a fire.

He stood there, stirring the burning papers with his foot, until all that remained was a tiny heap of ash, which was soon scattered by the wind. He had a strange sense of loss, as though his life, his entire identity, was blowing away, lost in this strange, foreign wilderness.

What was it the Reichsmarschall had called Kurt and the others? *Dead men on leave.* Well, now he had joined the club. He smiled, a small, wry smile, and then went to help Moshe with the explosives.

4

Constable Boyd turned the envelopes over with one hand and scratched his tawny hair with the other. He looked up at George Hatch and sighed.

"Some sort of nuts, are they?"

"They're killers, man!" said George impatiently. "I tell you, they shot down a passenger—I saw them, I was there."

"I don't mean that," said Boyd. "I mean these. These letters. You've seen who they're addressed to, haven't you?"

"I brought them in! Of course, I've seen them. What are you going to do?"

"Bide a minute." Boyd fiddled with the envelopes again. The names written on them seemed to dance before his eyes.

To the Prime Minister of Canada, Mr. MacKenzie King

To the President of the United States, Mr. Franklin Delano Roosevelt

To Mr. Abraham Sondheimer, Chairman of the Jewish Relief Agency, Montreal

He sighed again and put the letters down. "Right," he said in a brisker tone. "Sit down over there. I'll be requiring a full statement from you in due course."

"I've got to get a train to Montreal. I've got passengers to think of!"

"Hold on a while, will ye? Can't you see I'm on my own? Hold on, please." Boyd picked up the telephone and drummed on the table, waiting for the operator to answer.

George took a chair to one side of the tiny office. He wondered about the poor devils stuck in that coach. There would be no food unless they had supplies of their own and, now the rest of the train had gone, no heating. When night fell, the temperature would fall to below zero. He thought of this and thought of the dead man and shivered.

His mind drifted back to Boyd. The constable had got through at last, and by the respectful note in his Scots voice, he was clearly speaking to a superior. And it soon became obvious that the man at the other end of the line was finding it difficult to believe what he was hearing. Boyd had to repeat it.

Which really wasn't any wonder, George reflected.

A train holdup, a murder, passengers being held as hostages. It was like a film, except that this had a chilling reality that frightened him.

And the sound of a church bell tolling in the distance reminded him that it was all happening on Good Friday.

5

Gradually the coach took on the aspect of a prison. First, Wolf moved along the side, humming happily to himself, covering all the windows except two with coats of dark brown paint. He worked quickly and sloppily, using a wide brush; the paint splashed onto the seats and ran down the glass like dribbles of treacle but this only seemed to add to his enjoyment. The passengers, watched by Moshe, were herded from one side to the other coughing as the sharp, acrid smell filled the air and stabbed at their lungs. As he finished each section, Wolf tore the rose-colored curtains from the windows. When he had finished he looked round, gave a grunt of satisfaction, and went out.

A few minutes later, Kurt came in. He looked around and then took a stick of chalk from his pocket. He drew a thick line on the floor, across the gangway between the seats. On his side, toward the rear, there was an area of about one-third of the coach, lit by the two unpainted windows.

"Now, pay attention, please," he said. He pointed to the white lines. "You will not cross this line without permission. Beyond it, on your side, you may move about as you wish, except at night when you are forbidden to leave your seats. You will not touch the windows, try to remove the paint, or try to look out; the door behind you has been sealed. Don't attempt to force it—explosives have been wired to the catch and you will only succeed in blowing yourselves up. Anyone wishing to use the toilet will come to the white line, stop, and proceed only when given permission. You may talk but you will keep your voices down at all times. You will obey the instructions of your guards to the letter, without dissent or argument. Anyone failing to do so will be shot."

"May I please ask a question?" said Pastori nervously.

"What is it?"

"Why do you hold us like this, like prisoners?"

"You'll find out—in due course."

"Another question, please?" said the little Italian.

"The last one. Yes?"

"You had a list of names. Our names. You keep us and let the rest go. Why is this? Why are we important to you?"

"Well," said Kurt, "let me put it this way. Taped to the underside of this coach—under your feet—there is enough high explosive to blow you all back to New York. You are sitting on a bomb. That's how important you are. Does that answer your question?"

It was impossible for them not to look at the floor. Their eyes went down to the innocent gray-green carpet, staring as though it were full of menace.

"A question," said Alma Manasse.

"No more questions!"

"It is cold in here," she protested. "Later it will get colder. Our luggage is in the compartment behind you. May we please have our coats at least?"

"I will consider the matter." He turned away, stopped, and looked back at her. "You."

"Yes?"

"Come with me. I will show you something."

She followed him out to the platform at the rear.

The Major and Wolf were sitting on the two tip-up seats normally used by the train staff. They looked up but said nothing. Kurt jumped down onto the track, put up a hand, and helped Alma down.

A light, chill wind stirred her hair. The sun was no more than a blur of red and yellow on the horizon; the fading light had the mellowness of amber. Kurt took her along the track, halfway down the length of the coach. He stooped down and indicated that she should do the same.

"I want to show you that I was not bluffing. Look—and then go back and tell the others."

He turned a flashlight on the underside of the coach, and she saw the sinister-looking cylinders of explosive that he had placed at various points. They had been taped onto the bogey and to the floor of the coach and linked by lengths of black fuse wire.

As she straightened up, she staggered slightly, and he put a hand on her arm to steady her. For an instant, their eyes met, then she shook herself free, as though his touch repulsed her.

"You see?" he said. "It will take me thirty seconds to fit the final fuse assembly. Another thirty to get clear. And then—" He spread his hands. She turned away, but he checked her. "Wait."

"Yes?"

"You are a Czech?"

"I was," she said, an edge of bitterness in her voice.

"And you are Jewish?"

"What of it?"

" It's simply that . . ." He hesitated, and fiddled with the flashlight. "We have no quarrel with you. You are free to go."

"Free?" In the half-light he saw her eyes widen with astonishment.

"The nearest depot is just a few miles up the track. Just follow the rail."

"Why me? Why just me?"

"Look," he said harshly, "don't argue. Go! Just go!"

He heard her draw in a breath, as though gathering strength. Then, shaking her head, she said: "No. Thank you, no. I cannot leave my friends."

"Friends?" He mocked her with the word.

"May I go back inside, please?" she said quietly.

"As you wish." He turned away in disgust.

She moved toward the door, then checked. "I am grateful for your offer. But you must see, I can't accept. And I'm sorry if my refusal makes you feel guilty. But—"

It was as if she had touched a raw nerve. He swung round on her, his face tense with anger. "Get inside! Get inside."

She had to pull herself up into the coach. He made no move to help her.

FOURTEEN

1

Abraham Sondheimer answered the ring at the front door with a sigh of irritation. The Sabbath had just begun, he had endured a hard grueling week, and he had been looking forward to a nice quiet evening. A man was entitled to a little time to himself, he thought angrily.

He slipped the catch and jerked the door open, ready to pounce on whatever intruder had dared to interrupt his privacy. The anger choked in his throat as his eyes met the bright red tunics of the two officers from the Royal Canadian Mounted Police, and his hand went to his mouth in surprise.

"Mr. Abraham Sondheimer?"

"Yes, I am he."

"I wonder if we might come in for a moment, sir?" The Inspector's tone was scrupulously polite, but before he had finished speaking he was already across the threshold, with the tall, granite-faced Sergeant close on his heels.

"Of course. Please. Come in." The invitation was unnecessary since they were already in. Sondheimer blinked, closed the door, and scuttled before them into a small study. "This way, gentlemen, this way. Kindly take a seat. Tell me what is the problem?"

The Inspector remained standing, and the Sergeant waited with his back to the door, almost obscuring it. "This is a matter of some urgency, Mr. Sondheimer," said the Inspector.

"Of course, of course. If I can help . . . "

The Inspector held out an envelope. "This is addressed to you, sir."

"A letter? To me? I don't understand. . . . "

"As you will see, sir, we took the liberty of opening it and perusing the contents. I would like you to read it, sir, if you wouldn't mind."

"Yes, yes. First, I must find my spectacles. Reading glasses, you understand. Excuse me. I will not keep you a moment." He hurried across to a writing bureau and searched frantically under a mass of papers. He abandoned this after a while and began to rummage among the cushions on a couch.

"I had them in here a few minutes ago." He gave the Inspector an apologetic smile.

"Would these be the ones, sir?" said the Sergeant. He indicated a small table. By the side of the telephone there was a pair of spectacles.

"Ah! Ah!" Sondheimer snatched them up, looked round for the letter, and found it in his hand. He smiled at the two policemen and began to read. They watched his face as it moved from bewilderment to astonishment.

"It can't be true," he said. "Is it true?"

"I'm afraid it is, sir," said the Inspector. "The train from New York was held up. A man was killed. Hostages are being held."

"It doesn't seem possible!"

"Do you know the man who signed the letter—Kurt Reiss?"

"No. I have never met him."

"You are sure?"

"Certainly!"

"Why would he write to you?"

"I don't know. Possibly because of my position in the Jewish community here. I really don't know. But the man is clearly mad or sick. To murder someone—and all this talk of explosives!"

"We can't be certain that explosive charges have been attached to the coach, sir. But as you say, they appear to be desperate men, and we cannot take chances with the lives of innocent people."

"Who are the hostages?"

"They would seem to be a group of scientists, sir, on their way to Montreal for some sort of conference."

"But what I can't understand is why these criminals—these train robbers—should want to speak with me."

"We don't think they're train robbers in that sense, sir. They could simply be cranks, madmen. Or there could be some other motive."

"What sort of motive?"

"That is what we wish to find out, sir. We're moving men up to the spot, of course, and by morning the area will be sealed off. We can't take the risk of a direct assault on the train—"

"Of course not! Those poor people . . . "

"Although it may come to that in the end. We wondered if you—"

"Would talk to them. Naturally! This is quite incredible, really incredible."

"I ought to warn you, sir—"

"No need, no need!" said Sondheimer. "You were going to say it may be dangerous, correct? Well, we'll worry about that afterward, eh? You want I should come now? Of course, of course. Two minutes. I must change, tell my family I have to go out. Make it five minutes."

Shaking his head, he hurried out, muttering to himself. "Incredible. Really incredible."

2

Planchonnet, the Frenchman, seemed to be the only one on the coach to sleep that night. The old man curled up in his coat, wrapped a couple of curtains round his legs, and in a few minutes he was away, chin on chest, nose almost buried in the luxuriant gray beard. For the most part the others found it impossible to rest. They had coats also, and some had travel blankets, but even so the cold found its way through, piercing the flesh with its damp chill.

The tension was not now so great as in the first hour, but even so it was still there, an invisible presence in the frigid air, like a noose around each neck.

And, curiously, it was Kurt's group that seemed to feel this most. With the exception of Kurt himself, they seemed to have used up all their reserves of calm. Wolf and Moshe, in particular, were almost neurotic in their reactions; alert for the slightest sound, irritable and at times even vicious with the hostages, irritable with each other. Wolf hardly sat down all night; he paced the coach like a restless animal, cocking and uncocking his gun as if he were impatient to use it.

Craig, one of the Englishmen, came in for the harshest treatment. He shuffled to the white line several times during the long night, putting his request for the toilet in an embarrassed whisper. Earlier that day he had eaten something that disagreed with him, and he had developed severe diarrhea. In the light cast by the two lanterns at the far end, his face appeared to have the color and texture of putty.

Toward dawn, Kurt came in to take over as guard, sharing the duty with Wolf, while the others rested.

"All quiet?" he asked.

"Too damned quiet!" said Wolf. "Christ, what a night—it seems to be going on forever. What's it like outside?"

"I'm not sure. They've brought up a train, I think. I put my ear to the rail and definitely heard something. And I thought I saw lights in the timberland on either side. They're probably moving up trucks."

"What are you going to do—just sit here and wait for them?"

"Wolf," said Kurt, "you know what we're going to do. We agreed. Take it easy."

"It's the waiting," said Wolf, "the bloody waiting!"

"Easy, I said. We may have to wait a lot longer yet."

"And we may not! What's to stop them opening up with a cannon and blowing us to hell?"

"That's the gamble. We're gambling that they won't want to kill this lot."

"A load of *schleppers*!" said Wolf contemptuously. "Look at them! Maybe we've been fooled, did you think of that?" He made a motion of the hand toward the prisoners. "What's so special about them?"

"They're very special, believe me—I'm not fooling. When the Major handed me that list back in Montreal, I made it my business to find out what I could. What we have here, my old friend, is a collection of some of the greatest physicists in the world."

"Excuse me for my ignorance," said Wolf acidly, "but I wouldn't know one end of a physicist from the other."

"There is a thing called splitting the atom," explained Kurt. "Scientists have been talking about it for a long time. These people have found a way to do it."

"And when you split an atom, what do you do with it, may I ask?"

"I'm not sure. But I read that it would be possible to use this knowledge to make a new secret weapon.

Imagine one bomb, one single bomb, that could destroy Berlin and its environs. One bomb that could burn and kill hundreds of thousands of people."

"And these people—these *schmucks*—could make such a bomb? A bomb to wipe out Berlin?"

"Any city. I am told that it is only a matter of time."

"Christ!" said Wolf, running a hand through his thick hair. "Maybe we would be doing the whole world a favor if we did kill them off."

"The thought has occurred to me," said Kurt.

"The bastards!" muttered Wolf. "They must be bastards to think of such a thing."

One of the hostages rose from his seat and moved toward the white line. It was Craig again.

"No!" shouted Wolf angrily. "No!" His voice was so loud that it roused the other passengers, even the sleeping Planchonnet.

"Please," said Craig feebly.

"No!" shouted Wolf again. In his anger, he dropped the poor English and fell back on his native German. "After what I've heard you can shit in your trousers!" He jerked his gun in the direction of the seats. "Get back to your seat, you hear me?" Craig went back, his head lowered in embarrassment. "That goes for all of you from now on!" roared Wolf. "You can shit yourselves for all I care!"

Alma Manasse got up and went to the line.

"Get back," said Wolf.

"That man is ill," she said quietly. "Mr. Craig is ill. Let him through."

"You heard me! Get back!"

She made no movement. He cocked his gun, the metallic click grating on the silence.

"Your last warning!" said Wolf.

And then Kurt was at his side, pulling the gun down, shoving the big man aside. Wolf spun round as if to attack him, and then, quite suddenly, he dropped his arms, the anger fading as quickly as it had flared. He gave Kurt a shamefaced look and turned to Craig.

"You," he said in English. "Come. Come."

He led Craig out, glancing once more at Kurt as he left.

"I am sorry about that," said Kurt. "He is a good man—"

"He doesn't give that impression," said Alma dryly.

Her tone angered Kurt. "You're in no position to judge!" he said sharply. "If you knew him, if you knew what he has been through—"

"Tell me," she said.

"You wouldn't understand," he muttered.

"Perhaps not," she said with a certain gentleness. "I'm sorry."

"Do you know what made him so angry—at that moment?"

"He is under great strain. That is obvious."

"More than that. I told him—I told him that it won't be long before you and your friend here make a new kind of bomb. What do you call it? A nuclear bomb, an atom bomb. I told him that just one of these bombs could destroy Berlin and kill thousands of people. He didn't like that. He is a Berliner, you see—whatever happens, it is his city."

She looked at him in astonishment. "What do you know of this—this so-called bomb?"

"Is it a secret?"

"It has been discussed only by a few people. Are you a physicist?"

"No, thank God. If I were—and I were asked to make such a weapon—I'd cut my throat."

She shook her head. "We don't even know yet if it is possible."

"But you think it is."

"Perhaps. But we also have doubts—not about the possibility, but the principle, the ethics." She paused, and shook her head again, as if to make some order of her thoughts. "That is the reason then? That is why you selected us, why you are holding us here?"

"Work it out for yourself."

"Jews." She breathed the word. "Jewish people! And you work for the Nazis. You hire yourselves out to them as assassins! And you dare to preach to us of morality! What happened—did you strike a bargain? Your freedom, in return for a little murder on the side?" Her voice rose as she spoke, until it reached almost to the pitch of hysteria. "That man—that good man—your friend who is so anxious about Berlin. Doesn't he know who rules in Berlin now? Don't you know?"

"He also rules in Czechoslovakia," said Kurt icily. He caught her arm as she moved to strike him. "Lady, if you ever get a chance to make your bomb, drop it on Prague, eh? How would that suit you?"

He released his grip, turned, and moved away. A voice checked him. It was the old Frenchman, Planchonnet.

"Young man, wait, wait. A moment. Don't be in such a hurry!" Kurt swung round, and Planchonnet rose stiffly from his seat. "I heard what you said. Every word. I am not quite deaf, not yet. And I must ask you this. Have you heard of Sixty-nine Unter den Linden in Berlin and what is going on there?"

"No."

"Then before you criticize Dr. Manasse and the rest of us, find out."

"I've no time to—"

"Don't waggle that gun at me!" said the old man. "At my age, do you think I am afraid of death? I look at you, and what do I see? Not a Nazi, no. I know those types. But I see an idiot nevertheless, a real idiot. Do you truly believe that if you kill us—me and my colleagues—that you will bring nuclear research to a halt? Rubbish! We don't want to make bombs, young man. We are scientists, not armament manufacturers. But we have come here to put our knowledge at the disposal of the free world because, if we do not, that world will be destroyed. By whom? By a gentleman called Hitler. It's a race, young man, between civilization and barbarism, and if you don't see that, you are even more of an idiot than you look! At this moment, at this very moment, there are scientists at Sixty-nine Unter den Linden who are constructing a uranium machine. All the resources of the Reich are behind them. In time, they will discover the way to build the sort of bomb you speak of. And that bomb will not fall on Berlin or Prague—it will destroy London or Paris. And after that there will be other bombs, for New York and Washington. Do you see the significance of that, or are you too stupid?"

"You want to make the bomb first," said Kurt. "You want to beat them to it."

"Is there anything wrong with that?"

"To fight one kind of evil with another?"

"Unfortunately, this is the kind of world we live in. We have to make value judgments. We have to decide not between good and evil, but between the greater evil and the lesser. It's the dilemma of our age. We have no other choice. Do you see a choice?" He smiled. "After all, isn't that exactly what you are doing, in another way? Do your means justify the ends you seek?"

3

Day came at last, and with it, a clear sky and a bright sun, which made the frosted rails glitter like crystal. Through the field glasses they could see clear evidence of movement in the woods on either side, and Kurt placed the team on full alert. They were steadier now that the night was behind them and the prospect of action lay ahead.

He went to the box in which they had brought the explosives and took out one prepared length of safety fuse and one of instantaneous. He had already capped them with aluminum detonators, but he tested the crimpled necks with his teeth, biting hard, just to make sure of the fit. Then, blowing some warmth onto his hands, he taped the two lengths of fuse together and got to his feet.

He glanced at the Major and took a deep breath. "Cover me," he said.

He dropped onto the track and crawled quickly under the coach. Turning on his back, he eased the detonator assembly into the center of the explosive and taped it in place. It wasn't an expert job, but it had worked well enough in Spain and he thought it would serve their purpose.

When he had finished, he rested for a few moments, and he thought of what the old Frenchman, Planchonnet, had said. How ironic that those people in the coach were faced with the same sort of dilemma that had haunted him since the day the Reichsmarschall had first proposed his devil's bargain. . . .

He roused himself, crawled back out, paying out the fuse, got to his feet, and, helped by the Major, climbed back on board. Taping the end of the fuse around one of the steel handgrips, he stood back. His hands were still cold, but there were beads of sweat on his forehead.

"No cigarettes," he said. "No smoking, no naked flame." He saw the Major's eyes go to the fuse and rest on it, and he added: "And no tricks, Major. No heroics. I think you'd better go inside and look after the prisoners. Send Wolf out to me."

"You still don't trust me," mocked the Major. "Well, the feeling is mutual. Remember that."

"It is engraved on my mind," said Kurt.

The Major went inside, and a moment or so later, Wolf came out. He was still subdued, still conscious of his earlier irrational behavior.

"Wolf," said Kurt, and indicated the fuse, "you are to watch this. Every second. No one is to go near it, especially the Major. You understand?"

"That bastard! We made a mistake when we brought him along," growled Wolf.

"We needed him. I couldn't have taken that locomotive on my own."

"We don't need him now. Let me put a bullet through his head."

"He may still be useful. If that ship doesn't sail we may have to get a message through to the German consul and get him to convince them that we mean business." He smiled and put a hand on Wolf's shoulder. "We've been in some scrapes in our time, eh, Wolfie?"

"Never anything like this."

"No. Never anything like this."

"Do you think we'll pull it off, Kurt?"

"It won't be for the want of trying."

"Last night—" Wolf began.

"Forget it," said Kurt, trying to cut him off.

"No. I behaved like a *nebekh*. Worse. But it was strange. Waiting there, hour after hour, things got on top of me. I felt—I felt as if I hated everybody, everybody in the whole world. I mean, here we are, in this crazy situation. And why? Simply because a madman has taken over in Germany, simply because we have the misfortune to be Jews. And then when you told me that they were going to blow up Berlin—Christ, they must be madmen also! I could have shot them all and then turned the gun on myself."

"Stop it, Wolf," said Kurt. "I didn't say they were going to blow up Berlin, I said—well anyway, stop beating yourself!"

"I'll tell you something else," said Wolf. "To clear my mind. Coming back on that train to Montreal the other day, I felt the same way as Maxie. I was thinking I might quit like he did, make a run for it."

"But you didn't. You're here," said Kurt. "And now, that's enough. Watch that fuse, and watch the Major."

"Right." Wolf turned away, looked toward the fringe of trees to the west, and stiffened suddenly. "Hey! Look. We've got a visitor."

Kurt snatched up the glasses and focused them. A tall, thin, bearded man wearing a black suit and a black wide-brimmed hat was moving toward them. In one hand he carried a piece of white cloth tied to a stick. He moved carefully, picking his way through the loose timber on the slight incline. Kurt studied the area behind the man, and then on the other side, and he fancied that he could see the outline of an armored car, but he could not be sure.

"Get one of the prisoners!" he ordered.

"Which one?"

"For Christ's sake, any one." And as Wolf moved inside, he shouted: "Bring the woman—the woman!"

He turned again to watch the man in black, who was now only about two hundred yards from the coach. He raised a rifle to cover him, waiting until he was a little nearer, and then shouted: "Wait! That's enough. Who are you?"

"Pardon?" The man stopped and cocked his head.

"Your name!"

"Sondheimer. I am Abraham Sondheimer."

"Put your hands above your head and move forward."

Sondheimer seemed to hesitate, as though wondering what to do with the white flag, and then he raised both arms as bidden and moved on again.

Wolf spoke at Kurt's elbow. "Here she is."

Kurt turned to find a strange-looking Alma Manasse. She had been caught in the act of grooming her long chestnut-colored hair, and instead of being pinned up on her head, it was flowing gently around her shoulders. He had not thought of her as being young, but now, with the hair framing her oval face, she looked almost like a girl.

"Kneel down," he said. "Here, by the opening, where they can see you." She gave him a quick, frightened look and then obeyed. He tossed the rifle to Wolf. "Stand behind her. Hold the gun to the back of her head. They'll be watching. Let them see you, too."

"What are you going to do?" Alma looked up at him, the rich hair swinging over her breasts.

"Don't worry. A little show of strength."

Alma closed her eyes, clenching her hands as the fear writhed in her stomach. As the cold metal pressed into her neck she had to bite her lips to prevent herself from screaming, and the teeth drew blood. Gradually the spasm passed, and a feeling of resignation took over. How strange she thought, that she had escaped from one sort of persecution, only to find another. And to find it at the hands of her own people!

Kurt took out his automatic and jumped from the coach to face the approaching Sondheimer.

"That's far enough," he said briskly. "Keep your hands up! Are you armed?"

"Armed? Certainly not! In your letter you expressly said—" He paused. "You are the person who wrote the letter?"

"Yes. And you are Sondheimer?"

"I am he, yes. Please, may I put down my hands? It is most uncomfortable and tiring. I promise I shall offer you no violence."

The thought of this frail, elderly man offering violence to anyone brought a little smile to Kurt's face. He waved the automatic. "Very well. Lower your arms—but don't touch your pockets."

"That is most kind," said Sondheimer. He looked beyond Kurt, saw Alma and Wolf and frowned. "Dear me, is that quite necessary?"

"Never mind that," said Kurt. "You got my message. What's the answer?"

"Before I give it," said Sondheimer tentatively, "I have been instructed ... er ... asked ... to assure myself that the ... er ... prisoners are unharmed."

Kurt turned to Alma. "Tell him."

"No one has been injured, if that's what you mean. Not since yesterday afternoon when a man was killed out here on the track. We saw it through the windows. It was plain murder." Contempt glittered in her eyes.

"You can believe her," said Kurt. "She's a good Jewish girl. Or you can go inside and see for yourself."

"No. I am under instruction to remain in view at all times. I will take the young lady's word." And then Sondheimer added, more severely, "You know, you really should give up this foolishness before any more people are killed. There are troops and police on both sides of you. They have guns trained on the coach, armored cars, I believe I even saw a tank. So you see, you have no hope of escape. Why not let these poor people go, and give yourselves up? I'm sure the authorities will take such a gesture into account. Besides—"

Kurt interrupted him brusquely. "In my letter, I asked you for some information. Have you got it?"

"Yes, yes. That's what I was about to say, you see. It's all very puzzling. You asked me to find out whether a Norwegian ship had sailed from Hamburg."

"And?"

"She has. The S. S. *Helga* sailed on Thursday, bound

for Cuba, with nearly one thousand Jewish persons on board."

"Are you sure of this?" Kurt's voice was a whisper, full of disbelief.

"Quite sure. Of course. I made a careful check. Would I lie on such a matter?"

"You might, if you thought it would help the people in there."

"I have in my pocket a copy of the relevant parts of Thursday's *New York Times*, which I procured for this purpose before coming here. If you will allow me to bring it out—"

"Get it!" said Kurt.

Sondheimer patted one pocket and then another and finally produced some sheets of newspaper from inside his overcoat. As Kurt snatched at them, he said: "First, look at page five. At the right, toward the bottom. There is the full story."

The item was brief. The S. S. *Helga* had sailed from Hamburg, with 977 Jewish passengers on board, and Dr. Joseph Goebbels, Reich Minister of Propaganda had managed to get into the act after all. He had informed the world's press that Germany was releasing the Jews as as act of goodwill. It was part of a general housecleaning operation, and he would be prepared to let more Jews leave the country—if they could find someplace to go. Now, he said, the democracies, who have been screaming their heads off about Nazi persecution had the opportunity to match their words with deeds. Germany would be interested to see how they responded to the Führer's unique gesture.

Kurt felt the anger drum in his temples. The bastards, the bastards! They had tricked him again, turned the whole thing into a propaganda exercise! He crumpled the paper, mashing it in his hands, as the anger gave way to a sense of despair.

"There is another item," said Sondheimer timidly. "Under the 'Shipping News.' It confirms the sailing."

"It doesn't matter." Kurt shook his head.

"Forgive me," said Sondheimer. "I am puzzled. Why did you wish to know this particular piece of news?"

"I have my reasons," Kurt said. "Tell me," he added bitterly—"you are a Jew. Does it make you happy?"

"Happy. Happiness is like medicine: it comes in small doses and often leaves a bitter taste. Nine hundred and seventy-seven people? Now much, but yet it is something after all. At least they are free. So when I read about the ship—yes, I was happy for them."

"Yes," said Kurt, "As you say, it is something." He was beginning to feel better and allowed himself a small, wry smile. After all, what the hell did it matter what Goebbels said? He and Wolf and the others had won another small victory: including the children from the orphanage, they had got over a thousand people out of that prison called Germany.

"You smile," said Sondheimer, "which suggests that the news pleases you also. May I be permitted to say that I am still puzzled? I see that girl kneeling there, a Jewish girl, and I ask myself—is he a Nazi perhaps? But then I tell myself—no, Abraham, that is not possible. He is concerned about a ship full of Jews, happy that it has sailed. So, what can I make from such confusion, I ask you?"

"It would take too long to explain. I am not a Nazi; you can set your mind at rest on that score. Nor are my friends. As for the girl, it isn't what it seems. There is an old saying: white bread can grow from black earth. Do you know it?"

"I know it," said Sondheimer frowning. "It is a Jewish saying." He gave a sigh of resignation. "Oi vey! If a man understood everything he'd no longer be a man." Another sigh, and then he continued: "So. You have the news. Are you satisfied? Is that what you want? Will you now release the hostages?"

"Not yet, not quite yet," said Kurt.

"What more do you want?"

"I want everyone on board that ship to be issued with a visa to enter the United States or Canada."

Alma lifted her head, forgetful of the rifle at her back, her eyes wide with astonishment. Sondheimer stared at Kurt, as he could not believe what he had heard.

"That is impossible!" he stammered.

"Why?"

"Only the other day the United States government announced that it could not increase the quota."

"I am not asking them to increase the quota! I want them to use it! Do you know that for the last four years there have been thousands of unfilled places on that quota?"

"I am aware of this—yes. But there are strict rules."

"I know. One of them is that anyone applying for a visa has to supply a police certificate to prove that he has been of good character for the past five years! Can you imagine what the Gestapo would say to a Jew who asked for such a document?"

"We know these things, of course we know them!" said Sondheimer, with a note of protest in his usually gentle voice. "You speak as if we do nothing, as if we are idle in the matter. We raised thousands of dollars and sent it to Germany so that people could buy their way out."

"What's the use if they have nowhere to go?"

"Many of the people on board the S. S. *Helga* bought landing passes for Cuba with money we sent."

"Landing passes that may be useless."

"You don't know that."

"I know that the Cuban government is considering

the issue of a decree that would make those passes invalid. It's called Decree Ninety-three. A man named Zellner told me that a few weeks ago in Berlin—don't tell me you—" Kurt checked suddenly, realizing what he had said. Trying to cover, he added lamely, "Anyway, there it is. Cuba may turn them away."

It was too late. Sondheimer's mouth was open, his lips were moving although no sound came. He seemed to be trying to pump words from a reluctant throat. Eventually one surfaced, in a sort of croak. "Berlin?"

"That's not important. Forget it."

"You met Zellner in Berlin? Joseph Zellner? Zellner of the Jewish Council? I know him. I mean, we have been in touch, many letters. A fine person. He even wrote about the ship to Cuba. But what have you—"

"Mr. Sondheimer, it's a long story and very complicated. I've said more than I should. But perhaps you understand a little better now." Kurt took his arm. "Come. I want to show you something." He led the bewildered man to the side of the coach. "Look under there and tell me what you see."

Sondheimer stooped with difficulty and eventually lowered himself carefully to his knees. He peered under the coach for a long time and then looked up at Kurt.

"Explosives?"

"Explosives." Kurt helped the old man to his feet. "Now, Mr. Sondheimer, I want you to go back. I wrote three letters altogether. Tell them that I expect a positive response to the other two by six o'clock this evening. If the answers have not come by then, or if they're in the negative, I intend to blow up this coach and everyone in it."

"You could not do such a thing!"

"You had better convince them otherwise. They need those people in there—I know it, they know it.

Well, after six P.M. they won't have them. And while you're at it, you'd better point out that if they start firing or any funny business like that, I won't need to light this fuse—they'll do the job for me." Kurt smiled. "I would shake your hand, but they will be watching and it might not go down well. Perhaps we'll meet again, perhaps they'll send you back with some good news. Shalom."

Sondheimer stood for quite a long time without moving, looking as if he had been stunned. At last, with a long, slow shake of the head, he turned and walked away, holding the white flag down by his side like a fallen banner. Kurt watched him for a few moments, then he ducked down and slid under the coach. When he emerged and went back to the doorway, he was surprised to find Alma still kneeling, with Wolf's rifle covering her.

"Sorry to keep you," he said. "You can go back inside now." She gave him a quick, wondering look, as if she were seeing him for the first time, and went into the coach. As Kurt climbed up to the platform, Wolf dropped the rifle, enveloped him in a bear hug, and gave him a great, bristly kiss.

"For God's sake!" said Kurt, struggling to get free. "There's probably a dozen people watching us through glasses. What the hell are they going to think!"

"Who cares! You've done it, brother, you've done it!"

"We've done part of it, Wolf. Part of it."

"The ship has sailed. That's the main thing. They'll have to give the visas now."

"Don't be too sure."

"If Cuba turns the passengers away, they'll have to let them come here or to the States. They couldn't send them back to Germany."

"Wolf," said Kurt. "You should know that in this world there are people who are capable of anything.

We'll learn soon enough. In the meantime, say nothing to the Major."

"Why?"

"The Major is a man of duty. If he realizes that the ship has sailed, he will expect us to deliver the bodies."

4

On the instructions of Mackenzie King, Prime Minister of Canada, the letter addressed to President Roosevelt had been opened. It was found to be almost identical in its wording to the one he had received himself, and it contained similar demands. He ordered, as a matter of urgency, that its contents should be telephoned through to the White House in Washington, D.C., together with an up-to-the minute version of events. An hour later the President, Franklin D. Roosevelt, came on the line.

"Good morning, Mac. I got your message."

"Morning, Franklin. Sorry we opened your personal mail."

"Glad you did. It's an odd business. What's your position on it?"

"Obvious. It's blackmail. We can't give in to the threat of force."

"Good. That's my reaction. What do you intend to do?"

"Play it cool. These people are armed, they've already killed one man. And we're pretty sure that they've got the coach wired with high explosives. So if we try any sort of direct assault, we run the risk of getting the hostages blown to smithereens. On the other hand, they can't move, and we've got them surrounded. So we'll try and starve them out."

"Call their bluff?"

"That's it. Starve them out. As far as we know, there was no food on the coach, and they must be running short of water."

"Suppose they call your bluff and blow the coach when the ultimatum expires?"

"I don't think they will. For the simple reason that they'll have to blow themselves up with it."

"Maybe they're just desperate enough to do that."

"It's a chance we have to take. I'm not being black-mailed."

"What about the hostages? Anything about them I should know?"

"Scientists. On their way to a congress in Montreal. A slight problem. Some of them are from overseas. Top men in their field—physicists. But I don't think we should allow that to affect our judgment."

"I agree. Do you know their names?"

"I can let you have them."

"Fine. As soon as you can—just in case I get asked any questions." The President paused, shuffling the mail on the desk with his free hand. "Mac, have you any idea who these people are? The holdup gang, I mean."

"No. They've obviously got Jewish connections."

"Seems that way. You know, I'm surprised something like this hasn't happened before. The Jews are having a hard time. Well, keep in touch, Mac. And if you want any help, call me direct."

"I will. Thanks, Mr. President."

"Bye, Prime Minister. Have a good day."

The President put down the telephone and began to leaf through the mail. He stopped at one letter that had a green label marked MOST URGENT affixed to the top; on the label there was a short written message that was in the unmistakable handwriting of Alexander Sachs, one of his most respected advisers. The message read: *It's long, it's difficult, it's incredible. But please study it. If we don't act now, we could lose out. Alex. PS. Look at the signature first.*

The President turned to the last page. There it was. *Albert Einstein.* He settled back in the wheelchair and began to read. Twenty minutes later a secretary brought in a telephone message from Mackenzie King's office. It listed the names of the people who were being held on the train. The President recognized one of them, and that only vaguely. He laid the list aside and continued with Einstein's letter.

When he had finished, he sat thinking for a long time. Measured by the clock it was just over six minutes, but the value of time is variable. A man can take six minutes to choose a shirt but in thirty seconds he can save a life or take it. He did not know then, he could not know, but the six minutes that Roosevelt spent considering the implications of Einstein's letter were destined to set mankind on a new course; that brief space of time was a bridge between two eras, and the world would never be the same again.

When he reached a decision he placed three calls. The first was to Alexander Sachs. He went straight to the point. "Alex, I've read Einstein's letter. I'm impressed. Point taken. Now, listen. I've a list of names here. I'll read them to you. And you tell me about them."

He read out the names on the memorandum, spelling out the more difficult ones. When he had finished, he said: "Well?"

"Mr. President," said Sachs. "You have just named ten of the leading physicists in the world today."

"Experts in—what do you call it—nuclear fission and so forth?"

"The best. Mr. President, they're the people who persuaded Einstein to write to you. At least two of them have detailed knowledge of the experiments that have taken place in Germany."

"Thank you, Alex. You've told me what I need to know. Have a good day." He hung up. Within moments, Mackenzie King came on the line.

"Mac," said the President, "I have a favor to ask you."

"Anything, Franklin."

"Don't be too rash. Those people on the train. The hostages. I've just learned exactly who they are. I need them alive, Mac. I need them real bad. We all need them."

"Well, of course, we'll do our best—"

"I want more than that, Mac. I want them so bad I'm prepared to accede to the hijacker's demands. That's how important it is."

"You'll grant entry visas to the people on that ship?"

"Yes. Mind you, it would make it easier for me if we could split it fifty-fifty. We'll take half, if you do the same."

"I take it you have a good reason."

"I never had better."

"What about the terrorists? They've asked for safe conduct and a free passage to Argentina."

"If you have to, you have to. That part is up to you. I don't care a cuss about them. But, Mac, right now I need those passengers as bad as I need a two-ocean navy."

"Okay. If you say so. But what in hell makes them so important?"

"I'll tell you next time we meet. Another thing, Mac. How is the press on this thing?"

"Slower than usual, since it's a holiday. But they're on to it."

"How much do they know?"

"So far—what we've told them."

"Do me another favor. Keep it that way. Play it down. A train robbery, nothing else. And listen, when you get those passengers out—"

"*If* we get them out."

"You've got to. Mac, I'm laying it on the line. Hook or crook—get them out alive. And then send them back here under plain cover. Forget the Montreal conference. Send them back here. We'll look after them."

"Like I said, I'll do my best."

"And the visas?"

"It's a deal. Fifty-fifty."

The final call was to the President's military aide, General Edwin Watson. "Pa," said Roosevelt, "I know you're enjoying a nice, relaxing weekend. Well, I'm here to tell you it's over. Get your pants on, and get in here. Fast. And I mean, fast. I've got a job for you, and it won't wait."

When he put the phone down at last, the President wheeled himself to a cabinet and took out a bottle of Napoleon brandy and a glass. He poured a measure and sat for a few moments, cradling the glass in his hands. He thought that it might be appropriate to drink a solitary toast to the future, but he decided against it. Then he considered drinking to Einstein, but he rejected that also. He couldn't help thinking that, as a result of what had happened that morning, there would come a time when the President of the United States would have to make a decision more awesome than any that had faced his predecessors. He didn't want to be that man.

In the end, he drank just for the hell of it.

5

The Major was facing a more immediate decision. The atmosphere on the coach had changed; he could sense it, almost smell it. Kurt had told him that the talk with Sondheimer had been inconclusive and that he had extended the deadline to 6:00 p.m. The Major was not convinced. It was difficult to define, but the air had suddenly become charged with hope; it was reflected not only in the attitude of Kurt and the others, but more remarkably in that of the passengers. By some mysterious alchemy, they seemed to have crossed sides, to sympathize with their captors, even to identify with them.

He sat in the rear of the coach, watching and wondering. A group of them were playing a word game, and Moshe, his submachine gun slung carelessly over his shoulder, was standing by Pastori, prompting him. There was a steady hum of lighthearted chatter and occasional laughter.

He thought of the fuse. But Wolf and Kurt were out on the platform and it would be difficult, if not impossible, to get near it. Moshe was an easier target; he could get behind him, knock him out with the butt of his gun, and mow down the hostages with the machine gun before the two men outside could intervene.

Yet he hesitated. This wasn't war; there was no provision for this sort of situation in the *Luftwaffe Manual of Operations*. In a sense, flying was an impersonal affair: when you had dropped your bombs you turned your head for home, you didn't see the dead bodies below, or hear the screams of the maimed. It was simply marked down on your record as another operation. And again, it was hard to think of these hostages as enemies of the Reich, harder still to generate the degree of hatred necessary to execute them. The fuse would be easier: a match, a touch from a lighted cigarette, and an unseen death would come suddenly, even mercifully, for all of them.

These dark thoughts were still tormenting his mind when Kurt came in, with Wolf behind him, to meet an astonishing reception. Led by Pastori, the hostages rose to their feet and applauded him, clapping their hands and murmuring as if they were greeting a hero. The Major looked on in astonishment, and Kurt himself stood staring in amazement. Pastori raised his hand and the applause faded.

"Signore Reiss," said Pastori. "I am speaking for us all, everyone here." He waved a hand in the direction of Alma. "Dr. Manasse has informed us about the ship and of what you and your colleagues are trying to do for the people on that ship. Signore, we applaud you, we wish to express our admiration." His voice took on a graver tone. "Naturally, we cannot condone yesterday's killing, but perhaps we understand the pressure that prompted it."

"Get on with it!" growled Planchonnet.

"I will come to the point," said Pastori.

"Good!" said Planchonnet.

"We have discussed this among ourselves, at some length. Naturally, we do not wish to die, to be killed. And we assume that you feel this way also, no? No, naturally not—everyone wants to live. So we have a proposal. Let three of us leave the train and go to the authorities. We will explain the situation and urge them to grant the necessary visas. It is possible that they will listen to us. We will ask for U.S. or Canadian visas for all the passengers on the ship and that you and your colleagues be treated with the utmost clemency. And whatever happens, we give you our word, our solemn word, that we will return and place ourselves once more in your hands. We have elected Professor Planchonnet, Dr. Manasse, and myself for this purpose. Now, what is your answer?"

The long silence that followed was broken by Wolf, who pushed forward, leaving his post by the door. "Why not? Kurt, why not? What can we lose?"

Kurt spun round as he heard the sharp click of metal. The Major was on his feet, automatic in hand, back to the door.

"Nobody move," he said, "nobody."

He reached behind for the door catch, and as he did so Wolf threw himself forward. The Major fired once, twice, a third time, but the big man seemed unstoppable. He fell on the Major, hands reaching for the throat, tightening on it, squeezing, squeezing, until the gun dropped from his hand, the eyes popped, and he fell. The Major's hand reached for the gun, fingers brushing the ground, as Wolf sagged against a seat. He found it, tried to lift and point it, but this time it was Kurt who fired. The Major gasped; blood gurgled from his mouth; he twisted and lay still.

They laid Wolf on a seat and put a cushion under his head. A last flicker of life stirred in him, and he opened his eyes.

"Wolf, you fool, you fool. Oh, Wolf, you fool!" Kurt almost crooned the words.

"Well," whispered Wolf. "They say that fools don't get gray. They're right." His eyes closed again.

"Shalom," whispered Kurt.

6

Alma, Planchonnet, and Pastori came back to the coach an hour later. Alma had wanted to leave Planchonnet, but the old man refused, insisting that he had given his word to return. They found Kurt, Moshe, and the others sitting in a silence that was heavy with grief. Kurt raised his head wearily.

"Well?" he asked.

"The Canadian government has a representative out there," said Alma in a low voice. "We talked to him.

They have set up a direct radio link between him and the Prime Minister." She seemed reluctant to get to the point.

"What's the verdict?"

"The visas will be granted. The refugees will be allowed to enter the United States and Canada."

"Naturally, they made the usual point that this must not be taken as a precedent," said Pastori. "But you have won your point. We spoke to the Prime Minister himself. We have his pledge."

"Good," said Kurt without enthusiasm. "So that's it. You can go now." They hesitated, and he added savagely, his voice ringing round the coach: "You can go! All of you! Don't you hear me? Are you deaf?"

No one moved.

"There is the question of your own position," said Pastori gently. "I am afraid—"

"There's no need to go on," Kurt said. "I can guess what they said. In any case, it's unimportant."

"Nevertheless," continued Pastori, "I think you ought to hear it. A safe conduct out of the country is out of the question. They insist that you surrender yourself to the police and stand trial."

"But they promised that they will take full account of the circumstances," said Alma quickly. "And we will testify on your behalf."

"Please go," said Kurt. "Ask them to wait an hour. We'll think about it."

"You should come," Alma said. She touched his cheek with cool, gentle fingers.

"We'll see," said Kurt. "Now go."

The passengers filed out, murmuring embarrassed farewells. There was no show of relief at this release: their experiences had been too shattering, and each felt a certain sense of guilt that they were thus privileged, that they were about to walk to freedom.

Moshe and Kurt went to the platform and watched them pick their way toward the line of policemen who were now openly showing themselves. From the area behind there came the flash of cameras.

Alma turned and looked back. She did not wave, and Kurt was reminded of another moment, when Emmy had stood with the children on the deck of a ship leaving for Sweden. They had not waved then. A posse of policemen surrounded the group as soon as they reached the trees, and they were hustled away.

The two men sat in silence for a long time. Then Kurt said: "Well, Moshe, my friend."

"Yes?"

"What do you think?"

"How do they execute people in this country? Do they use the electric chair or the rope?"

"The rope, I think."

"What difference? Either thing is distasteful."

"In any case," said Kurt, "I don't think they will put us on trial. It would be too awkward. They wouldn't want us shooting off our mouths about this nuclear business."

"Oi vey," said Moshe. "What a world! If it isn't Hitler, it's the atom bomb!"

"I should like to have given Wolf a proper burial," said Kurt, after a pause.

"And the Major," said Moshe. "In a way, he was a victim also."

"We couldn't dig," said Kurt. "The ground is frozen."

There was a long silence. Kurt got up and jumped to the track. Once again he crawled under the locomotive. When he returned, Moshe looked up at him, an inquiry in his eyes. "I disconnected the assembly after Sondheimer left," said Kurt. "I didn't want to take any chances."

"The Major didn't know this?"

"No."

"But Wolf—"

"It would have made no difference. If the Major had emptied a magazine into that stuff—"

Moshe nodded. "You've reset it."

"Yes. It'll take thirty seconds for the fuse to burn. I timed it exactly. I'll give you five minutes to get clear."

"What are you saying?"

"It's a sort of burial for Wolf—even for the Major. I think they would prefer it."

"And you?"

"The rope, the chair, a lifetime in jail. Is that a future?"

"I feel the same. Kurt, we did something, didn't we? I mean, it was something."

"It was something."

Moshe took out a cigarette and lit it. He drew on it deeply, until the end glowed red. Kurt watched him in silence. Moshe strolled over to the fuse and turned, smiling.

"Shalom, you old bastard."

"Shalom to you."

Moshe touched the end of the fuse with the cigarette. It caught at once and began its steady, spluttering run. . . .

7

The newspapers were full of photographs and stories of the incident next morning. For the most part, however, the authorities had done their job well, whisking the scientists away in a covered truck before they could be questioned.

So it was reported as a train holdup near Lacolle. The criminals were said to have demanded ransom for the release of certain passengers, but in the face of the firm attitude taken by the government, they had released their prisoners unharmed. Explosives had been set under the coach, and it was thought that the hijackers had accidentally ignited this and been killed in the subsequent explosion.

What was not reported was that blackmail persisted to the end of the story. Abraham Sondheimer and the scientists were warned that any hint of the truth might endanger the security of the United States and Canada. There was a hint that if they stepped out of line, the visas would not be issued, and there would be a further tightening of the immigration regulations.

In the circumstances, they remained silent.